A Place in the Country

A Place in the Country

Published by The Conrad Press in the United Kingdom
2018

Tel: +44(0)1227 472 874
www.theconradpress.com
info@theconradpress.com

ISBN 978-1-911546-33-7

Typesetting and Cover Design by:
Charlotte Mouncey, www.bookstyle.co.uk

The Conrad Press logo was designed by Maria Priestley.

Printed and bound in Great Britain
by Clays Ltd, St Ives plc

A Place in the Country

ROB STUART

To Janine

All the best

To Liane

1

On a Saturday morning in late May, Mitchell Dever sits with his wife, Jocasta, in his new metallic blue BMW, which he's parked in front of Yew Tree Cottage, the thatched residence they've bought in the Hampshire village of Itchen Prior.

Mitchell closes his eyes and listens to the ticking of the car's engine in the soft spring air as his pride and joy cools down (his car, not Jocasta, although he regards his wife as the love of his life) following the long drive from London down the M3.

'Oh dear, the place looks quite dilapidated,' says Jocasta, doubtfully. 'Much more of a wreck than it was in March.'

'Nonsense, my love,' Mitchell replies, optimistically. Like the new car, which was a thirty-seventh birthday present to himself, this move to the country is very much his pet project; an escape from the daily commute on overcrowded public transport.

'Let's remember what the estate agent said, darling,' Mitchell adds. '*A dream cottage for a new rural lifestyle.*'

'But the garden's a jungle!' exclaims Jocasta.

'*A bucolic haven*, he told us,' Mitchell adds.

'I thought bucolic was something babies got.'

'Darling, he meant it's a pastoral idyll, and he was right. It'll be marvellous. We'll have chickens, a goat, maybe even a sheep. It's going to be *such* an adventure.'

'But we don't know a thing about rearing animals.'

'Exactly! It'll all be a totally new experience. Our new life. No more London, no more risking your life on your bike in the rush hour, or being crammed onto the tube with our noses pressed into armpits.'

Mitchell looks pleadingly at the woman he loves. He hardly ever ceases admiring her beautiful green eyes, her blond hair tied back into a pony tail, her picturesque face with its strong, very feminine features. He feels a rush of the warmest emotions. He knows perfectly well that Jocasta thinks he's engaged on a mid-life crisis, what with the new car and this new rural life he craves. But he also knows she loves him and is prepared to indulge his whims, and he in turn loves her for being prepared to indulge them.

'And don't forget the dodgy plumbing,' she adds.

'Darling, we discussed that,' Mitchell replies gently. 'Pavel and Karol have promised to come down asap to start work.'

Jocasta purses her lips, her usual expression when she isn't convinced.

'Darling,' says Mitchell, 'once we get Harriet's interior designers in you'll have free rein to stamp your mark on the place. We can afford it, after all. It's all going to be lovely. We can even have a conservatory with workstations for each of us. Working from home, with wonderful views. Why didn't we think of it before?'

Harriet is Jocasta's younger sister.

Jocasta gives a shrug. 'Well, I suppose it *might* work.'

'No, love, it definitely will.'

Mitchell smiles. He feels happy; very much in love with the cottage and with Jocasta. They sold their Victorian terrace in Chiswick for almost a million and bought this cottage for just over half that, so they still have more than enough for the renovations.

Mitchell is sure a door has opened; life in the countryside beckons in the company of the salt of the earth, a close-knit village community, with (he imagines) village fetes, flower shows, a village pub, a cricket team etc.

The countryside! He wants it to be like the Archers, but all the time, not only in fifteen-minute segments.

Mitchell opens the driver door and gets out of the car. He takes deep breaths, expanding his chest to accommodate the wonderful smog-free air.

'What's that awful smell?' Jocasta exclaims.

Mitchell coughs and shuffles his feet.

'I'm not quite sure, love,' he says. 'Silage, manure, and that kind of stuff I suppose. It's the smell of the countryside. Ah, my little city girl, you've a lot to learn about the ways of the country.'

'And you're some kind of expert, are you? You've never lived out of West London in your whole life until now. You're about as rustic as Earls Court Station!'

Mitchell doesn't deny this, but with a sudden impulsive sweep of his arms, lifts Jocasta off her feet and staggers with her in his arms in the direction of the front door. This bold romantic gesture ends when he has to put her down to get the door key out of his pocket. The lock is stiff and Mitchell struggles with it.

The door opens reluctantly. They are hit by a smell of mildew and must. The estate agent has assured them this will vanish, following a good airing.

2

About a hundred yards down the lane from Yew Tree Cottage, Ashley Warren, forty-three, plump, her brown hair in a bun, is kneading dough in her kitchen. Her strong hands are covered with flour and flecks of dough.

Her partner Seth, forty-five, closes the front door behind him with a firm slam. He is a small, dark man with bright eyes and sharp movements that always reminds Ashley of one of the five ferrets he keeps in the shed outside.

Ashley wonders what Seth has got himself overexcited about this time. She can see that his eyes are wild and that he's shaking with excitement and bursting with news.

'Incomers!' exclaims Seth, as if announcing the outbreak of World War Three. '*Incomers!* From outside the village!'

Ashley looks at him calmly and says nothing.

'Didn't you hear what I said?' Seth demands. 'Incomers! To Itchen Prior! Remember when Major Wallop came? When were that? Six year ago? Not been such excitement since. Not even when Cole Henley got crushed by that traction engine at the village fete.'

'Well, he shouldn't have been abusing himself against the back wheel,' says Ashley, still stoically pummelling at the loaf. 'He wouldn't be told. It was his own stupid fault.'

'Never mind him, Ash. Incomers! I've seen them!'

Ashley pauses in her punching of the dough, delivers a series of elbow strikes, flings it in the air and smashes it down onto the table. Almost gently, now that the battle is won, she brushes the top with milk from a jug and commits the body to the Aga.

'Where were they?' she asks.

'At Yew Tree Cottage.'

'You mean the ones who paid Penton Mewsley half a million quid? They must be mad. The place is falling down.'

'He's done well though, the canny bugger. He's talking about jetting off to that Thailand and buying himself a Thai bride or two.' He pronounces it 'Thighland' and 'Thigh'.

'If you ask me,' Ashley opines, 'he's likely to end up with half a dozen of them girlyboys.'

'Oh, I see,' says Seth vaguely. He is puzzled as to the exact nature of girlyboys. Ashley prides herself on being the worldly one of the family and has read books and watches all those fact programmes on the TV during the daytime. Seth is more of a sports and soaps man. He is convinced that *Eastenders* is an accurate portrayal of urban life. He has never been a great traveller, hardly ever going beyond the local market town of Westleigh, and never having been to London at all.

'What, like that Eurovision singer whatsisname?' asks Seth.

'Yes, I expect so.'

Ashley's own idea of normal human relations has always been that if you keep it in the family, you can't go wrong. This has been a Warren tradition for centuries. She is also Seth's younger sister, the stock of cousins having dwindled away. Other people, Ashley thought, had such complicated lives. You only had to look at that stuck-up cow Gwendolyn St John who was no better than she ought to

11

be seeing as her father had been the shepherd on the estate. Goodness knows, the things he got up to with the sheep, whenever he got ill he was as likely to call in the vet as the doctor.

'Half a million quid,' Seth muses. 'What we could do with that!'

'Such as?' Ashley says, glancing at him.

'Oh, lots of things.' Seth says vaguely, going over to the cider jug and taking a good slug. But his imagination stops at the bounds of Itchen Prior, which Ashley knows he will never leave.

Ashley draws up the old carver chair to the table and plonks herself down.

'Pass the jug, you daft old sod. Like o' us, we ain't never going be rich.'

She sighs and pours herself a generous measure of cider into a cracked mug.

3

Compared with most of the stately homes of Old England, St John Hall could be described by the National Trust as modest, but the present owners - Gwendolyn St John, thirty-four and her fifty-three-year-old husband Sherborne St John (it's always been 'St John' not 'Sinjun'; they're a literal kind of family) - regard it as a place they could never imagine not living in. Not unless Sherborne were to die and Gwendolyn were to sell it, anyway.

St John Hall is a Jacobean red-brick residence, built onto an earlier building dating from 1540, when the St John of the time saw a chance to capitalise on the Dissolution of religious houses and bought it cheap. The main feature of architectural interest are the two high chimney stacks twisting their way skyward from the west end of the building, and the motto of the St Johns (*nihil debit:* meaning that an accused defendant says nothing) carved on the lintel of the Great Door (said to be by the legendary Grinling Gibbons). The St Johns have made a point of presenting a modest persona to the world ever since a narrow squeak in 1571 when they became involved in a dodgy wool deal with John Shakespeare, a glove-maker from Stratford, whose son would go on to make a name for himself in London.

Wool had been the making of the St John family, ever since the days when John St John (yeoman of the parish) dragged himself into the ranks of the minor gentry in the

Fifteenth century by the cunning ruse of dealing equally with both Yorkists and Lancastrians in the War of the Roses and cheating both without prejudice. By keeping their heads down for the next two hundred years the St Johns managed to keep their heads on their shoulders.

The present estate itself is the product of centuries of skilful land acquisition and runs to around three hundred and fifty acres of farms and woodland. Helpful farm subsidies care of the soon-to-be-discarded European Union, creatively accounted, a number of properties in the village, a half share of the St John's Arms and the income from tenant farmers means the current incumbent of St John Hall, Sherborne St John is a man of comfortable wealth, modest ambition and a traditional outlook on life in the country, much given to wearing tweeds and walking the estate with his dogs.

Not so his wife Gwendolyn (*nee* Abbas). She still burns with a yearning to rise higher in county society, to mingle with the Great and the Good, to appear in *Hello* magazine in a variety of designer clothes displaying the charms of her admittedly lovely home; and handbagging the generous fee thus earned. She is a woman who knows she will never have enough money, no matter what she does, and spends most of her waking non-horizontal moments scheming to acquire more.

Her plans to stage the Itchen Prior Rock/Folk/Indie/Hiphop Festival of Music have been fiercely vetoed on several occasions by Sherborne, but Gwendolyn still nurses dreams of strolling the grounds arm in arm with Sir Mick Jagger and Sir Paul McCartney (headlining on Saturday and Sunday respectively). Her dreams have also embraced an Itchen Prior Romantic Literature Festival; a visit from the Antiques Road Show; the Itchen Prior Film Festival (George Clooney to chair the judges) and her latest idea, the Itchen Prior Horse Trials.

Gwendolyn has an almost erotic love of horses. She keeps several in the stables behind the Hall and keeps Crux Easton (twenty-two, tall and broad of shoulder, fit, and prone to doing workouts with his top off in all weathers) to look after them.

And her.

His predecessor, another stable lad of about Crux's age, having spent close to two years submitting to Gwendolyn's particular interpretation of *noblesse oblige*, had staggered, sexually shattered, off into the dark late one November night to find refuge - after months of convalescence with his mother in Weston super Mare - in the powerful arms of a fifty-year-old fish and chip ship proprietress on the sea-front whose large breasts and insatiability reminded him of Gwendolyn, whom he'd started to miss.

Gwendolyn admits to being 'in my late thirties, my dear. In my prime!' She is economical with the truth about her actual age as about most things, seeing this as nobody's business but her own. She habitually dresses in tight jodhpurs, black riding boots, and black riding cap and invariably carried a riding crop, from time to time giving herself a little slap on the thigh and when riding Crux Easton from above, often thrashing him with it on the thighs or buttocks.

Gwendolyn's father, who had the sobriquet of 'Itching' Abbas, had been the estate shepherd. The young Gwendolyn, having been expelled from secondary school for an unspecified incident involving the Geography teacher (who had hitherto been a respectable married father of two) was determined to rise above her humble station. She stalked Sherborne with the skill, determination and attention to detail of a Highland ghillie. When coy glances and fluttering lashes had no effect on the slightly unworldly and unmarried gentleman farmer, she contrived to be caught sunbathing topless on top of a haystack after the Harvest Home picnic. And in the weeks that followed she contrived to put herself in Sherborne's path at every opportunity. Soon Sherborne was putty in her hands, apart from the few occasions when he rose to the challenge. After that it was a simple task to hint at pregnancy and the shame of a little St John burdened with the name of Abbas; and then there was her father's unfortunate reputation to think of.

Several of Sherborne's ancestors have played their part in shamelessly populating the immediate area with their offspring, the St John nose being a prominent feature on the faces of a number of both men and women in the village.

Reader, he married her. And that was more or less the end of his conjugal relations, and the start of Gwendolyn turning her attention to her stable lads.

'Have you heard the news, old girl?' Sherborne asks Gwendolyn over breakfast, eggs, bacon and sausage for him, quinoa and black coffee for her. It's Sunday morning, the day after Mitchell and Jocasta arrived at their dream home.

Gwendolyn hates to be called 'Old Girl', which always seems to her too horsey, but she smiles and says:

'What news is that, my sweet?'

'Couple from London have moved into Yew Tree Cottage. Used to belong to old Penton Mewsley.'

'But it's a total wreck!'

'Supposed to have paid him half a million for it.'

Gwendolyn is stunned. She starts to do calculations in her head. If someone is prepared to pay £500,000 for a dilapidated cottage, what would they pay for the St John estate? Figures with *lots* of zeros swarm around in her head.

Of course, she is well aware that the slight obstacles to this scheme are that Sherborne is a) still alive; b) would never sell it, even though he has no immediate offspring to whom he could leave the estate. There is a nephew in Australia (there always is), but *if* Sherborne was to die, who would inherit? Obviously, the widow.

With a sound like the pinging of a pinball machine, *Hello* cover-spreads bursts, not for the first time, into her mind:

> *Gwendolyn St John, the wealthy widow, seen here
> aboard her fabulous yacht in the marina at Cannes.*

and

> *Gwendolyn St John, seen here in the
> Winners' Enclosure at Royal Ascot*

and

> *A stunning exclusive of the wedding of
> Gwendolyn St John to Johnny Depp.*

'Are you all right, old girl?' Sherborne asks. 'You've got a funny look in your eyes.'

'What?' replies Gwendolyn innocently. 'Oh, I was just thinking. Darling, I can't believe anyone would pay that much for Yew Tree Cottage, not when it needs so much work. And they've got that awful Warren family next door.' (Seth Warren, in a rare breach of the Warren family code, had been Gwendolyn's first lover, just after she turned thirteen. She hopes Ashley never finds out; Ashley Warren is not the forgiving kind.)

'A chap was telling me the other day that most of London is now owned by Russians, Chinese and Nigerians,' Sherborne continues. 'Hardly any semis even in Zone Four sell for less than a million nowadays. Even the Arabs are moving out. Makes you think.'

'It certainly does,' Gwendolyn agrees.

4

Tristram Clatford is the vicar of Itchen Prior and of several of the surrounding villages. He sees himself as the leading light in parish affairs, as in fact he is, although attendance at religious services is on a steep decline. Sherborne St John, though, is a regular worshipper at the church, driven by his sense of duty as the squire to set a good example to the village, but his wife is not.

On the Wednesday following the arrival of the Devers in the village, Clatford is astride his bike, pedalling in the direction of Yew Tree Cottage. It is his first parochial visit to see Mitchell and Jocasta Dever. Clatford habitually wears a rain cape when out on his bike. This flies behind him, giving him, he likes to think, the look of Zorro or the Caped Crusader riding out to right wrongs.

In the garden of Yew Tree Cottage he spots a youngish man with cropped blonde hair, Sunday stubble, and wearing a tee shirt with the slogan *Let's Do It In The Country* on it and a pair of blue jeans. The young man is staring wistfully at the jungle that is the front garden.

'Hello there,' Clatford calls out. 'I'm Tristram Clatford. Vicar by trade, of this parish and many others.'

'Oh, hi. I'm Mitchell Dever,' the younger man says.

Clatford wobbles to a halt and dismounts, advancing on Mitchell with his right hand thrust out like a sword.

'Quite a job you've got there.' He shakes Mitchell's hand vigorously.

A lovely young woman wearing cut-off shorts and a man's blue shirt comes to the door of the cottage; she, too, is blonde and Clatford sees, very beautiful. She is holding a feather duster that is heavily coated with cobwebs.

'I can't believe how grimy this place has become since we saw it with the estate agent,' she remarks to her husband.

'It's not for me to speak ill of an ex-parishioner,' says Clatford, 'but I suspect old Penton never lifted a finger once you'd signed on the dotted line. He's gone off to live in foreign parts.'

'I see,' says the woman. 'I'm Jocasta Dever, by the way.'

'Welcome to Itchen Prior, my dear,' replies Clatford, shaking her soft hand with its smooth, nicely manicured nails. 'Will I be seeing you both for Morning Service? Evensong? Holy Communion? We're a very friendly church here.'

Mitchell and Jocasta look at each other. 'Er, we're not really very religious… we're just…' they say, in a pretty much simultaneous way.

'No rush, no rush. Find your feet first I expect. Anything I can do to help?'

'Well, we *are* rather snowed under,' admits Jocasta. 'Camping out, really. Renovations on hold. Builders called away to an emergency. But we are coping, thanks.'

'They'd only been here one day!' Mitchel says, complaining to Jocasta as much as to Clatford.

'They'll be back, darling,' Jocasta tells him, consolingly. 'They said they would be, after all. Remember what a good job they did for Edward and Corrine?'

'That took six months!' Mitchell exclaims.

Clatford shuffles uneasily; he is in no position to take sides.

'If there is anything…' he proffers.

'No, but thanks for offering,' says Jocasta, shouldering her duster.

'I saw the neighbours yesterday,' Mitchell says to Clatford. 'I waved and said hello but they just ignored me.'

'Sorry to hear that. They're the Warrens. Local family. Been here for generations. Keep themselves to themselves. Seth, he's the father, is a local character. Does a bit of this and a bit of that.'

'Is he a builder?' Mitchell asks hopefully.

'I don't think so. More of a poacher, if I'm honest. He's a real country man. Odd jobs on the farms.'

'Might be useful when we get the livestock, then.'

'Have you kept livestock before?' Clatford asks.

'No, not as such. But how difficult can it be?'

Clatford wisely says nothing.

'Anyway, that won't be for a while yet, the way things are going,' says Mitchell.

'Well then, if there is anything I can do to help you can always find me in the vicarage. You can't miss it. Big house next to the church. Far too big for me, really. Needs a chap with a brood of kids to fill it. Do you and Jocasta have any children?' he asks, eying the cottage dubiously. *Anyone trying to bring up children in that rat's nest needs to be reported to Social Services without delay*, Clatford thinks.

'No,' Mitchell says. 'We've decided there are more than enough people in the world without us adding to the burden. I had the snip!'

'Oh, I see,' says Clatford, only vaguely aware what this means.

'I'm sure I could get you a cup of tea, vicar,' says Mitchell, 'though to be honest the kitchen's rather a bomb-site at present.'

'Very kind of you to offer, Mitchell,' says Clatford, 'but I need to be on my way. Be seeing you around.'

'I look forward to that,' says Mitchell, sincerely enough. 'We're going to love being part of village life.'

'It's good to have you in it,' replied Clatford, affably, feeling quite sure that Ashley and Seth wouldn't say the same. 'Yes, we'll be seeing you both.'

And he mounts his bike, give Mitchell and Jocasta a wave, and peddles erratically back in the direction of the village.

5

Marjory Hinton Daubrey is Clatford's right-hand woman and plays the organ for his church services. She also plays the piano every morning at the village school where she is the teacher. She is in her twenties, regarded by all in the village as almost the archetypal image of the school marm. She favours twin sets with a cultured pearl necklace, wears her hair drawn back in a bun, wears glasses and sensible shoes. She is unmarried and insists on being call Miss rather than Ms.

She is strict in the classroom and brooks no nonsense but is scrupulously fair and gives praise where it is due. The parents think highly of her and the school is rated 'excellent' by OFSTED. Her SATS results are impressive and parents from the surrounding villages would dearly love to send their children to her, if there were space.

As Clatford passes the school, the children tumble out, their lessons done for the day. He dismounts and leans his bike up against the railings. Inside he finds Marjory tidying up her desk.

'I've just met the incomers,' Clatford tells her. 'City folk with city ideas! Livestock! Won't have any children so they don't destroy the planet!'

'Calm down, Tristram.'

'Well.'

'We need new blood in the village; they ought to have children to bring up in the country.'

'He told me he'd had a vasectomy. Came right out with it.'

'But what about her?' Marjory asks gently, and for some not yet explained reason of her own. 'She might be able to have children.'

'True enough,' says Clatford thoughtfully.

6

In the St John Arms the landlord, Gordon Turgis, is struggling to deal with the lunchtime rush. Propped against the bar, gently caressing his second pint of Old Bishop (abv 8.6) is 'Ragged' Appleshaw, retired part-time farm labourer and village elder.

Seated by himself at a table by the large fireplace (the fire is not alight this warm early spring day) is Henry Grey, lately retired from Shearwater Agricultural College (or, perhaps, the victim of Further Education cuts), author of a well received, by its hundred-odd readers, of *Traditional Country Lore*, Itchen Prior's answer to *The Golden Bough*. He drinks sherry, although in the privacy of his own snug lounge he is a neat gin man. He is reading today's copy of *The Daily Telegraph* and making mysterious notes in a small book he has brought with him for this very purpose.

Paul Hartley, local arable farmer (and tenant of Sherborne St John) and Jed Smith, owner of the garden centre just outside the village - he styles it the Itchen Prior Horticultural Centre - are deep in conversation lamenting the banning of DDT and the lunatic opinions of all 'green lefty liberal city anti-GM know-nothing bastards' who have 'no business poking their noses in where they are not wanted', which is, as far as Hartley and Smith are concerned, anywhere outside the M25.

Apart from these, the saloon bar of the St John Arms is empty. The pub itself is old, dating back to the days when Old Mother Candover brewed ale in her hovel back in the 1600s: free ale to any visiting witch finders, who left forgetting what they had come for, a feat for which Old Mother Candover was held in high regard by the villagers, who depended on her to charm away murrains from their cattle and brew love nostrums and place a curse on their neighbours.

The present building was built by Hubert St John, a man with an eye for any business opportunity to screw more money out of his tenants. Sherborne St John still has a fifty-one percent interest but is more than happy to leave the day to day running to Turgis. Gwendolyn has suggested an upmarket make-over involving a cocktail lounge and happy hour but this has been firmly opposed by Turgis, who finds pulling pints and pouring from bottles quite taxing enough. Sherborne has wisely let the idea hang in limbo. However, in keeping with the trend for pub grub, the St John Arms does now offer a range of pickled eggs, crisps and pork scratchings.

Next door to the pub is the small village shop, also owned by the St John family. As well as newspapers (*The Daily Mail*, ever a best seller, *The Daily Telegraph*, *The Daily Express*, *The Sun* and on one occasion a copy of *The Guardian* - which stayed on the shelf for two weeks before being returned to the distributer to be pulped), it offers a range of ready meals, mainly traditional fare like Chicken Tikka Massala and lasagne, basic groceries like baked beans and spaghetti hoops, stamps and an extensive range of patent medicines that can be used, interchangeably, to cure the ills of both human and animal patients.

When she is not helping Gordon Turgis to cope with the rush in the pub, the village shop is run by Natalie Somerfield, a woman in early middle age and the font of all gossip and rumour (some of it, as gossip and rumour often are, based on fact) in the village. She has never heard of an EU Directive and still clings happily to Imperial measures and a manual till.

The Devers' BMW draws up in the pub car park, disgorging Mitchell and Jocasta. Today they are dressed in unisex overalls with embroidered bibs, his with a pig, hers with a rabbit. Jocasta heads for the shop while Mitchell enters the pub.

Hartley and Smith fall silent and glare at him. Here is the living embodiment of all that is wrong with the world. Grey looks up from his paper for a moment and then goes back to his scribbling. Sensing an opportunity, Appleshaw downs what is left of his pint and eyes the stranger hopefully.

'Good morning,' Mitchell calls out brightly as he approaches the bar.

Turgis heaves a sigh as only one who thinks he carries the weight of the world on his shoulders can.

'What'll it be?' he asks.

'I'd like a half of bitter, please. I'm driving,' explains Mitchell. Hartley and Smith, who regularly drive home with one eye shut to compensate for double vision, exchange knowing glances.

'So what beers do you have?' asks Mitchell, feeling bold. He is used to gastro pubs and craft ales, guest beers and a range of continental lagers from places like Moldova and Latvia.

Turgis scowls at the two pumps.

'Old Bishop, and Badger's Tail. Badger's Tail needs changing but I ain't had time since last week.'

'A half of Old Bishop it is then.'

'In a fresh glass?'

'Yes, please, if that is no trouble.' This is not the hail fellow, well met reception Mitchell had expected from his new local. But perhaps this is part of the charm of rural life, or a test for the newcomers?. That must be it, the landlord is teasing him.

It isn't. This is Turgis at his most affable.

Ragged Appleshaw clears his throat loudly and peers into his empty glass. Mitchell sees his chance to ingratiate himself with a local.

'Care to join me?'

'That's right kind of you. A pint.' Appleshaw hopes to sink his pint before the incomer can drink his half and benefit again from the mug's generosity.

Turgis plonks the glasses down on the bar and goes back to staring morosely at the door. Any more trade and he will have to get Natalie to shut the shop and help out.

Meanwhile, Jocasta has gone into the shop.

'Hello,' she says to Natalie. She looks around at the shelves stacked with goods that seem to have been there for years: small blue bottles with faded labels, tins with long forgotten brand names, ancient small bottles of vanilla essence dating from the 1950s, boxes of soap flakes and packets of Vesta ready meals. Jocasta wonders for a moment if she has entered a museum until she sees a freezer stocked with a modest range of frozen veg., oven chips, pizzas and burgers.

'You're that incomer,' says Natalie, a note of accusation in her voice.

'Yes. We love the village and the house was *such* a bargain.' Jocasta is determined to establish her credentials as a patriotic member of village society. 'We hope we are going to be very happy here.'

'Well,' says Natalie, grudgingly prepared to meet her, if not half way then at least some distance down the road, 'what can I do for you?'

'Have you got a tub of hummus?'

Natalie looks at her blankly.

'I've got the *Daily Mail*,' she answers.

'No. Hummus. The paste made from chickpeas.'

'I've got frozen peas. And mushy peas. In a tin.'

'OK.' Jocasta is not prepared to admit defeat and tries another tack. 'A tin of anchovies. In olive oil.'

Here Natalie is on safer ground. 'I've got rubbing oil. *Crippen's Embrocation.* The vetin'ry swears by it.'

'No, not quite what I had in mind.' Jocasta is not yet prepared to abandon hope. 'Taramasalata? Milano salami? Ciabatta? Focaccia? We are having an *al fresco* picnic in the garden to celebrate clearing a patch in the garden. Edwin and Corrine are coming down from Town.'

Natalie has given up listening; Jocasta's words drift over her head. This strange woman is obviously speaking in a foreign language for some inexplicable reason and Natalie doesn't do foreign.

'Nah,' she says. 'You might try Westleigh. They've got one of them foreign shops there. Lots of foreigners in Westleigh. Coming over here……'

Jocasta beats a retreat before Natalie launches into a racist rant and meets Mitchell coming out of the pub.

'Any luck?' he asks her.

'I might as well have been speaking Double Dutch,' she replies.

At last she and Natalie have something they can agree on.

7

Crux Easton and Sally Fairfax, his sexual partner of choice, are scrunched up together on his single bed, enjoying a post-coital spliff. Sally's curvaceous body and firm, large breasts are pressed against his back. She has blue-green eyes, a pretty nose, a rather large mouth and a tongue that has a small gold ring through it, near the front. Her head, with its long, bright blue hair, rests on Crux's shoulder. Sally changes her hair colour every few months, depending on how she is feeling about life and thanks to the efforts of Hair N Nails of Westleigh, next door to Ink Inc, the tattooist where Sally got the small lizard that is now a permanent resident on her right shoulder.

Crux lives in a studio apartment annex to the stables. He lives rent-free as a perk of the job. This means that Gwendolyn can usually find him when the mood (and a reluctant Crux) takes her. It is this that the lovers are discussing.

'You've just got to tell her NO,' says Sally.

'How can I?' demands Crux. 'I'll be out on my ear like a shot. Remember what happened to the last stable lad but one?'

'The one who ran away?'

'No, I mean the one before that. Half an hour's notice, pack yer bags an' on yer bike.'

'Well, tell Sherborne then.'

'He won't believe me. Thinks the sun shines out of her arse.'

'Well, *you'd* know!'

'That's not fair! Do you think I enjoy having to shag her on demand?'

'You're a bloke, aren't you?' she says, giving his willie a vicious pinch.

'Where would I live? Me ma won't have me back. An' then there's me record. Who's going to give me a job round here?'

These two facts are linked. Crux used to have a lucrative occupation growing weed in his mother's old greenhouse and selling it on at £10 a pop to his disreputable mates in Westleigh. He had told his mother he was developing a strain of Jamaican Funnybush, a plant new to the United Kingdom, with a view to supplying Jed Smith's garden centre. Mrs Easton, sensing a coup at the annual Itchen Prior Flower and Produce show, had entered a particu-larly fine specimen, confident of sweeping the board and triumphing over her rival's offerings of chrysanthemums and carnations and other such run of the mill no-hopers.

Unfortunately, one of the presiding judges was Sgt Barton Stacey, of the Rural Neighbourhood Policing Team. A visit by the Westleigh Drug Squad to Mrs. Easton's glass-house resulted in the apprehension of over fifty fine spec-imens of Jamaican Funnybush, an impressive result for them and a six-month custodial sentence for Crux.

On his release and return to Itchen Prior, Gwendolyn St John, who had just fired her stable boy for going on strike, as it were, saw an opportunity of ensnaring a young pris-on-fit lad with no immediate prospects. Crux moved in to the stables and a life of sexual servitude. He has been her captive for a year and has had enough.

'You could try asking Jed Smith for a job. After all, you're good with plants.'

'I tried. He only employs Eastern Europeans and pays them less than the minimum wage. They all live in those two ropey old caravans in the field behind the garden centre. An' he charges them rent out of their wages.'

'Well, this can't go on. It's got to be me or her. I ain't sharing you.'

'You're not sharing me,' Crux protests. 'That other is part of me job. It's like you saying you ain't sharing me with the horses.'

'It's different.' Sally protests. 'You ain't doing it with the horses.' She pauses for a moment as a thought enters her head. 'Are you?'

'Don't be daft. Besides, they're nearly all geldings. Apart from Molly, an' I don't fancy her.'

'You're a dirty bastard, Crux Eaton.'

'But I'm *your* dirty bastard,' he replies. 'Give us a kiss.'

8

the ashtray and a line of ... spending the day been ...
happier in a seedier bar ...
you could say adding Pat Smith ... ...tion. After all ...
you're good with people.

The builders have finally returned to Yew Tree Cottage; a skip full of assorted rubble and scrap blocks the drive. The sounds of banging and rending issue from the house. In the garden a tall, slim young man, stripped to the waist, is wielding a scythe. He is a garden designer who is busily making true the Devers' promises of water features, rustic benches, espaliered fruit trees and year-round flowering plants in a natural meadow. All plans for livestock have been suspended for the present. At last Mitchell and Jocasta can see their rural dream start to come alive and the possibility of a hot tub in the garden for the summer seems very real.

The Warrens have finally come down the lane to pay a neighbourly visit. They are all dressed in denim of one sort or another; Seth in jeans, cowboy boots, tartan shirt and denim waistcoat; Ashley in an ankle-length denim skirt and blouse. The twins, Hare and Hatch, are in their mid-teens and have been excluded from school long ago. Hare wears very short cut-offs with a cropped halter top that leaves her mid-riff bare. Over her navel she has the word *bruv* tattooed.

Hatch has the word *sista* hidden under his dirty t-shirt that proclaims his love of the band *Slipknot*. He wears ragged jeans and a denim jacket. Both wear expensive trainers and have extensive body piercings as well as other tattoos scattered about their bodies. Both, too, are wearing earplugs and compulsively check their smartphones.

Ashley carries a jug of cider, covered by an old tea-towel.

'Anyone home?' calls Seth while Ashley and Hare stop to admire the gardener in full Poldark action.

Mitchell and Jocasta come to the open door of the cottage.

'We brung you some cider, seeing as it's such a warm day,' explains Ashley.

This is the first real contact the Devers have had with their neighbours and they are deeply touched at this kind thought. Jocasta thanks them and takes the jug inside for the workmen.

'That's a tenner,' says Seth.

'An' we want our jug back,' says Ashley.

The twins have started rooting about in the skip looking for salvage. Mitchell is completely wrong-footed and fumbles in his wallet for a note.

'Ta,' says Seth, pocketing the money with a smirk. *Incomers*, he thinks, *bloody townies!*

'How you be settling in, then?' asks Ashley.

'Well, as you can see, it's a bit hectic at the moment but we're getting there,' says Mitchell.

'You ever need a cleaner,' says Ashley, 'our Hare is available for a very reasonable rate.'

Hare at that moment disappears into the skip and pulls out a length of copper piping, scattering rubble onto the ground.

'This is worth having, Pa,' she calls.

'Good girl,' Seth replies. 'Keep looking.'

'Er, we were going to send that to the tip,' explains Mitchell, as Hatch dumps a load of builder's waste into the garden.

'No harm,' says Seth, 'only a few old bricks. Make you a nice border.'

'I don't want a nice border,' says Mitchell, beginning to get annoyed, 'I've got a garden designer for that.'

'No need to get aireated,' says Ashley, 'the boy don't mean no harm.'

'He's tipping waste all over the ground!'

'Nah, it's only a bit of dirt.'

'It's concrete!'

'Keep yer hair on,' Seth says. 'Hare, Hatch, come out of there now,' he calls. The twins with their earphones cannot hear him and keep disgorging spoil.

Mitchell has had enough and goes to pull Hatch out of the skip. He reaches for the boy's arm but before he can make contact Hare is waving a Stanley knife in his face, her teeth bared in a feral snarl. He backs away in alarm, stumbling over the spilled rubble.

'Don't take no notice of her,' says Ashley. 'She's very protective of her brother. They love each other.'

Mitchell, wondering exactly what this means, finds he is trembling slightly. In all the time he lived in London he never felt threatened. This is not what the country is supposed to be.

Jocasta comes out of the house, blissfully unaware of what has been going on.

'Thanks awfully for the cider. I'll get your jug back to you asap.'

Hare has magically made the knife disappear and looks the picture of innocence. Her parents beam at her.

'We'll be off, then,' says Seth as if nothing has happened. The twins shoulder the piping and other bits of scrap metal and set off in the direction of their home.

'Welcome to Itchen Prior,' calls Ashley over her shoulder. 'Don't forget that jug. It's valuable and we'll have to charge you if you damage it.'

'That was nice of them,' says Jocasta.

'I wonder how you go about getting a shotgun licence?' says Mitchell, hitherto a lifelong pacifist.

'What?' asks Jocasta, unsure she has heard properly.

'To protect us from the neighbours,' Mitchell replies grimly.

He fills Jocasta in with the details of the Warrens' visit.

9

Farleigh Wallop (maj. Rtd) is a tall and, he likes to think, a sprightly bachelor of sixty-two. He drives an ex-MOD Land Rover Defender painted in desert camouflage with the words *Paintball Patrol* on the side panels.

This is the business he owns on land leased from Paul Hartley, which, as the name implies involves paintballing fun. In an area of set-aside on Hartley's farm is the replica of a village as might be found in Helmond Province, Afghanistan. However, instead of mud bricks this village is mainly constructed of plasterboard and 2x2 wooden struts.

Next to the village is a most un-Afghan copse of distinctly English deciduous trees. The object of the exercise, he explains to the corporate bonding teams out on a weekend HR jolly and the boozed-up stag parties who make up the bulk of his customers, is to take the village and 'give Terry Taliban a good seeing to.'

To the defenders he says that they are holding the village against a sneak attack by the sneaky Afghans. Generally, neither side gives a toss who they are supposed to be as long as they have a good day playing at soldiers with minimum risk to life and limb. Farleigh Wallop and his small team actually run the Paintball Patrol sessions while Hartley takes a cut for the use of his land.

Farleigh Wallop was a career soldier who joined up in time to see service in South Armagh, Desert Storm, Bosnia, Basra and latterly Camp Bastion in Afghanistan. In all of these hell-holes he had played a vital role in ensuring that the troops were fed three square meals a day. That he *was* a major on retirement was certainly true but he did not advertise that his service had been entirely spent in the Catering Corps and he had never actually discharged a weapon in anger.

The image he presented to the world of Itchen Prior and the potential clients of Paintball Patrol, was that of a rugged ex-killer whose modesty prevented him from talking about the terrible sights he had seen, and, indeed, been a perpetrator of.

He detests Hartley, his landlord, who he regards as a parasite, but was careful never to let his loathing show. The revenue from Paintball Patrol was a nice little fillip to his generous Army pension and without the use of Hartley's land the business could not exist and this galled Farleigh Wallop like a canker.

But this is nothing compared to the unspoken trench warfare over Alice Lacey. Alice is a widow lady of forty-eight, comely in appearance and twinkling of eye. Monday and Thursday she cleans bachelor Major Wallop's detached new-build in the little cul-de-sac at the edge of the village on St John land; Tuesday and Friday she can be found cleaning the divorced Hartley's nineteenth century farmhouse on Hartley land.

Alice is playing both men with consummate skill, seeming to favour first one and then the other. She has no intention of committing to either but has so far trapped them into an escalating price war over her wages as both men believe that money *can* buy them love, or at the very least the services of a live-in housekeeper.

Both men are perfectly civil to each other face to face, as befits business partners and stalwart members of the local community, but spend dark hours plotting the downfall of the other and the subsequent joy of *Schadenfreude* at the others crushing defeat and humiliation. As a military man, Farleigh believes he has the tactical edge but Hartley has spent years dealing with DEFRA and its predecessors over farm subsidies and is no slouch in the cunning department. At the moment the war is in stalemate.

10

'Long' Sutton's family can be traced back in Itchen Prior as far as the Warrens and the St Johns. The Suttons have always been retainers of the St Johns and pride themselves on their sense of duty to the family. They have felt no shame in their faithful adherence. During the years they have performed the duties of footmen, grooms, coachmen, gardeners, chambermaids, cooks, parlour maids and once reached the dizzy heights of butler in the 1850s, although that particular Sutton was said to be closely related to Ebenezer St John and the scullery maid Mary Sutton. They accompanied Ensign George St John to the Peninsula, they died with Richard St John in the trenches.

Long Sutton is long in every way. He stands six feet four inches; he is thin with arms that nearly reach his knees; his face is long and lugubrious, his feet are long and his hands are long. But for all his ungainly appearance he is extremely agile and silent of movement. He is the current gamekeeper on the St John estate.

He has known and disapproved of Gwendolyn Abbas all her life. Indeed, he is one of the rare males in the village and surroundings of Itchen Prior *not* to have known Gwendolyn Abbas in a biblical sense. He thinks she has risen above her station and has no business with her airs and graces and Lady Muck ideas. She takes especial pleasure in ordering him to perform menial tasks for her, particularly in her husband's hearing. Long can do little but grind his teeth and obey. He hates her and prays for the day when she will get her comeuppance. Like Sherborne, Long Sutton is the last of his line and feels they are all living in the twilight of a glorious past. Were something unpleasant to happen to Gwendolyn, Long Sutton would go to his grave a happy man.

11

Itchen Prior Horticulture (prop J. Smith) is bisected by a line of tall leylendi trees. On the public side, accessed from the B823, lie the shop and gift centre and the various greenhouses open for the public to browse around. Behind the trees is the working guts of the business; the propagating sheds and the poly tunnels where Jed Smith grows soft fruit. Also situated behind the anonymity of the screen of trees is the accommodation for the seasonal live-in staff. This consists of two very old two berth caravans arranged in a 'V' and propped up on bricks. Behind the caravans there is a portaloo. Smith recruits his labour from the Balkans and pays strictly cash in hand at way below the minimum wage and works them way above a forty-eight hour week. He deducts fifty pounds per person per week for rent. This arrangement lasts from March through to July, when he can pick up the services, free of charge, of local school children on 'work experience'.

Being a conscientious employer, Smith likes to keep his employees' passports safe by locking them away in the safe that he keeps in his office for the duration of their stay in Itchen Prior.

Jagoda Doboj, a Bosnian, is boiling a kettle for her evening meal of pot noodles. Nevena Stolac, who shares the caravan, is already tucked into her sleeping bag; she has been picking strawberries since six o'clock in the morning and too exhausted to eat. She will have bread and jam in the morning.

Two young men, Mirko Knin and Vukodin Punta, share the other caravan.

Jagoda hears a knock on the door. Mirko is outside holding a bundle.

'Can I come in?' he asks, in Serbo-Croat.

Once inside he unwraps the bundle to reveal a dead rabbit.

'Can you cook this?' he asks her. 'I've got some potatoes and carrots and some salt and some herbs.'

'Where did you get it?' Nevena has revived enough to sit up at the prospect of a real meal.

'Vukodin and I went out last night and set some traps in the woods. We often hunted rabbits back home. I've had enough of living on noodles and potatoes and packet soup.'

Jagoda's mouth is watering.

'You skin it and joint it and I'll cook it,' she says. 'Oh, real food at last.'

Mirko gets to work while Jagoda fills a rusty old saucepan from the standpipe outside. Soon the rabbit and vegetables are simmering on the one ring calor stove and they are joined by Vukodin.

'I'd like to skin that bastard Smith,' says Mirko, 'like he is skinning us.'

'Just don't get caught,' says Jogoda.

A sentiment they all agree with.

12

It is the second Saturday of June, a hot day. Gwendolyn St John is holding her annual garden party. A marquee and a beer tent stand on the lawn in front of St John Hall with Gordon Turgis, assisted by Natalie Somerfield dispensing drinks. Crux Easton, wearing, on Gwendolyn's instructions, a pair of tight black jeans that show off his bum and a cut-down black tee-shirt that shows off his six-pack abs, is serving drinks on a tray. He hates it.

He has managed to get Sally Fairfax a job for the day dispensing canapés. She is dressed in pale jeans and a white tee shirt but Gwendolyn has insisted she wear a frilly head-dress and apron. She hates it.

Mitchell and Jocasta are paying their first visit to St John Hall and are eagerly looking forward to meeting village society and integrating into their new life.

Mitchell is wearing tweeds and has a Burberry checked flat cap on his head and Jocasta is wearing a long skirt and embroidered peasant blouse. Her hair is hidden under a Hermes scarf. A pair of wellington boots peep out from under her skirt.

Gwendolyn herself is wearing her usual black riding kit; Sherborne St John is wearing a pair of very baggy and very old trousers, a blue shirt and sports jacket circa 1965. The Rev Tristram Clatford is in working gear of dog collar, dark jacket and trousers. Henry Grey wears corduroy trousers and a tweed jacket (less expensive than Mitchell's) with leather patches on the elbows as befits a retired academic and sandals with a pair of Argyle socks; Major Farleigh Wallop (rtd) has come wearing what looks suspiciously like a combat smock and a tee shirt bearing the legend Paintball Patrol - he is never one to miss a chance of a bit of advertising.

His rival for the affections of Alice Lacey, Paul Hartley, has his feet neatly tucked into a pair of polished brogues and wears a sleeveless puffa vest over a check shirt.

Marjory Hinton Daubrey is crisply dressed in a knee length denim skirt, court shoes with a flat heel and a white blouse over which hangs a gold cross on a chain.

Jed Smith has on a grey business suit, shirt and tie with black shoes to show that he is a serious business player in the local community.

Hovering at the very periphery of the gathering and feeling very uncomfortable, he is a retainer, after all, is Long Sutton. He is there on the insistence of Sherborne St John and much to the annoyance of Gwendolyn. He is unsure of his role and has resolved to stay out of the way as much as possible. There are a number of other guests who are acquaintances of the St John's and are there as a matter of form and who will reciprocate with functions of their own over the course of the summer.

No-one in their right minds would dream of inviting the Warrens to a gathering like this; they are likely to steal the silver.

'How are the renovations coming on in your dear little cottage?' Gwendolyn asks Jocasta.

'Quite well now,' Jocasta replies, sipping her glass of Chardonnay. 'Most of the heavy work is finished and at last we have a proper bathroom with all the mod cons. I've got an interior designer who did some work for my sister coming down from London to give the inside its character and we are having a hot tub built into the conservatory '

'How delightful!' exclaims Gwendolyn, successfully masking her jealousy. She has been trying to persuade Sherborne to bring St John Hall into at least the Twentieth century. The plumbing creaks and gurgles; the Aga in the kitchen was new when Agas were first invented; the furniture is old and shabby despite the fact that some pieces are valuable antiques. Sherborne calls it 'comfortable' and refuses to change a thing. The sooner I can get shot of the place, the better, thinks Gwendolyn.

'And how do you like living here in the country?' Gwendolyn asks. 'A bit quiet for you after the hectic life in London?'

'We love it,' enthuses Mitchell. 'The peace and tranquillity! The scenery!'

'I miss some of the shopping,' admits Jocasta. 'There are *so* many things you just can't *get*. But we can shop online, of course. When the broadband's working, that is.'

'And have you both retired?' Gwendolyn asks. 'You both look awfully young to have given up work?'

'No such luck,' Mitchell says. 'We're both still hard at it. But most of the time we can work from home.'

'How do you manage?'

'On line, again,' Mitchell says, 'though yes, Jocasta's right: the broadband can be a bit temperamental. We have to go up to London now and again, of course. But that gives us the chance to catch up with friends who haven't made the move yet. And to go to a show or an exhibition. You know the sort of thing.'

Gwendolyn has not been to a show or exhibition (not that that is really her thing) for many years; now she distinctly feels she has been missing out. All that will change, she thinks, when...

Crux Easton approaches carrying a tray of drinks. The Devers refresh their glasses. Gwendolyn notices Jocasta giving Crux an appreciative once-over and glares at him. He gets the message and strolls over to where Tristam Clatford is chatting to Marjory and Henry Grey.

'They do seem a nice young couple,' Marjory is saying.

'Yes, we must draw them into village life a bit more,' Henry says, 'now that they've had time to settle. I'll have a word with them. See if I can interest them in the local history. Perhaps the local folklore of the area.'

'You do that, Henry,' say Tristram. 'Let me know if you want any help.'

'Perhaps they might be interested in the Campanology Group?' Marjory suggests.

'Worth a try,' Tristram agrees. 'Go over and have a chat.'

Sherborne is bored, he always is at these things. Still, Gwendolyn seems to be enjoying herself chatting to the newcomers Mitchell Whatsisname and his very dishy wife.

Sherborne promises himself that he'll have a word with them, welcome them to the village. That sort of thing. He feels it is expected of him in a lord of the manor kind of way. Not that he really holds with that guff. Bit antiquated. He spots Long Sutton out of the corner of his eye shuffling his feet and looking miserable. He would far rather be talking to Sutton about the estate than talking to these people that he does not really like and whose company he would not automatically seek out. Let them gather once a year to drink his booze and trample his lawn and that is his duty done. Gwendolyn expects him to put on a bash and she doesn't get much fun, poor old girl. He beckons Sutton over.

'Now then, Long, how're tricks?'

'I found some snares out in the north of St John's Wood, Master Sherborne.'

'Seth Warren up to his old game? Teaching his boy Hatch the craft?'

'Didn't look like his work. These snares were a bit different, like.'

'Is it serious, Long?'

'I don't reckon so, Master Sherborne. Perhaps someone catching conies for the pot. Could be anyone.'

'Well, keep your eyes open. Maybe take a stroll in the woods at night. I won't prosecute for the odd rabbit but if it's serious we will have to take steps. Can't have the birds disturbed at this time of year.' The shoot is a useful earner for the estate.

'I'll get right on to it, Master Sherborne,' says Sutton, grateful for an excuse to make his exit.

In the beer tent Gordon Turgis is having a well earned break and Natalie Somerfield has taken over pulling the odd pint and opening the bottles of wine. Somehow Ragged Appleshaw has sneaked into the marquee as he always does on these occasions and is drinking a pint of Old Bishop's Bits. The other regulars of the St John Arms are in attendance. Having announced their presence to their host and hostess they see no reason to mingle with the other guests, none of whom they actually like.

'How's the flower business this year?' asks Paul Hartley.

'Can't complain,' says Smith, who is in fact doing very well in this mild late spring weather. 'You?'

'Terrible,' complains Hartley, who looks set for a bumper crop all round and is thinking of buying a new Range Rover – farm equipment to be offset against tax.

'Never met a happy farmer,' comments Turgis.

'Nor a happy publican,' replies Smith.

'Never a moment's peace,' grumbles Turgis.

Natalie says nothing as she wipes down the bar and washes the glasses, ready for Crux Easton to do another circuit of the guests

'So why did you go into bar-keeping?' Smith asks him.

'Better'n working for a living, eh, Gordon,' Hartley gibes.

'What do you know?'

'You should try getting up at all hours an' all weathers.'

'I thought you had old Ragged for that.'

'It's called *delegation*. Like you and Natalie there.'

'I calls it *division of labour*.'

I calls it *exploitation*, thinks Natalie, but wisely says nothing.

'Did someone offer to buy me a pint?' Appleshaw has heard his name mentioned.

'No!' they answer in unison.

'Miserable buggers,' he mutters to himself and goes back to sip his pint slowly.

Farleigh Wallop has buttonholed Mitchell who has become separated from Jocasta.

'Farleigh Wallop. Major. Retired now. Run Paintball Patrol. Corporate events, don'tcha know. What line are you in?'

'I'm in publishing, actually.'

'Read lots of books, then?'

'Er, yes.'

'Military history and such?'

'Not as such, no.'

'Big market for military history. Thinkin' of writing my memoirs.'

'Oh, really.' Mitchell stares around frantically for Jocasta and rescue; she is nowhere in sight.

With his keen military acumen Wallop senses his prey is about to retreat and casually catches hold of his sleeve.

'Saw plenty of action in my time. Paddies, Serbs, Towel Heads, Terry.'

Mitchell is immediately uncomfortable in the face of these racist epithets.

'I'm sorry. Not my area.' He tries to extricate his arm from the Major's grip but Farleigh is having none of it.

'So, know any military publishers?'

'No, I'm afraid I don't. We tend to publish literary novels and a small portfolio of poetry.'

Farleigh changes tack.

'Does your lot go in for corporate bonding? You know, team building? Out in the open air. Team on team. Combat.'

Mitchell thinks of his co-workers at the publishing house and shudders. The very idea of rampaging through the countryside splattering each other with paint in the name of 'team bonding' seems ludicrous to him. Literary luncheons with fine wines and Michelin starred catering is more to his taste.

'No. I'm sorry. I don't think so.'

'Don't say never. Here's my card. Pass it on to your boss.'

Mitchell's boss is an aesthete middle aged bluestocking with a First from Cambridge; she would rather run naked through Bloomsbury with her pubic hair dyed purple then spend a second in combat dress and a visor.

At last Mitchell spies Jocasta talking to a young woman in a sensible skirt and sensible shoes.

'Er, I just need a quick word with my wife.' He tugs his arm free and scoots off in Jocasta's direction.

'This is Marjory. She's the school teacher here in Itchen Prior,'

'Pleased to meet you,' says Mitchell. 'I've just had the most awful experience,' he says to Jocasta.

'I saw you talking to Major Wallop,' says Marjory.

'Ah, is he a friend of yours?' asks Mitchell, afraid he has committed a faux pas.

'No, don't worry,' Marjory reassures him. 'He can be a frightful old bore. Jocasta tells me you're in publishing. Did he try to sell you his memoirs?'

'Yes. As a matter of fact he did,' says Mitchell.

'No-one's ever seen them!' Marjory laughs. 'I don't really think they exist.'

'Marjory's been telling me about all sorts of village groups and societies. We must get involved, darling. Really become a part of village life.'

'Become Village People!'

The two women look at him blankly.

'Joke,' he explains. 'The Village People. *YMCA*,' he attempts to sing.

'Anyway, there's the Campanology Group....'says Jocasta. 'Marjory has been telling me all about it.'

'See what I mean,' says Mitchell triumphantly, 'the Village People.'

'It's all about bell-ringing,' explains Jocasta.

'I knew that really.'

'Have you met Henry Grey?' Marjory asks. 'He a retired academic. He wrote a book all about folklore. We call him the Village Intellectual.'

'I suppose every village has to have one, balances off with the Village Idiot' Mitchell mutters. Jocasta gives him a disapproving look. She senses Mitchell is in a skittish mood and wonders how much he has had to drink; between them Crux and Natalie are doing sterling work keeping the booze flowing.

'There are so many people we haven't met yet,' says Jocasta, 'that's why we were so glad to be invited to this party.'

'I haven't seen the Warrens,' says Mitchell, gazing round nervously.

'Er. Well, you won't. The Warrens can be a bit...' Marjory says, not wanting to speak ill of an old village family.

'Like an army of invading Huns. With hangovers.' Mitchell snaps.

'Oh,' says Marjory, 'they're not *that* bad.'

'Tell that to our builders,' says Mitchell. 'A cement mixer went missing.'

'We don't know *for sure* it was the Warrens,' says Jocasta. She doesn't want to cast aspersions on a long established village family.

'No, it might have been a roaming band of building bandits down from London on the off chance,' says Mitchell bitterly. 'That came off our bill. And set the work back a week! I learnt a lot of interesting Polish words when the builders found it missing.'

'Well, perhaps they shouldn't have left in in the front garden,' says Jocasta, still trying to pour oil on very disturbed waters.

'No. I suppose we should have kept it in the living room. With a Rottweiler chained to it.'

'Oh Mitchell. Give it a rest.' Jocasta has had enough of the Warrens.

'Look,' says Marjory, trying to change the subject, 'here's Henry coming over. I think you'll like him. He's ever so interesting.'

Grey indeed is making his way over to them, hand extended.

'Henry Grey,' he announces. 'I hear you're in publishing.' He grasps Mitchell's hand and pumps it vigorously. 'And

I believe you, my dear, are something to do with dear old Aunty?'

'Yes,' replies Jocasta. 'I'm a freelance researcher.'

'Glad to see the average IQ of the village has shot up a few notches. How do you like the place?'

'Charming,' Jocasta answers. '*So* tranquil after London. All our friends are so jealous.'

'To be honest, we can be a bit rural.' Grey sounds almost apologetic.

'So I've noticed,' says Mitchell. Jocasta gives him a Final Warning Look. 'But, on the whole, it is just what we were after' he adds hurriedly.

Crux is back with the tray; Mitchell takes fresh glasses for them all and Crux heads off back into the throng of guests, the ladies admiring his taut rear.

'That chap's got an extra finger,' Mitchell exclaims.

'Ah, yes,' says Grey. 'Comes from an old village family. 'Itchen Prior used to be a bit cut off for centuries. The gene pool tended to become a bit, shall we say, stagnant. Fascinating study.'

'Like the Warrens?' Mitchell is like a dog with a bone.

'Yes. In a way,' Grey agrees.

'*Mitchell.* JUST LEAVE IT!'

'I'm sorry, my love. I was only wondering.'

'Marjory was just telling us you're an expert on local folklore.'

'In a small way,' Grey replies in a self-deprecating tone. 'I wrote a little volume called *Traditional Country Lore*.'

'Who's your publisher?' asks Mitchell, showing a professional interest.

'Oh, just a small local publisher.' Grey doesn't like to admit it was self-published and has yet to receive a single (independent) review on Amazon. In his own review of the book, under the name of Downton Black he gave it five stars and praised it highly. To date his review has not sparked much interest but a small pile of copies are available in the village shop.

'If you are interested in local folklore, we have a gathering once a month in the classroom at the school,' says Marjory. 'And Upton gives talks to the WIs all around.'

'We mustn't miss it,' says Mitchell.

Jocasta is not sure if he is being sarcastic, but just in case he is she will make sure that they go.

After two hours of handing round stuffed vol-au-vents and prawn tartlets and snaffling the odd surreptitious drink, Sally resolves to confront Gwendolyn, who is talking to a group from the WI.

'Can I have a word?'

Gwendolyn is more than happy to escape.

'Has the food run out?' Gwendolyn asks. 'The caterers assured me that there would be enough to feed the five thousand.'

'It's not that,' Sally says. 'It's Crux.'

'Looking unusually fine today, don't you think?'

'He's mine!' hisses Sally.

'My dear girl, what *do* you mean' asks Gwendolyn, genuinely mystified.

'He's my boyfriend. I love him.'

'You silly girl! He belongs to the stables. He's part of the estate and that means he belongs to *me*.'

'You can't have him, you old witch. You're old enough to be his mother.'

It is the use of the word 'old' that particularly stings Gwendolyn.

'Listen you little trollop,' she says, with a fierce glare. 'Our mutual friend Crux knows a good thing when he sees it and he's not about to walk away. Where would he go? With his criminal record, where would he get a job? I'd see him blacklisted throughout the county.'

'You can't do that.'

'Oh, I assure you I can. Look around you at these people. That's Influence. We *are* the county.'

She may be Gwendolyn St John, lady of the manor but she used to be Gwennie Abbas, Village Scrubber, and she knows how to fight dirty. It is not as if she is particularly attached to Crux; there would be - and she knows it - plenty more eager young men to step into his shoes and her knickers and take his place in the bed in the studio; she's sometimes thought she might go for something more exotic next time.

At that moment Crux passes with his tray of glasses three-quarters full of wine. Sally snatches one and flings its contents - a rather good 2012 Californian merlot (the long, warm, growing season that year created a supple wine with a ripe, rich flavor) - into Gwendolyn's face.

'You nasty old bitch!' yells Sally.

Gwendolyn wipes her face with her hand. Crux stands frozen. He has no idea what has happened, but he knows it doesn't look good.

'*Get out,*' Gwendolyn barks at Sally. 'You can forget your wages. And if I see you anywhere on this estate I will prosecute you for trespass. And as for you,' she turns on Crux, 'I'll speak to you later.'

'What am *I* supposed to have done?' Crux protests.

'You'll find out soon enough,' Gwendolyn says, then turns with a glorious elegant sweep to Sally. 'Now *you* get out of my sight before I have you physically thrown out.'

The realisation of what she has done hits Sally and she flees, sobbing.

Gwendolyn, with great aplomb, returns the the circle of WI ladies.

'She must have the painters in,' she explains.

The WI ladies, post menopausal to a woman, nod sagely.

In the beer tent Paul Hartley finishes his sixth pint and decides that is time for a well earned slash.

'Gorra see a man about a dog,' he tells Smith.

'No stamina. Thatza trouble,' Smith slurs at him and weaves to the bar for a refill, knocking over a chair on his way.

'Bugger'em,' Hartley growls, suddenly feeling belligerent. He staggers his way to the portaloos that have been discreetly set up a short distance behind the beer tent. Gwendolyn has learnt from previous garden parties to on no account allow the good folk of Itchen Prior to use the facilities in the Hall. An unfortunate discovery in a Ming Dynasty vase in the entrance hall two years ago was the last straw. Alice Lacey, Wednesday and Saturday, has still not managed to entirely dispel the vague odour.

And it is with thoughts of the fragrant Alice Lacey on his mind that Hartley spies his bitter rival for her love.

'Awright, General,' he calls. 'Howza playing at soldiers?'

Farleigh Wallop is an abstemious drinker but takes his paintballing seriously.

'It's called *team building*. Something you'd know nothing about. You're drunk.'

'What if I am. At least I'm happy.' But then he realises that he is not; he will not be happy until Alice Lacey becomes Alice Hartley. The drink overcomes his inhibitions and unleashes his hitherto unspoken rivalry with Farleigh Wallop.

'An' a 'nother thing. Stay away from Alice. She's mine.'

'The lady is no such thing. She has far more taste than to take up with a drunken sot like you.'

'Who you callin' a drunken sot?'

'Look at your self, man. You can hardly stand. You're a disgrace. I'd put you on a charge if you were in my unit.'

'Yeah, well I not. Thank God.'

'On your way. Go on.'

'Don' you tell me what to do, you old shit.' Hartley takes a step nearer to Wallop and bunches his fists. 'I'll show you.'

He swings his fist at Wallop who easily dodges the punch. Hartley's momentum swings him around and he loses balance and topples to the ground. He feels a sudden release and a warmth spreading down his trousers.

'Oh hell. I wet meself.'

Farleigh Wallop walks away whistling a victory march. He knows the story will be all around the village by morning. Alice Lacey will be his for the asking.

That evening Sherborne St John and Gwendolyn are eating a light supper in the gloomy dining room of St John Hall. The guests have departed. Tomorrow the contractors will come to take away the portaloos and Long Sutton and Crux Easton will dismantle the marquee and beer tent.

'I think that went well, old girl. Don't you?'

Gwendolyn smiles through gritted teeth.

'Yes, darling. Like it does every year.' This will be the last, she promises herself. She loathes all the people tramping about her lawn and swigging down any profit that the estate might make. Yes. This year will *definitely* be the last.

13

It is nine pm on Friday - pay day at Itchen Prior Horticultural. The front of house staff, the cashiers and the nurseryman, those who are legitimately employed and pay National Insurance and PAYE have been paid and have gone home. Now it is the turn of the four Bosnian students. They are crowded into the small office in the rear of the main building. Jed Smith hands out four old fashioned brown pay envelopes.

'There must be some mistake, Mister Smith,' says Nevena Stolac. 'It says £53. It should be at least £85 after we pay rent.'

'No. that's right, Nevena,' says Smith. 'Short week.'

'What do you mean 'short week'?' demands Mirko Knin. 'We worked a full week. From six in morning to six at evening.'

'Yes. But production levels are down,' explains Smith. 'The strawberries are not quite ripe and the rush for daffodils is over. Right now your work is just maintenance. Non productive, you see.'

'But still we work twelve hours,' objects Jagoda Doboj.

'No, no. It's all about productivity,' Smith insists. He thinks he is explaining this perfectly reasonably; why can't these bloody foreigners understand?

'We have contract,' says Vukodin Punta.

'Yes,' Smith agrees, 'but no work permits, unfortunately.'

'That is not our fault. You told agent you would arrange.'

'He must have misunderstood. And you did enter Britain in the back of a lorry!'

'Then give us back our passports and we go back home,' says Jagoda.

'Well, you see, I can't do that.' Smith is not at all apologetic. 'As you say, you have a contract to work for me until the end of the summer.'

'*Stanje!*' says Vukodin.

'*Jebo te!*' Nevena adds.

'What was that?' demands Smith, although he has a pretty good idea.

'Nothing,' says Mirko.

Their situation is hopeless. Smith has them over a barrel.

'At least reduce the rent for those horrible caravans,' Joagoda suggests.

'Oh, I can't do that either. That's part of the contract, see.'

'You are not a good man, Mister Smith. You are a cheat and a liar.'

'And right now I'm your boss, so take your pay and get out.'

Left with no option, the four young Bosnians troop back to the broken-down caravans. They sit in the boys' caravan, cramped up on the two beds with their thin mattresses.

'What are we going to do?' says Vukodin, in his native Serbo-Croat.

'What *can* we do. That bastard has got us trapped. We can't go to the authorities because we are not supposed to be here. He has our passports so we can't get home and we haven't got much money to buy tickets anyway. We're screwed.'

'We fight back. Remember the Partisans! We fight back!' says Mirko.

'How?' asks Jagoda.

'Sabotage! Theft!'

'How?' Jagoda asks again.

'We will find a way. For the moment Vukodin and I will go back to the woods and catch food. That rabbit we caught was good, wasn't it? We live off the land and save our money. Austerity is the plan. And somehow we stick it to that bastard Smith.'

'We could go on strike,' suggests Nevena.

'No,' says Mirko. 'We don't go *on* strike. We *strike back*!'

'Yea,' they all cheer, fired by the spirit of resistance.

14

St John's Wood covers over two hundred acres of the St John estate. It is a mix of ancient deciduous woodland and managed woods. Since the time of the Tudors a Sutton has done the managing on behalf of the St John family. The large spinney brings the estate a healthy income from timber and game birds, slaughtered on the annual shoot for a very nice fee per gun and sales to up market providers of game. In recent years Sherborne has added a small herd of semi-wild fallow deer, not enough to cause serious damage to the trees but enough to make life interesting, notwithstanding complaints from Paul Hartley who is worried about depredation to his crops.

Long Sutton has known these woods since he was a small boy, in the days when his uncle was the keeper. He loves the woods and he loves the wildlife even though part of his job is to keep the birds alive long enough to be blown to bits.

But at this moment he is not a happy man; snares have been set at the warrens on the edges of the woods and the word 'Warren' is uppermost in his thoughts.

Just as the Suttons have always managed the wood, the Warrens have always poached them. Over the years an understanding has evolved; don't be greedy and take too much and the 'keeper will turn a blind eye. Recently, however, Seth has been turning his attentions to other forms of nefarious income and left the woods alone. Now he seems to be back. With a vengeance. Sutton will have none of it. The odd snare, fair enough. Rabbits are pests, when all is said and done. But the birds are sacrosanct and the snares have started to appear in the woods.

Long Sutton hammers on the door of the Warren's cottage where the skeleton of an old Ford Anglia rusts away on its plinth of bricks like a piece of art from the Tate Modern.

'Hello, Long.' says Seth, answering the door wearing a pair of striped pyjama bottoms and a wife-beater vest. He has not had a shave for several days and is unlikely to have had a bath recently either. 'What can I do for you?'

'You can lay off, that's what, Seth Warren.'

Seth is mystified. He tries to think back to anything any member of the tribe might have done to upset Long Sutton and can think of nothing.

'Give us a clue.'

'Don't come the innocent with me,' Long Sutton thunders.

'I really don't know what you are talking about.'

'Who is it, Seth?' Ashley Warren calls from indoors.

'It's Long Sutton.'

'What's he want?'

'Buggered if I know.'

Sutton is standing on the doorstep tapping his foot in its hobnailed boot. He discarded the button up gaiters at Sherborne's insistence some years ago as too feudal and antiquated; he has not felt really properly dressed since.

'I'm talking about the snares, as if you didn't know.'

'Nothing to do with me,' Seth says automatically and then thinks it over. 'Really. Long. Nothing to do with me. I ain't been up the woods since I don't know when.'

'What about your boy, then?'

'Hatch?'

'Him.'

Seth thinks about it. Hatch is a law unto himself, as are all the Warrens, but Seth has seen no evidence of poaching. That's my lad, he thinks proudly. Never leave no evidence.

'Naw. He's a good lad, he is. Law abiding.'

They both know this is a blatant lie but Sutton has no proof to the contrary.

'So what snares are these, then?' Seth asks, the picture, on this occasion, of innocence.

'Someone's been setting snares in my woods and you Warrens have got form.'

'Not me, Long. I'm not in the frame for this one.'

'Well, just take this as a warning. I've got me eye on you. And that lad of yorn.'

Feeling a righteous job righteously done, Long Sutton walks back to his beloved woods, whistling.

Seth goes back into the cottage.

'What did he want, then, Seth?' asks Ashley.

'Some nonsense about me poaching his precious woods?'

'An' were yer? You've not brought nothing back for the pot as I've seen.'

'Nah. Given me an idea, though,' he says thoughtfully.

15

By the end of June, Yew Tree Cottage is transformed: the garden designer has worked his magic. Where there was a wilderness, money has spoken. A latticework porch now frames the front doorway with jasmine threaded through it. 'Lovely scent in the warm evenings' the garden designer assured them. Flower beds have been dug and planted with euphorbia, peonies, lupins and geraniums, with edgings of violas and pansies. It is a picture. Mitchell and Jocasta are ecstatic with the result and plan to invite all their London friends down to see it and to make them insanely jealous.

Seth Warren is standing at the gate in the new wall that now protects the front garden. The chocolate Labrador puppy ('Bartholomew') that the Devers have settled on in lieu of the chickens, goats and alpaca that reality has made them realise was a fantasy, barks and yelps in frantic excitement. Mitchell comes around the garden to see what all the fuss is about. He spies Seth and moves warily, like a man surrounded by a pack of hungry wolves on the Siberian tundra.

'You awright, boss?' Seth greets him as if they were life-long friends.

'What can I do for you?' Mitchell asks suspiciously.

'It's what I can do for you,' Seth replies, a broad smile of innocent bonhomie on his face.

'And that is…?'

'Natalie Somerfield down the village shop tells me your missus is forever asking her for all sorts of posh food that there is no call for here in the village.'

This is true; Jocasta persisted in asking Natalie for items like walnut oil, Kalamata olives, anchovies, wholemeal bread flour, kimchi and oyster sauce. All to no avail and to Natalie's utter confusion. Jocasta has given up and either orders on line or goes up to London for shopping expeditions to Waitrose or Marks.

'Yes?' Mitchell has no idea where this is going.

'I reckon I can do you a favour.'

'Really? In what way?' Mitchell is guarded; the last time Seth Warren did him a favour it ended up costing him ten pounds.

'Your missus likes fancy cooking, does she?'

'Jocasta is a very good cook. She went to lessons with some very good chefs. Michelin starred.'

Seth wouldn't know what a Michelin star was if it bit him on the bottom but that doesn't stop him.

'Would she be interested in game?'

'Game? What sort of game.'

These bloody townies really have no clue what day it is, thinks Seth. Speaking very slowly so that Mitchell can keep up he says:

'Not a *game* like. It's what we here in the country call rabbits, an' pheasants an' such.'

'Yes,' says Mitchell testily. 'I know what game is. I asked, what *sort* of game.'

'Oh, yeah, right you are. I meant rabbits an' pheasants an' such. Mebbe a bit o' venison.

'Why?' Mitchell trusts Seth about as far as he could throw Waterloo Station.

'I might be able to help you out.'

Mitchell is less than convinced that he wants Seth Warren to help him out with anything.

'At a very reasonable price,' says Seth as if this was the deal clincher.

'I'll have a word with Jocasta and let you know.'

'Fair enough, but don't hang about, the season don't last forever.'

'I'll let you know,' Mitchell repeats. He makes a lunge for the puppy that is dancing round his legs, scoops it up and retreats into the house. Moments later he is peeping out of the front window to make sure Seth is not stealing anything before he goes.

'Ungrateful sod,' Seth mutters as he goes back home.

16

Crux Easton is under a cloud. Gwendolyn is less than impressed to find out she has been sharing his services with a rival and is determined to keep him on a tight rein, literally if necessary. Long Sutton is under orders to shoot to kill if he finds Sally Fairfax anywhere on the estate, an order he has taken with a bucket of salt. Crux creeps out of the studio soon after midnight; he knows that even Gwendolyn is unlikely - or fairly unlikely, anyway - to come amorously calling this late. He phones Sally on his mobile.

'Oh, it's you, is it?' she answers.

'It's not my fault.'

'Then whose is it?'

'Let's not fight, Sally. You know I love you.'

'You're *having sex with her!* I can't deal with it no more.'

'It's part of the job description. You don't think I *like* it do you?'

'It's her or me,' she says emphatically.

'You don't mean that. I love you.'

'Then stop seeing her.'

'How can I? I work on the estate. I have to see her every day.'

'Then tell Mister St John.'

'Are you out of your mind? He'd never believe me. And she'd kill me. And then fire me. Where could I go? I'm trapped.'

'That's for you to sort out. You say you love me; prove it!'

'I could play the Lottery. That might do it.'

'Pigs might fly.'

'Well what then?'

'I don't know,' says Sally, 'but I'm not going on like this. There are plenty more fish in the sea.'

'Not in this village there ain't. Who do you fancy? Hatch Warren?'

'With Hare Warren on the loose. I'm not mad.'

'Listen, why don't we meet up and have a proper talk. Face to face, like. You never know what might come up!'

'Not if that bitch has been riding you it won't,' she says.

'Don't be like that. Look, we could meet up in the woods. Away from the house. At night.'

She begins to soften: she does really love Crux and doesn't want to lose him. And a midnight, moonlit tryst *does* sound romantic. Providing it doesn't rain.

'When?'

'A couple of day's time. I'll phone you. I love you.'

'Bye!'

'Bye!'

He creeps back to the studio apartment in the stable block and opens the door. To his horror he sees Gwendolyn lying on the bed in her riding gear.

'Where have you been, you naughty boy!' She gives the mattress a hard thwack with her riding crop.

'Naughty boys must be punished!'

Crux gives a small moan of terror as she pulls him down onto the bed.

17

After his contretemps with Paul Hartley at the estate garden party Farleigh Wallop is uncertain about the future of his business partnership. It would be typical of Hartley to cancel their arrangement, cutting off his nose to spite his face. The face in this case being Wallop's. Although they have a legal contract leasing Wallop the use of the land for Paintball Patrol and the mock Afghan village, Wallop knows that Hartley is an unscrupulous swine and far from being a gentleman. Unlike Wallop, who is both an officer *and* a gentleman. Measures must be taken. Forward planning, that's the military way. Outguess your enemy and take him unawares. Undermine his morale. That's the way to do it. Sadly. Farleigh Wallop was never selected for staff college so the finer nuances of strategy escape him. He must resort to low cunning; the kind Hartley is a master of.

If the Afghan village is Plan A, his USP, then he must come up with Plan B. What do other paintball businesses offer? Free style open air combat. Infantry versus infantry in swift moving action. Stalking and killing. The hunter in his (or even, nowadays, her) natural element. The Native American (why did they stop being Red Indians?) moving silently through the Great North Woods to strike their enemies unawares. The bold Forgotten Army fighting the Japs in the jungles of Burma or Myanmar or whatever it is called now. Or the classic jungle of Nam. That's the thing. St John's Wood. Surely Sherborne St John would be up for it for the same cut as he gives Hartley. St John is a decent chap, after all. Salt of the earth. Yeoman stock made good. Thoroughly good fellow.

Intelligence. That's what is needed. A reconnaissance is called for.

18

For three nights now the Bosnians have been secretly stripping the caravans of anything they deem useful and hiding it in a tiny clearing that Mirko and Vukodin found in an ancient part of St John's Wood. They have also stolen various gardening tools; spades, forks, twine, poles and plastic sheeting from the garden centre. They have not been getting much sleep but nor have they been working with much effort during the day.

It is one o'clock in the morning when they begin the long hike to their new home. They are laden down like a soldier in the Great War with backpacks containing their clothes. Mattresses and sleeping bags rolled up and bound with twine slung over their shoulders. The two men also carry cylinders of calor gas while Nevena carries the ring. The weather is warm and they will not need a wood fire, while calor does not produce any betraying smoke. Jagoda is festooned with pots and pans wrapped in clothes to stifle any noise.

An hour's hard walking through the wood along a path they re now familiar with gets them to their lair where the gear they shifted earlier is hidden. Swiftly they rig up a shelter from the plastic sheeting and poles, partially hidden by bushes and overhanging branches. Satisfied that the camp is not immediately obvious to the casual observer the two men leave the women to settle in before they make

the return trip to the garden centre; there is one more
thing they must do.

19

Jed Smith becomes aware that something may be amiss when the noise of the sirens wake him up. He stumbles out of bed and draws the curtain. He sees the smoke coming from the direction of the garden centre and frantically pulls on some clothes. He is halfway out of the door when he realises he is not wearing shoes and has to stop and struggle into a pair of old trainers he keeps by the back door. His bungalow sits a short distance along the road from the garden centre from where he can now, clearly, see smoke and flames in the early light. He runs faster than he has run in years and arrives wheezing and gasping and cursing a lifelong smoking habit of twenty a day.

The fire engine has ploughed up the nursery beds and fire fighters are busily trampling down what is left of the summer plantings. They direct their hoses at the burning caravans that hiss and crackle under the jets of water; they are totally destroyed.

'Are you the owner, sir?' asks Cliff Maybank, the Fire Chief.

'Yes,' Sutton gasps, beginning to feel the effects of shock. 'Itchen Prior Horticultural,' he adds inconsequentially.

'Lucky someone saw this and phoned it in.'

'Who?'

'Didn't leave a name, sir. Anybody using the caravans?'

Oh yes, thinks Smith. Like I'm going to tell you I had four illegal immigrants living there and working for less than the minimum wage. I don't think so.

'No.' Oh God, what if there are four charred bodies inside. No, they must have got out, mustn't they? But what if? He needs a get-out.

'Somebody might have broken in. A homeless person.'

'What, here in Itchen Prior? In Westleigh perhaps, but it's highly unlikely you'd get homeless people out here in the sticks,' says Maybank, puzzled.

'Well I don't know. As far as I know the caravans were empty. They're old. Been here for years. Not really fit to live in.' And that's the truth. *Please* don't let there be any crispy corpses in the ruins; that would be awkward to say the least.

'Clear, boss,' a fire fighter calls.

'Anything?'

'No, but I'd put money on arson.'

'Where they insured?' the Fire Chief asks, suspicion dark in his voice.

Smith is stunned; he hadn't thought of that.

'No,' he replies indignantly. 'Like I said, they were basically wrecks.'

'You made any enemies, Mister…?' Maybank asks.

'Smith, Jed Smith.'

'As I said, you made any enemies?'

'No,' says Smith, all wounded innocence. Those ungrateful bastards, he thinks.

'There will have to be a proper investigation. If it was arson, we'll have to file a police report.'

Smith sinks into a world of hurt. His business will not stand up to close investigation. The regular staff know about the seasonal illegals he employs each year, bribes might be necessary. And Natalie Somerfield has served them in the village shop. Altogether too many people know his business. And, oh please, don't let the ladies and gentlemen from HMRC start poking their noses in where they are not welcome.

He stands among the pools of water in the trampled flower beds with the stink of smoke and burnt plastic in the air and starts to cry.

Mirko and Vukodin are back in the woods in their cosy bivouac. They smell faintly of smoke and paraffin.

'That'll give the *psihopata* something to think about,' says Mirko. *Psihopata* is Serbo-Croat for 'psychopath.'

'Strike one,' Jagoda smiles.

20

The night is a perfect, warm night at the end of the month of June and the moon is beginning to wane. Seth Warren and his son, Hatch, armed with small wooden stakes and lengths of thin wire, steal into St John's Wood. Their purpose is nefarious. Like Long Sutton, they have spent a lifetime exploring these woods. As the Suttons have always been gamekeepers, the Warrens have traditionally been poachers, although in recent years Seth has not been a regular in the woods. Sutton's visit and warning-off has kindled atavistic urges in Seth and he feels it is high time to initiate the next generation into the art. Hare, much to her anger, has been left behind on this occasion and is making Ashley's life a misery with the queen of a teenaged strop. Deafening heavy metal is shaking her room and Ashley has to turn the television to top volume to watch her recorded reality show. The noise is keeping the Devers awake but Mitchell is disinclined to venture a complaint. Seth rightly thinks this will establish an alibi should he be challenged as to his whereabouts.

'Yer pheasant is a suspicious bugger,' Seth tells his son. 'Soon as they hear you, they're off. But they're ground birds, see, so we got to find their scrapes where they are nesting an' fix our traps nearby. Old Long keeps his eyes open, so we got to be so much smarter. An' quiet as the grave. So when we gets in, no speaking. Watch my hands for signals.'

Hatch nods. 'What we going to do with them as we catch, Pa?'

'Neck 'em, son.'

'Yeah, I ain't stupid. But then what?'

'Sell 'em to those daft townies what moved in down the lane.'

'I thought you told Ma they weren't keen.'

'That was the bloke. I reckon I can talk his missus into it. Tell her they're real country food. A delicate, like. She's daft enough to go for it.'

'How much, then?'

'Tenner a bird.'

'Nice one, Pa.'

'Now shut up an' follow me. Keep your eyes an' ears open. We don't want to run into old Long Sutton. 'He wouldn't take kindly to a bit of free enterprise.'

21

Not far away from where Seth and Hatch are stalking through the woods, Crux Easton meets Sally Fairfax. He has been forced to dine on mutton and now he fancies some lamb. He feels as randy as a stoat and cannot wait to drag Sally onto some handy mossy bank where the wild thyme blows and oxlips and the nodding violets grow. Actually, as long as it isn't overgrown with brambles and poison ivy and is tolerably dry, he's not that fussy.

They kiss and Sally strokes his buttocks. Crux winces in pain. He still has the welts of his last encounter with Gwendolyn.

'Oh my poor baby,' says Sally but he cannot tell if her sympathy is genuine.

It isn't.

'Serves you right' she says, pushing him away.

'It's *not my fault!*' he says.

'Then whose fault is it. I told you. It has to stop if you want to stay with me.'

'Of course I want to stay with you. I love you.'

'You've got a funny way of showing it.'

'Come here an' I'll show you right now,' he says, his voice suddenly thick with lust.

'Patience, lover boy, patience. We need to talk.'

'Talk later. Shag first!'

'No, no, no. I'm serious. We need to talk.'

'Well let's take a walk in the woods and then we can discuss it,' he suggests. And look for somewhere suitable for a little lie down, he thinks. He takes her by the hand and half pulls her into the shelter of the trees. Feigning reluctance, she allows herself to be led. If the truth be told, she is not averse to a little nooky under the stars. A girl has needs too.

They follow a path into the woods halting now and again for an encouraging canoodle. Crux knows his luck is in and he is on a promise. He spies a perfect spot and pulls her down to him.

'So what are you going to do?' she asks, deliberately spoiling the mood. He is in no mood to have the mood spoiled.

'Whatever you like,' he promises.

'Really?'

'Really. Now take your jeans off!'

'Some one might come,' she says coyly. Crux is hoping that that someone will be him.

'Not here. Not at this time of night.' He pulls his tee shirt over his head and starts to wriggle out of his trousers.

Minutes later, in the throes of passion she digs her nails into his bottom.

He screams.

'What was that?' asks Hatch Warren in an alarmed whisper.

'Dunno. Didn't sound like no animal I know.' Seth whispers back. 'Let's get outta here.'

22

Long Sutton is out prowling 'his' woods. He *knows* Seth Warren is up to no good. He is determined to catch Warren in the act of taking game and he will haul him up before the magistrate. Who just happens to be Sherborne St John. He hears the scream. Sutton knows every sound and cry, every bark, peep, whistle, trill, squeak, squawk, chatter, grunt, pipe and howl uttered by the denizens of the wood and this is not one he has heard before in his many years as a gamekeeper.

He sets off in the direction of the scream.

In accordance with Plan B Farleigh Wallop is on a night reckie for his new Jungle Fighter Experience. He is wearing camouflage smock and trousers (genuine Army Surplus), a black balaclava, rubber soled boots and black gloves. His face is covered in black face paint. He is carrying a stubby paintball marker set on rapid fire and he is living a Special Forces fantasy as he darts from tree cover to tree cover. Even if he does not lose the land he leases from Hartley he decides to integrate the Jungle Fighter Experience into the Paintball Patrol portfolio of adventure. 'Fight Terry Taliban by Day; Fight Charlie Viet Cong by Night!'

Oh yes.

He stops periodically to take aim at invisible targets, crouching and sighting along his weapon. He is fit and agile for a man of his age but right now he is a little boy playing at war.

He hears the scream and freezes. What the hell, he thinks and considers making off swiftly in the opposite direction.

'Pull your self together, man,' he says out loud. 'What would the SAS do?'

He sets off in a series of spurts from cover to cover in the direction of the scream.

Much deeper in the woods Jagoda, a light sleeper, wakes up. She dreamt she heard a wolf howl but that was just a dream, surely? There are no wolves in Britain, she is fairly sure. She turns over and goes back to sleep.

Crux Easton, buck naked, is hopping in pain. All thoughts of consummation extinguished. Sally Fairfax, also naked, is rolling on the ground in fits of laughter. This is not doing a lot for Crux's hurt feelings, not to mention his lacerated bottom. He manages to stub his toe on a rock, grab his foot in his hand, topple over, land on his bottom, leap up again from the pain there and falls on his face, banging his nose, which he now cups with his other hand

'Please stop,' Sally gasps, clutching her aching side, 'I can't stand any more.'

'Iz not bloody funny,' Crux is nearly in tears.

'Oh it is, it is.' Sally *is* actually in tears.

'You're a heartless bitch!' he shouts.

They are making so much noise and are so preoccupied that they are unaware of Long Sutton's approach.

Sutton has seen many strange things in the woods and has observed the mating rituals of many of God's creatures but this is a first for him. Why is Crux dancing on one leg and holding his nose and foot in his hands? Is this something peculiar (in every sense) to the younger generation?

'What are you up to?' he demands.

Still sobbing with laughter, Sally makes a lunge for her clothes and rolls onto her stomach to belatedly protect her modesty.

'I banged me foot an' then I banged me nose,' Crux explains.

'You're bollock naked,' says Sutton, stating the very obvious.

'We were just…' says Crux and then realises it is pointless trying to find an excuse.

'I can see what you were 'just',' says Sutton and then adds, 'them's nasty marks on yer arse. Looks like you been horsewhipped.'

He has a shrewd idea who inflicted the damage. He has seen many a stable lad walking gingerly over the years. She's a terrible woman, he thinks for maybe the thousandth time, leading poor Mister Sherborne a dance like that. Something's got to be done about her.

Crux has stopped jigging about and starts to get dressed when he screams again. A large blue stain appears on the fly of his underpants. He clutches his groin and falls down again. Moaning. This is really not his night.

Other paint blotches hit Sutton and Sally.

Farleigh Wallop materialises out of the trees.

'I'm sorry. Instinctive reaction. Honed military skills.'

What he means is that he was so surprised to see a half naked nymph (Sally) in the woods his finger squeezed the trigger of its own accord and involuntarily ejaculated a burst of paintballs.

'And what are *you* up to, you soft bugger?' Long Sutton demands, not a happy bunny for being shot at in his own woods. 'Look at the mess you've made.'

'It'll wash out,' says Farleigh lamely.

'But what are you doing here, creeping around in the middle of the night playing at daft sod soldiers?'

'It's a new idea for Paintball Patrol,' Farleigh explains.

'What, going round shooting innocent folk all unsuspecting like?'

'It was an accident. Anyway, those two were naked.'

'Doesn't give you leave to hunt 'em.'

'It was a shock,' Farleigh explains

'It was a shock all right. Nearly gave me a heart attack. Don't do it again,' Sutton warns him.

'What's that!' Sally suddenly shouts. She is still topless with splashes of blue paint trickling down her impressive breasts. She points into the trees where she has seen the flash of a white face.

There comes a crashing in the undergrowth as something large starts to move swiftly followed by a stream of swearing as Seth, for it is he, trips over a root and twists his ankle.

Quick as a ferret down a rabbit hole, Long Sutton dives into the bushes and drags him out.

'It's like Westleigh bus station on a Saturday (the most crowded thing Sutton can imagine) in here tonight,' he says in wonder. 'And just what are *you* doing here?'

'She a fine-looking girl,' Seth explains. 'I were just admiring the view.'

'So you just so happened to be takin' a midnight stroll in the woods hoping to get an eyeful of some nudie woman who just happened to be lying down with her kit off?' Sutton is not usually strong on sarcasm but tonight he is buzzing.

'Sommat like that, yeah.'

'Is that a poacher's coat you're wearing. One with deep pockets on the inside?'

'A man can wear what he like, can't he?'

'Turn 'em out!'

By great good fortune Seth has given the pheasant they found in one of Mirko's snares to Hatch to take home to Ashley. Seth's fall and capture has given Hatch time to make his escape. Seth instilled in his son the first rule of criminality: don't get caught and if the other bugger does, leg it for home. Hatch has done just that.

'See,' says Seth triumphantly, 'nowt.'

'The moon's just off the full but the place is still full of nutters. Get lost, the lot of you an' if I sees any of you running about in my woods at night I'll take the shotgun to you. Now go on, get lost!'

23

Jocasta and Mitchell have sent out invitations to their official housewarming for the first weekend in July with the enigmatic instructions to '*bring swimwear*'. All will be revealed to the guests when the Devers unveil their pride and joy – the eight-seater hot tub on the newly erected patio decking. Sharing pride of place is the rotating garden pod, bought on-line from John Lewis. The garden is a riot of buddleia, lilac and verbena to attract butterflies; where old Penton Mewsley had allowed the garden to revert to a wilderness the Devers' garden designer – Dennis 'Possibilities' Jackson – has torn it down and replaced it with very expensive artificial meadow grown on a roll of wire. The effect is much the same as Mewsley had achieved by studious neglect. A water feature ambles through the bottom of the one-acre garden, crossed by a Chinese bridge. This has been carefully aligned to maximise the positive aspects of the feng sui. A statue of the Buddha lurks in a stand of bamboo beside a 'rustic' bench made out of old railways sleepers.

Inside, the old Aga has been replaced by a new version; a wood burner stands ready to heat the lounge in the winter. A neat pile of chopped wood (bought from Seth Warren by Jocasta (much against Mitchell's better judgement) and stolen from St John's wood is stacked outside. A comfortable corner unit in brown cord throws its arms around the lounge facing the 52' curved smart TV. Sadly, broadband reception is not all that it might be.

The Devers have invited a selection of village worthies (but DEFINITELY NOT the Warrens) and their former neighbours from London so they can show off their new home and preen.

Auguste and Ann Marie Cuthbertson and their two children, Maud (12) and Thomas (13) arrive first. They are both lecturers at the Institute for Middle and Far Eastern Studies. Auguste is an expert on Middle Period Akkadian and Ann Marie on Song Dynasty Court Painting. They take themselves seriously, as befits academics and intellectuals. They are both forty-somethings; he tall, slightly balding and in a tweed jacket; she plump and with a head of corkscrew curls beginning to go grey. The two children are welded to their smart phones and wear smart trainers.

Mitchell has fired up the barbie; a trestle table covered in a white cloth (a souvenir from a weekend break in Tallinn) sags under the weight of salads, breads, cheeses, coleslaw, pickles, relishes, fruit and all the assorted party snacks Marks and Waitrose can offer. Mitchell has managed to negotiate with Gordon Turgis for a barrel of Old Bishop's on the understanding that he, Mitchell, should collect and return the barrel himself.

Coolers of white wine, both still and fizzy, are perched on a second table that also holds bottles of red and a huge assortment of glasses and soft drinks for the designated drivers: this does not apply to the good folks of Itchen Prior but the Londoners might be more squeamish about drink driving.

Gwendolyn St John arrives alone and makes her apologies for Sherborne.

'He's a bit under the weather,' she explains. Hopefully with something terminal, she thinks, but suspects it is, disappointingly, just a summer cold. She ohhs and ahhs appropriately and assures the Devers they have performed miracles. She holds up a tiny bag.

'What is the mystery about the swimwear?'

Jocasta leads her off to the garden at the rear of the house'

'A hot tub!' Gwendolyn squeals in genuine envy. 'How divine.'

'And we've got just the weather for it,' says Jocasta. Indeed, they could not have asked for better. The last few days have been something of a heat wave with endless blue cloudless skies. The buddleia is fulfilling its promise and the garden is a haven for butterflies; bees buzz in the meadow. Bartholomew the chocolate lab ('Bart" to his owners) is running around in a frenzy.

Tristram Clatford arrives with Marjory Hinton Daubry and Upton Grey, who seem to form something of a Trinity at village events.

Mitchell introduces them to the Cuthbertsons.

'This is Tristram, our vicar; Marjory our school teacher and Henry our resident academic.' This piques the Cuthbertsons' interest.

'*Dr* Auguste Cuthbertson. Akkadian.'

Grey has no idea what he is talking about but smiles vaguely as he shakes Auguste's hand.

'You might have seen my television programme *Hammu-rabi the Law Maker*. It was on BBC Four. On a Thursday. At 11.30.'

'Er,' says Grey.

'*Dr* Ann Marie Cuthbertson. Song Court painting.' She is a bit miffed that she has not joined the ranks of the academic glitterati TV stars and has not yet been offered a television contract. She resents her husband's taste of fame.

Grey wonders whether Song Court was their address but dismisses the thought as unlikely. Why would you need to have a doctorate to be a house painter? Or maybe she is an eccentric GP? He is confused.

'And what's your game?' asks Auguste.

'I'm sorry?'

'I mean, what was your academic field?'

'Oh,' says Grey, 'folkloric studies. Of England. That sort of thing. I'm retired now.'

'Fascinating,' says Ann Marie and turns to the other two. 'Much call for religion out here? We are terribly secular nowadays, aren't we?'

'We manage,' says Clatford icily. 'You would be surprised.'

'Haven't Mitchell and Jocasta done well?' says Marjory, trying to change the subject. 'It was in such a state when the bought it. You'd hardly recognise the place.'

'Yes, they put 'before and after' pictures on Facebook,' says Auguste.

'Oh look,' says Ann Marie, grabbing her husband by the arm. 'Here are Toby and Rachel.'

The newcomers are also erstwhile neighbours from London. The Cuthbertsons shoot off to greet them and escape from the 'rustics'.

'So what's all this about swimming, Mitchell?' asks Marjory. 'I've brought my costume. This is *most* mysterious.'

'We are going to christen the hot tub,' says Mitchell.

'Oh, so I'm here in a professional capacity, am I?' laughs Clatford.

'Go through the house and into the garden. Jocasta has enough booze and snacks to feed an army. And talking of an army, here's Farleigh.'

More people arrive from the village and from London, mingle, divide, form tribes, consume food and drink. The smoke from the barbeque rises to heaven.

24

One person from Itchen Prior who is absent despite receiving an invitation is Jed Smith.

He awoke three days ago to find a note pushed under his door. It read:

You have our passports. We want them back. You have cheated us of our pay. We want one thousand pounds each. When we have these things we will leave England and go home. If you do not do these things then bad things can happen.

The note is unsigned but Smith knows exactly who it is from. He has no intention of forking out four grand to these idle layabouts and is toying with the idea of burning their passports. But like all bullies when the victim turns he is afraid; he has not had a proper night's sleep since receiving the note.

The Fire Service have returned a report of possible arson and Sergeant Barton Stacy has been round for a chat. Fortunately, he and Stacy go back a long way and Smith has managed to implicate some travellers who passed through recently; Stacy, who indeed knows Smith very well, has a niggling suspicion of an insurance scam but decides that it is not worth the time, effort and expense to pursue so pretends to be content with that and has not made much of an effort to interview the garden centre staff, who were pleasantly surprised to find a bonus in their pay packets and who got the message to keep schtum. Realistically, Sutton thought, what can the little scrotes do? But then who would have thought they would have torched the caravans? Memories of watching the horrors of the Balkan wars on TV in the 'Nineties when he was a kid gave him a frisson of apprehension. These people could be cruel savages. Maybe he could reason with them, strike a deal. But where were they? How to get in touch. The message gave no clue as to how or where they might be contacted.

The suspense was killing him.

25

The house-warming is in full swing; tasteful music is blaring out, not that awful rubbish Hare Warren plays when she is in a strop. Gwendolyn St John is in the hot tub, just about wearing a thong and the tiniest bikini bra.

Beside her sits Marjory Hinton Daubrey in a sensible one-piece swimsuit of austere black. Mitchell Dever sprawls opposite them in a pair of Bermuda shorts and an open Hawaiian shirt. He looks like an exotic fruit cocktail and smells like one too. He is a little to the worse for drink. He sings along, out of tune, to the Mumford and Sons song, 'The Cave'. Jocasta climbs out of the hot tub to check on the food and drink. She wears a nice little silver bikini she bought on their holiday in Phuket last year. Paul Hartley in his blue speedos sits ogling Gwendolyn and hoping that no-one will notice his very obvious appreciation. Toby Highbury from London is waxing lyrical about the joys of moving out to the country from London although he has no intention of leaving his mistress who lives in West Acton and whom he thinks his wife Rachel does not know about. Rachel herself sits next to him in the hot tub looking bored whilst calculating the divorce settlement.

Mitchell is suddenly aware of a foot probing the leg of his shorts, a foot that is inching towards his crotch. The song dies on his lips. He stares at the three women but none gives a sign that the wandering limb belongs to them.

He dismisses Marjory instantly. He knows about Toby's girlfriend and wonders if Rachel is out for revenge. The Gwendolyn winks at him. Has to be her. For a moment he is flattered and then sanity comes crashing in. He is very happily married to Jocasta and has no wish to endanger their new bucolic life for a quickie with the village bike (or so he has heard). He shifts uncomfortably. Instantly the foot is removed as if it never happened.

The two Cuthbertson children jump into the hot tub, shrieking although the water is the temperature of a warm bath. They hold their smart phones over their heads until they are in and seated and then go back to taking selfies and texting their friends about everything they have been doing in the previous five minutes.

Mitchell takes his cue and gets out. He finds Jocasta with a glass of cold chardonnay in her hand.

'Gwendolyn tried to shove her foot up my shorts,' he tells her. They have a totally honest relationship and confide everything to each other. Also, Mitchell thinks, better to tell her myself in case she finds out from someone else and then I'll be in deep do-do.

'What?'

'In the hot tub.'

'Are you sure?'

'Of course I'm sure. I may be a little bit pissed but I can tell when someone tries to grope me with their foot.'

'I mean, are you sure it was Gwendolyn?'

'Well I've known Toby for years and we used to play squash together and shower afterwards. In all that time he's never made a move.'

'Of course it wasn't Toby. Do you know he's got a girl-friend? He thinks Rachel doesn't know. She's going to take him to the cleaners.'

'Does everyone know about Toby?'

'Everyone except Toby.'

'The poor sod!'

'What do you mean "poor sod"? He's a philandering bastard. And he's your mate.'

Mitchell is not sure he likes the direction this conversation is going in; guilt by association is an age old technique of the finest organisations – the Gestapo, the KGB, the Spanish Inquisition and any spouse with an iota of suspicion about their partner's fidelity.

'No, no, you're quite right. Shall I circulate with a tray?'

Jocasta is not letting him off the hook so easily.

'So you think Gwendolyn tried to shove her foot up your pants, do you?'

'It could have been Rachel,' he suggests, 'getting her own back.'

'Rachel is one of my oldest and dearest friends,' Jocasta hisses at him. 'She would NOT do that to me.'

'It was me she might have tried to do it to,' says Mitchell, realising that he is digging his own grave.

'How can you say that?' Jocasta squeezes out a soulful tear. Just the one, to make her point.

'Perhaps it was Marjory,' he tries in desperation.

'You'd like that. The mouse that is a secret sex siren.'

'Look, darling. This is getting silly. Perhaps I just imag-ined it. I was a bit Brahms and Liszt. And I did come straight away and tell you.'

'You sure it wasn't Paul Hartley?' Jocasta is resorting to sarcasm; he has been forgiven.

'Paul Hartley has been staring at Gwendolyn's tits for the last ten minutes. He looks like he's trying to smuggle a parrot in his Speedos.'

Jocasta shudders at the image; she suspects she may well not be able to sleep tonight if she can't dispel it. She feels a rush of love for her poor Mitchell and resolves to stop being nasty to him.

'Well, aren't I lucky to have a sexy husband that the other girls fancy!'

And she gives Mitchell a kiss that causes quite a commotion in his Bermuda shorts too.

26

Deep inside St John's Wood (not the London one, but Gwendolyn's), the Bosnian students are sitting round a smokeless fire enjoying their evening meal of rabbit stew, vegetables courtesy of a number of gardens in Itchen Prior but never enough stolen to raise suspicions. They have also fashioned bows and arrows and dispensed with tell tale snares.

'It's time to turn the screw on that bastard Smith,' says Mirko.

'Another note?' asks Jagoda.

'I think not. Not yet. Time for more direct action.'

'What do you have in mind?' says Vukodin.

'We pay the garden centre a little visit tonight.'

'Yes!' says Nevena, who has turned into quite the little guerrilla.

27

Jocasta is hitting the chardonnay. The party has reached the free-for-all stage where the hostess no longer needs to circulate and encourage the guests to drink and try the nibbles. The Cuthbertson children have taken up residence in the hot tub and are joined by a procession of increasingly intoxicated adults. The designated drivers sip their soft drinks and gaze down their noses at the antics of the drinkers. Next time, if there is a next time (and they are sure there will be – Mitchell and Jocasta are sure to milk the social kudos of their little place in the country), it will be their right to get totally sozzled while their partner stays sober.

Bartholomew seems to be trying to kill a cushion by shaking it to death whilst uttering fearsome little growls. Jocasta recognises the cushion as belonging in the garden pod and wrestles it away from her pet. It tears in the battle and leaks feathers. Satisfied that he has eviscerated his prey the puppy loses interest and goes off to dig up a flowerbed. He is in doggy heaven; the centre of attention and more tidbits, almost, that he can eat.

Jocasta takes the corpse of the cushion back to the garden pod where it seems like a good idea to have a little rest and take stock of the situation. She finds Gwendolyn, still in her skimpy bikini, having a slurred conversation with Farleigh Wallop about transferring the activities of Paintball Patrol to St John's Wood. A cold war standoff with Paul Hartley is the current state of affairs and Alice Lacey is playing hard to get. Since the incident in the woods Long Sutton has been distinctly cool at the prospect of Farleigh leading troops of city yuppies crashing through *his* woods and upsetting *his* birds. Farleigh is hoping to get Gwendolyn onside to overrule her over mighty subject. Gwendolyn is well aware of Long Sutton's opinion of her and is well disposed to grant Farleigh's suit, if only to spite the gamekeeper. All she has to do is talk Sherborne into it. The prospect of a steady year round income would also come in handy.

'Fabulous party, darling,' she says as Jocasta stumbles in to the garden pod, '*So* much more fun than our dreary garden party. We *simply must* get a hot tub.'

At the mention of the hot tub Jocasta sees red.

'How dare you, you bitch!' Jocasta rarely swears but feels on this occasion she is fully justified.

'What?' Gwendolyn has often been sworn at but this time she has no idea of the cause.

'Don't you 'what' me.' Anger and an excess of wine make Jocasta sway alarmingly. She spills her drink, which fuels her anger.

'Look, darling, I've no idea what you are talking about. What have I done?'

Seeing as she has not much to lose, having spilled most of it, Jocasta throws the remains of her drink at Gwendolyn but her aim is shaky and she hits Farleigh Wallop instead. This makes her even angrier.

'You made a pass at my husband!'

'Mitchell?'

'He's the only one I've got,' Jocasta snarls, 'and I want to keep him.'

'I don't know what you are talking about.'

'In the hot tub. You stuck your foot on his balls.'

'I did *what*?'

'He *told* me.'

'Wishful thinking on his part, I think, darling.'

That is exactly the wrong thing to say. Jocasta launches herself at Gwendolyn but trips and falls onto Farleigh Wallop who has been trying to edge out of the pod. They crash to the floor and Jocasta starts to sob loudly. Farleigh hasn't a clue what to do but starts making 'there, there,' noises. Gwendolyn sees her chance and slips out. She really has no idea what that was all about; Mitchell, except for an emergency, is absolutely not her type.

28

As the twilight turns to night four figures carefully approach the garden centre. Jagoda and Vukodin break off to right and left to keep watch. Mirko and Nevena creep towards the staff kitchen/restroom. It is never locked as Smith only provides the minimum facilities for his staff. He encourages them to bring their own supplies but has grudgingly provided a kettle as long as they supply their own tea, coffee, milk and sugar. And teaspoons and mugs. Mirko fills the kettle and switches it on. Nevena goes to check on the poly tunnels. The strawberry season is nearing its end but there are still plenty of plants in the beds. Mirko comes in with a steaming kettle.

29

At Yew Tree Cottage the party is winding down. Jocasta is not the only one in an over-emotional state. Toby and Rachel have come to blows, the festering boil of Toby's infidelity has burst and Toby will be looking for a bed for tonight and for the foreseeable future. He is also too pissed to be able to drive back to London. Jocasta is in a vindictive mood and rebuffs Mitchell's suggestion that he could spend the night in their spare room but is prepared to let him sleep in the garden pod.

Paul Hartley has been sick in the bamboo grove.

Unseen in the dark, two people approach the hot tub where the Cuthbertson children are now turning into prunes, still on their smart phones. The newcomers quickly strip off and slide into the hot water.

'Hi,' says Thomas, glad at last to find someone close to their own age.

'Give me your phone,' says Hatch Warren.

'Why?' asks Thomas.

'Because I'll rip yer balls off if you don't,' Hatch informs him.

''An yours,' says Hare to Maud. ''An we'll 'ave them trainers,' she adds. They are probably too small for the twins but there is a ready market for 'second hand' trainers in Westleigh and these are state of the art and high fashion.

'No,' says Maud. 'I'll call Mummy,'

'Do 'an I'll 'ave yer. Give.'

The Cuthbertsons are nicely brought up middle class children from a nice middle class area in nice middle class West London. They go to a nice, middle class private school with other nice middle class children with names like Miranda and Justinian. They have, of course, heard of people like Hatch and Hare Warren but life has sheltered them from the actuality and they are at a loss how to react.

'Help!' Thomas shouts but in the general hubbub of the party wearing down and the befuddled state of many of the guests his crie de Coeur goes unanswered.

Hatch ducks him under the water, careful not to get the phone wet. Maud bursts into tears as Hare takes the phone off her while her brother relieves Thomas of his,

'Now piss off,' Hatch tells them.

The Cuthbertson children flee the hot tub.

'It's awright, this is,' says Hare as she stretches naked in the warm water and lets the bubbles massage her.

'Right,' her brother agrees.

Marjory Hinton Daubrey stands at the side of the hot tub.

'Hare, Hatch. Have you been misbehaving?'

Incredibly, the Warren twins hang their heads.

''S'only a bit 'o fun. Miss.'

'Give me those phones and go home.'

'Yes, Miss,' says Hatch meekly.

'Sorry, Miss,' says Hare with a very rare apology.

'Only a bit 'o fun. We didn't mean nuffing by it.'

'Now, Hatch, are you telling me the truth?'

'Jest a joke, Miss,' says Hare.

'Well. We'll say no more about it. Get out and *do* put some clothes on. Go home. And leave those trainers alone.'

Meek as lambs the twins emerge from the water, shaking themselves like dogs and pull on shorts and tee shirts.

As they leave the family Cuthbertson arrive with Mitchell.

'What happened?' says Mitchell.

'It was all a silly prank,' Marjory explains. 'They've apologised and have gone home.'

Mitchell is dumbfounded; these are the Warren twins, people the term 'feral children' was coined for.

'How...?'

'Oh, I've known Hare and Hatch a long time. They attended school for almost a year. They're good kids, really. In their own way,' she adds.

'What's that in the pool!' Ann Marie shrieks and points.

Floating amongst the bubbles and the foam is a large turd.

Hatch Warren wuz 'ere!

30

The morning after the Devers' housewarming Jed Smith is called to the polytunnels. Boiling water has been carefully poured over the strawberry plants, killing them. The dead plants spell out a message:

Pay Us

31

There is an air of *déjà vu* in the St John's Arms this evening, but then again there usually is.

Ragged Appleshaw nurses his pint at the end of the bar. Gordon Turgis stands, exhausted, behind his bar while Natalie Somerfield polishes a glass and nervously waits for the rush.

One summer two years earlier, a coach taking a full complement of trippers on the Tour of Scenic England (which usually passed through Itchen Prior at just above the permitted speed limit) had broken down and twenty four senior citizens, plus a glamorous lady tour guide had poured into the St John's Arms seeking refreshment, while they waited for the bus to be fixed. Ragged Appleshaw had erupted into the village shop.

'Gordon is going to have a stroke,' he announced.

Natalie hastily shut up the shop and ran to the pub.

She found Turgis in a near catatonic state behind the bar; the coach tour turned out to be a special for deaf and dumb pensioners who were frantically signing at Gordon for food and drink way beyond the limited resources of the St John's Arms. The guide was trying to interpret for her clients and only adding to Gordon's misery and confusion.

It was a traumatic incident that Natalie lived in fear of reliving.

Now, two years after that incident, Jed Smith comes into the pub and orders a double scotch with a double scotch chaser. His hand shakes as he carries his glasses to a table, spilling some of his drinks. He is unshaven.

'You awright there, Jed?' asks Natalie.

'Yes,' he snaps. 'Why wouldn't I be?'

'Just a bit early for you,' says Natalie, sorry she tried to show a bit of friendly interest.

Smith growls at her and downs his first glass in one. He wipes his mouth with the back of his hand and reaches for the second glass. Even Gordon Turgis, who normally evinces no interest whatsoever in his customers, takes notice. Gordon is aware that if Smith keeps knocking back the spirits at this rate, he, Gordon, could be on for a nice little earner for minimum effort.

'I ain't seen them foreign pickers of yorn for a while,' says Natalie. 'They were good customers in the shop. Always buying pot noodles an' milk an' yesterday's bread at a reduction. They gone home or summat?'

Smith jumps as if he has been tasered.

'Wha'?'

'Them nice foreign folk. They gone home, then?'

'Yeah… yeah. That's what happened. They went home.'

''How you managing, then? What with the season not yet over?'

'I'm managing, awright! 'S none of your bloody business!'

'Keep yer 'air on.'

'Gimme another double an' cut the cackle.'

Natalie brings over the drink and Smith fumbles the money out of his pocket and slams it on the table.

'Some folks, eh?' says Natalie to Turgis, loud enough for Jed to hear.

Turgis does not react; he has troubles enough to occupy his thoughts.

32

The following morning, not long after breakfast, Jocasta is working at her computer when the strident opening bars of Beethoven's Fifth Symphony blast out of her mobile.

'Oh, hi Jocasta. It's Marjory. Do you remember what we were talking about at your party last weekend?'

Jocasta has tried to put all memories of the disaster behind her. Toby has only just moved out of the garden pod and Rachel has hinted that she holds Mitchell and Jocasta somehow responsible for the breakup of her marriage; the Cuthbertsons retreated to the safety of West London, vowing never to set foot outside the M25 again. Mitchell has had the hot tub drained at great expense and threatened the Warrens with the attentions of Sergeant Barton Stacy should the twins ever set foot on his property again. The Warrens have not taken this threat unduly seriously; like Jed Smith, they go back a long way with Stacy.

'Sorry. Remind me?'

'The bell-ringing. You said you and Mitchell might be interested?'

Jocasta has a hazy memory of talking to Marjory just after her fight with Gwendolyn; her adrenaline was still pumping and the chardonnay was overriding all rational thought.

'Erm?' Jocasta asks.

'It's a real part of the village community. One of the bells goes back to the Seventeenth century.'

'Is that good?' Jocasta wonders.

'Oh yes indeed. It's part of the heritage of Itchen Prior. We are famous throughout the bell-ringing community for Old Tom.'

'Is he one of the bell-ringers? I don't think we've met him.'

'No, silly! Old Tom is the bell.'

'Do they all have names?' Jocasta feels that she is losing the will to live.

'No, only Old Tom. He's the tenor. The bells range in weight from the lightest called the treble to the tenor. Here at Itchen Prior we have a peal of six bells for ringing changes.'

'Bit technical for me,' says Jocasta. She can tell that Marjory can bore for England on the subject of bell-ringing.

'Well, it is a *teeny* bit. But it's lots of fun once you get into it. You should come along. I'll be there, and Tristram and Henry and Long Sutton and Ragged Appleshaw.' Marjory feels it politic not to mention Seth Warren as she knows the Warrens are a sore point with the Devers.

'Oh, I don't know,' says Jocasta vaguely.

'You must come. It's a lot of fun. And we all go to the pub afterwards.'

'Well. Maybe,' says Jocasta and immediately regrets it.

'Great!' says Marjory. 'I'll come round and pick you up at six.'

Bugger, thinks Jocasta as Marjory rings off. She is not sure how she is going to break the news to Mitchell.

33

On that same Wednesday Paul Hartley has got a contractor with a combine in to deal with the harvest and has decided he deserves to go for a lunchtime pint. He sees Jed Smith looking flushed and sitting in his chair like a poorly filled sack of potatoes.

'Jed! How's it hanging?'

Smith looks up, an expression of mingled hope and cunning creeping over his face.

'Paul, me ol' pal. Lemme buy yer a pint.'

Never one to turn down the offer of a drink, Hartley orders a pint of Old Bishop's and strolls over to join Smith.

'Ta very much, Jed.'

'Iz nothing for a pal,' Smith slurs at him. He lays a finger along the length of his nose and winks at Hartley. 'Can yer do a pal a small favour?' He breaths out a fug of whiskey fumes. So far he has downed half a bottle and Turgis has confiscated his wallet, having first checked the value of the contents. He removes the cost of Hartley's pint before Smith can change his mind.

'What's that, then?' asks Hartley, suddenly guarded.

'Len' me yer shotgun.'

'What you want that for, Jed?'

'Vermin!' says Smith emphatically.

'Whadda mean, vermin?'

'Inna garden centre.'

'What? Like rats?'

''Az jes' what they are. Rats!'

'Can't you put down poison? You sell it. Don't you.'

'Wanna blast 'em,' says Smith, a manic gleam in his eye.

'You'll blow 'em to bits.'

' 'Atz the idea.'

'Bit drastic, innit?'

'Blow 'em to bits,' Smith repeats to himself, liking the idea more and more as he mulls it over in his whiskey sodden brain.

Hartley is at a loss to guess what his friend is planning to do and is no hurry to make promises regarding the loan of a lethal weapon. Particularly not one that can be traced back to him.

Smith has lapsed into silence, dreaming dreams of blood and the solution of his problem with the Bosnians. Slow motion scenes of the shootout in *The Wild Bunch* play themselves across his imagination.

Dreaming dreams of mayhem and gore, his head sinks to the table and he starts to snore.

'I reckon he's 'ad enough,' says Ragged Appleshaw. 'But 'e did promise me a pint.'

'I didn't hear him,' says Natalie.

''At's 'cos you weren't listenin' proper. Take it out of 'is wallet. 'E won't mind.'

''E won't remember,' says Natalie.

'That's awright then, innit. I'll have one o' them whiskies an' all.'

'I'll get him home,' says Hartley, 'After 'e's bought me another pint.'

'Right you are, gents,' says Turgis, extracting the cash out of Smith's much depleted wallet. 'Natalie, do the honours. 'An' let's have one ourselves.'

34

Jocasta has promised Mitchell a resumption of normal marital relations after the period of freeze following the housewarming party if he will accompany her to the bell-ringing this evening.

'Why on earth did you tell her we'd go?' Mitchell complains. 'It's not your sort of thing and it certainly doesn't hold any attraction for me.' But he is really just going through the motions; the promise of a shag is very persuasive and he knows Jocasta can be very accommodating when she has a mind to be.

'I couldn't say no. Besides, I like Marjory. And you're always going on about how we need to integrate ourselves more into the life of the village. And she *did* manage to control those dreadful Warren children!'

Mitchell has no answer to this. Promptly at six o'clock the doorbell rings.

'Ready?' ask Marjory, brightly. 'It's a lovely evening, I thought we'd walk. And then you don't have to worry about driving home afterwards.'

'Yes, we're ready,' says Jocasta and takes Mitchell firmly by the arm. There will be no escape for him.

'What do you know about bell-ringing?' Marjory asks as they walk along the lane towards the church in the warm evening.

'It's proper name is campanology,' says Mitchell, showing off.

'Actually, it isn't. Campanology is the *study* of bells. Bell-ringers are called bell-ringers.'

We are in for a fun night, thinks Mitchell. *I think I'd rather stick hot pins in my eyes. While having root canal work without an anaesthetic. From an untrained dentist. With a drink problem.*

'Here we are. I think you know the others?' says Marjory as they arrive at St Bride's church.

Mitchell and Jocasta are not best pleased to find Seth Warren among the assembled company but they are here now and there is no plausible excuse for them to flee.

'Mitchell, Jocasta, welcome,' says Tristram Clatford. The others nod. Mitchell scowls at Seth Warren, who smiles back at him, putting Mitchell in a worse mood.

Once inside the church Henry Grey takes over.

'We come from the tradition of English bell-ringing. Hardly surprising, seeing as we are in England.' He gives a little laugh. 'It's called English change ringing and we start by ringing rounds, which consists of ringing the bells in order from the treble to the tenor. The bells are numbered in order from one to six, with the treble being one. Later on we will progress to call change ringing and Ragged will be our conductor.' He calls out which bell is to be pulled in which sequence. 'All the bells are hung in the "down" position until we start pulling them slowly from side to side to get them in the upright position when the stay and the slider are engaged and the bell goes through a circle of 360 degrees.'

'Do you have to be very strong to pull the rope?' asks Jocasta nervously.

'Absolutely not.'

'Let's get started. You two can watch,' says Ragged Appleshaw, who is a veteran of many years and the obvious authority figure here.

Henry Grey feels a little peeved; he was just warming to his lecture.

'In a minute,' says Clatford. It is *his* church, after all, and he wants to lecture the Devers as well. 'English bell-ringing has a long history and is intimately tied up with life in the country. It is used to mark the great passages of life – birth, weddings and death. It is as English as Morris dancing and the maypole.'

'I thought they were pagan,' says Mitchell, still with a hump on.

'So they are, dear boy. But still part of country life.'

'Can we get started?' says Ragged Appleshaw impatiently.

'The bell rope is called a sallee,' Marjory informs them as they go up to the ringing chamber.

'Don't touch anything. Just watch. You can have a go later,' says Seth Warren, leering at Mitchell.

'Wouldn't dream of it,' Mitchell replies. Jocasta gives him a look that says, *play nice! Or else all promises are off.*

35

An hour later they are all gathered in the St John's Arms. For once the pub is packed. Have the drinkers all been summoned by the bells? Natalie Somerfield is pulling pints and distributing packets of stale crisps. Even Gordon Turgis is playing the role of an almost friendly mine host.

'Wow,' says Mitchell. 'That was really *fun.*' He and Jocasta have been allowed to ring a change under the watchful eye of Ragged Appleshaw who commented 'not bad' at their efforts. 'Can I buy everyone a drink?'

'I'll have a pint,' says Appleshaw quickly, before the townee can change his mind. The other bell-ringers give Natalie their orders and retreat to a corner table to mull over the evening's performance.

'Think you'll give it another go?' asks Marjory.

'Oh yeah,' Mitchell is a man of sudden passionate enthusiasms and bell-ringing has just become his latest.

'If you'll have us,' says Jocasta, pleased that Mitchell has stopped sulking and actually seemed to be enjoying himself. Their integration into the life of the village community has taken a huge step forward. Mitchell even clapped Seth Warren on the back and said 'You're not so bad, mate.' Whether this spirit of brotherly love will last depends on what Seth and/or his brood get up to in the future. Jocasta has her doubts about this détente. Still, she too has enjoyed herself and resolves to give Mitchell a happy ending to the evening.

'I'm so glad you've enjoyed yourselves. People think these country traditions are a bit quaint,' says Marjory. 'But we think they are very important.'

'They give a sense of *continuity*,' Henry Grey chips in.

'Helps us keep in touch with where we come from,' adds Tristram Clatford.

'Reminds us o' the ancestors,' says Ragged Appleshaw.

'Always bin bell-ringers in Itchen Prior,' mutters Seth Warren. 'Any chance o' another pint?'

Full of the spirit of good fellowship and bonhomie and on a promise, Mitchell fishes out his wallet.

36

The peals of bells crashed into Jed Smith's hangover like all the demons from hell beating metal buckets with sledgehammers. He wakes up on his sofa with no idea how he got there. He crawls into the kitchen to find aspirins. Somehow a herd of wildebeest have managed to get into his mouth and crap there. He needs water. Or maybe the hair of the dog. He realises that it is actually night and not just the fact that he is having trouble opening his eyes. Night means the possible return of his tormentors.

'Oh God,' he moans and slinks back to his sofa.

In this state, what is the worst they can do to him?

Death would be a blessed relief, if perhaps, a little drastic.

But the night passes uneventfully.

37

Sherborne St John is an early riser. Up at dawn, whatever the weather, he can be found walking the estate, inspecting the home farm with his farm manager, discussing the shoot with Long Sutton or visiting his tenants in the village.

Sherbourne is a traditionalist; his tenants still line up at the Hall on Quarter Days to pay their rents. He is a man who has both an affinity and a deep love for the land that his family have owned for hundreds of years. He feels responsible for its well being and the one great sadness of his life is that he has no direct heir to pass the stewardship of the St John acres on to. He had hoped that by marrying the much younger Gwendolyn Abbas a brood of young St Johns might result, but Gwendolyn has not lived up to her earlier promise of a fecund earth mother sex goddess. In fact, in the sex goddess department she has been something of a disappointment. It has been at least a year since she invited Sherborne into her bedroom.

He supposes there must be an heir somewhere; previous St Johns had been very active in spreading their gene pool around but he has never had the inclination to investigate the matter. Now in late middle age, he supposes it is time to instruct his solicitors to locate an heir who he can train in the ways of the estate. It is a burden he finds heavy and is much on his mind this morning.

Gwendolyn St John is not an early riser. She has her own suite of rooms – bedroom, dressing room and sitting room – that she calls her 'boudoir'. These are decorated in swathes of bright swathes of fabrics: satin sheets, velvet curtains, lots of cushions, a collection of Beswick animals and a large television upon which she watches the shows she loves like *TOWIE* and *Made in Chelsea* as well as all the talent shows. She is a woman of certain aspirations, most of which she feels remain unfulfilled by her marriage to Sherborne St John. She does not love her husband. Indeed, she is uncertain what love *actually* means; the nearest she comes to feeling any tender emotion towards any living being is to her horses; to the emotions of the rest of the sentient world she is merely indifferent. Even in the act of sex she is only concerned with her own gratification, hence her use and abuse of the likes of Crux Easton and his legion of predecessors.

Sherborne and Gwendolyn meet, for what he calls brunch and she calls breakfast, at ten o'clock the day after the bell-ringing practice. He has eaten a light snack of toast and coffee before his rounds and is now ready for the full English cooked for him by Mrs Wellow, the live-in house-keeper. Gwendolyn has black coffee, muesli and fruit, with perhaps a small vodka and orange on the side.

'Sherborne, my love,' she says in a singsong voice that she believes is both appealingly little girl and sexy vamp but that Sherborne detests but is too polite to say.

'Yes, old girl?'

'Remember I told you about the party at the Devers?'

'Yes,' he says, tucking in to a sausage made from an erstwhile member of the Gloucester Old Spot community of the home farm.

'Remember I told you about the hot tub and how much fun it was?'

'Yes.' He knows where this is going.

'Can *we* get one?'

'No, I don't think so, old girl.' He cuts up a slice of fried bread and dips it into the yolk of his egg – laid by one of his own hens.

'Oh, Sherborne! Why not?'

'Because, my dear old girl, we are not made of money. These things don't come cheap, I should imagine.'

'Just a couple of thou, Sherborne. That's all. Be a darling. For me.'

'You know I love to spoil you, old girl, but I was talking to Mrs Whiteparish in the village this morning. Her house needs repairs to the roof.'

'That's her problem,' says Gwendolyn, resorting to her normal voice.

'No, I'm afraid it's *our* problem. We're her landlords. We have a duty to maintain the property.'

'If the lazy old bat got a decent job she could fix it herself,' says Gwendolyn.

'She's been on Invalidity Benefit since her husband died and she lost her leg in the car crash.'

'And?'

'She does try to make a bit extra stuffing fliers into envelopes but they only pay £3.50 per thousand, and with her arthritis she can't do that many. And if the DWP found out she might get into trouble.'

'She could always make a fortune running an 0800 chat line.'

'You've lost me, old girl.'

'An 0800 chat line. You know: *Call naughty mistress for a damned good tell off; young blonde housewife will talk dirty.* That sort of thing. Pays a fortune. So I'm told.'

'Mrs Whiteparish is in her late fifties!'

'The punters don't know that! Half the time it's young male students pretending to be women.'

'How do you know all this, old girl?'

'What?' say Gwendolyn, who has considered this as an option for making a bit of cash on the side but was worried that St John might find out. 'Everyone knows that. Really, darling, you are such an old fuddy-duddy.'

'No, I don't think poor Mrs Whiteparish needs to resort to that. Not when we can help her out.'

'But Sherborne...' The little girl voice is back.

'No. Sorry old girl but that's the end to it.' Sherborne St John likes to indulge his wife but he has certain responsibilities that must come before family. The arable harvest looks like being a bumper crop all over the country this year so prices will be down, and you can't give lambs away. As for milk, profits are continuing to nosedive. Thank God for farm subsidies – but how long will they last?

Sherborne St John finishes his last rasher and wipes his plate with the last fried slice. He is ready to face the rest of the day with a pleasantly full stomach. He is content. A final cup of English Breakfast tea and then it's off to go over the accounts with his farm manager.

'I'll see you later, old girl. Got anything nice planned for today?'

'I might go out for a ride on Prince of Darkness.' Prince of Darkness is her stallion, a gift from Sherborne for their tenth wedding anniversary; she got him a pair of cufflinks.

'Have a good day.'

'You too, darling!' Miserable old skinflint, she thinks as she smiles at him through gritted teeth. Time to do something about you.

38

Crux Easton is also an early riser. The stable chores are a hard taskmaster and Gwendolyn (a hard task mistress) expects everything to be spick and span when she turns up for her morning hack. Afterwards she usually goes for a ride on one of her horses.

Crux's romance with Sally Fairfax is going through a bad patch. She has issued a final ultimatum: her or me! Crux is frantic. He doesn't want to lose Sally but he wants to keep his job. He realises that something must be done about Gwendolyn, but something that will not jeopardise his position here at St John Hall.

A bit of hard graft mucking out does not hurt him and he has come to genuinely love working with the horses. Sherborne St John allows him to ride and exercise his charges, a pleasure he does not want to lose. He has free time and money in his pocket and the stigma of his penal past is fading, being put down to youthful folly. However, old habits die hard and Crux still cultivates a small patch of Jamaican Funny Bush out of sight in an old abandoned greenhouse for personal use. Horse shit makes excellent fertiliser and it would be a shame to let it go to waste. Gwendolyn is out on Prince of Darkness and Sherborne is out and about on the estate.

He rolls himself up a little number and settles back to mull over his problem. Perhaps if Gwendolyn were to have a little accident…

39

The same day finds Farleigh Wallop in full combat gear and with a swagger stick under his arm, giving a rousing pep talk to a group of marketing executives down from Bristol on a team building jolly.

'It's kill or be killed out there. This is Helmand. There is NO mercy. When I was out there we understood Terry Taliban; they hated us and we hated them. Every little village sheltered the enemy. We never knew who was a friend and who was a foe. No quarter asked or given. You have to be hard. You have to depend utterly on your comrades. One for all and all for one. Take no prisoners and don't leave your wounded behind. There is no air evac here! And you, Terry Taliban. These foreign infidels are here to take your country; to make you give women equal opportunities and give them ideas above their station; to educate boys AND girls in the wicked, corrupt ways of the West. To poke their noses into your opium growing operations. Do you want that? DO YOU?'

The designated players who will take the roles of the Taliban mutter 'No.'

'I can't hear you!'

'NO,' they shout in chorus.

'No what?'

'NO SIR!'

'Better. Now off you jolly well trot and get ready to defend your territory. Visors on. Don't forget. You have all signed the waivers. Load up your weapons and let battle commence.'

The very urban marketing executive, dressed in baggy trousers and long shirts whoop off in the direction of the fake Afghan village.

'Now,' says Farleigh Wallop to the remaining group, 'the honour of the British Army, the finest army in the world, depends on you guys. Are you up for the challenge? Are you?'

'YES SIR!' they holler.

'Off you go then. And give 'em hell.'

Farleigh goes off to his office, or Command HQ as he prefers to call it. As he plonks himself behind his desk the phone rings.

'Paintball Patrol. Major Wallop speaking.'

'Ah, Wallop.' He recognises the voice of Paul Hartley. They have not spoken since the St John's garden party.

'Hartley,' says Wallop in as friendly a tone as he can muster.

'It's about your lease. It's due for renewal.'

'I'm aware of that,' says Wallop guardedly.

'Bad news, I'm afraid,' says Hartley. Can Wallop detect a gloating edge to the man's voice? 'The rate has to go up. My overheads, you know.'

'What overheads? You don't pay a penny.'

'Cost of living,' replies Hartley smoothly.

'Two percent per annum.'

'Oh no. No, no, no.'

'Whadya mean: no?' Wallop is becoming alarmed. After the fracas in the woods 'Long' Sutton has been distinctly cool on the prospect of Wallop running The 'Nam Expe-

129

rience. He has made tentative approaches to Sherborne St John but St John is advised by Sutton and permission seems unlikely. Wallop, for the moment, is tied firmly to Hartley, his love rival and deadly foe.

'What I say,' says Hartley. 'If you want to keep your cockamamie Dad's Army on my land it'll cost you.'

'How much?'

'Shall we say an extra grand?' Wallop sighs in relief. His operation runs on pretty much a shoe string but an extra thousand he can just about manage. 'A month!' adds Hartley.

'You bastard!' shouts Wallop down the phone. 'You bloodsucker.'

'Take it or leave it, chum,' Hartley crows. 'Your choice. Otherwise it's a full retreat for Captain Mainwearing and the boys.'

He rings off.

Wallop sits with his head in his hands. This means the end for Paintball Patrol and the end for Farleigh Wallop's dreams. And probably the end for his hopes of romance with Alice Lacey who will have no truck with a broken man.

Pull yourself together, man, he orders. You are a trained military man. A trained killer. Albeit one from the Catering Corps. You laugh in the face of danger. Are you going to let a civvie street shit like Paul Hartley get the better of you? Never! Plan, man, plan! What would Alexander do? What would Napoleon do? Rommel (although he was on the wrong side)?

Farleigh Wallop sits and schemes.

40

In the converted stall in the stables that serves as a tiny office Crux Easton is busy searching online. He finds what he is after and places his order. This could be the drastic final solution to his problem.

Gwendolyn, too, is trawling cyberspace for information using the laptop that she keeps in a locked bottom drawer in her private sitting room. Her travels across the internet take her to some dark places but she is no stranger to these exotic sites. She makes notes in her large, untidy handwriting (school was never really her thing) and also makes some purchases using an account that Sherborne is unaware of and funded from what she can siphon off the allowance for the upkeep of the house. This fund she only uses for *very* private purposes. And this purpose is very private indeed.

41

It is Friday and in their camp in the woods the Bosnians are having a conference.

'We have made him wait and sweat long enough,' says Jagoda Doboj. 'And we've thrown stones at his windows at night. It's time to confront him. I'm getting tired of camping out. I need a proper shower, I smell.'

'We *all* smell, Jagoda so it doesn't really matter,' says Mirko Knin.

'It matters to *me*.'

'And me,' says Nervena Stolac. 'I agree with Jagoda. I want to go home. I've had enough. We are supposed to be back at university in six weeks.'

'Actually, I agree' says Vukodin Punta. 'I think now is the time to confront Smith.'

'Ok,' says Mirko, 'we do it tonight.'

42

Paul Hartley sits in the St John Arms drinking with Jed Smith.

'You look rough,' he says.

'Not been sleeping well,' says Smith. He does not mention the flurry of stones that hit his windows at unpredictable times in the night or his forays out into the darkness to try and catch his tormentors. Which he never does. 'But you're looking like the cat that got the cream.'

'I got old Farleigh Wallop by the balls,' Hartley gloats. 'I got 'im!'

A terrible vision flits across Smith's inner screen.

'Why's that, then?' Someone else's misfortune is always a tonic. Smith starts to cheer up.

'His sub-tenancy is up. I'm cracking an extra thousand on his monthly rent. He's no chance of paying it. That business of his only just limps along as it is.'

'So what'll that get you? Surely summat is better 'n nowt, as they say.'

'Satisfaction at seeing the bugger go under. Natural selection, that is. The strong and the weak locked in an eternal struggle for survival.'

Smith has never heard his friend wax so philosophically lyrical and wonders if he has taken something to stimulate parts of the brain not reached by the Old Bishop.

'Bloody hell, Paul! Where did that come from?'

'I'm not as ignorant as you think I am, Jed Smith. An' that's a fact.'

'But like I said, apart from satisfaction, what'll it get you. Cutting off your nose, if you ask me.'

'Alice!' Hartley sighs the name. 'All to meself. If he can't afford to pay her, she won't want to keep working for him, no way. But *I* can take her on full time, mebbe even live in!' He leers at Smith and winks, tapping his nose at the same time.

Smith gets the message; it would be hard not to.

'So all this is for you to get yer leg over.'

'Jed Smith, if you weren't me best mate and drinking buddy I'd deck you for that.' Hartley thinks it over. He grins. 'Actually, yeah.'

'Well, good luck, chum.'

'Two birds with one stone, so to speak,' says Hartley, rubbing his hands. ''Nother pint?'

'No, thanks all the same. Best be off. Got a business to run.'

'Got any replacements for them nice young Bosniaks,' calls Natalie Somerfield from behind the bar where she has been earwigging.

'They've gone, Natalie. And no, I haven't. And no, I'm not going to. And it's none of your business. Ain't you got a shop to run?'

'I've got to help poor Mr Turgis in the rush, haven't I?'

'Rush?' says Smith. 'There's Ragged Appleshaw. Who just about lives here, me an' Paul Hartley an' Henry Grey, when he comes in. Which isn't now.'

'You never know,' says Natalie defensively.

'I'm off.' says Smith. 'Sure you can manage?' He feels confident he has distracted Natalie from all thoughts of the Bosnian students who *are* still out there somewhere, lurking like Freddy Kruger at the edge of a nightmare.

43

Farleigh Wallop is reading his tattered and much thumbed copy of *On War* by that great German writer Carl von Clausewitz, who was on the right side at the time he wrote it. Wallop keeps this and a copy of *The Art of War* by Sun Tzu prominently displayed on a bookshelf behind his desk. He has read that Sun Tzu enjoyed a vogue as a business training manual and likes to reference it in his introductory spiel.

'Business is like war,' he lectures. 'Ruthless and competitive. Sun Tzu teaches us that. But you also have to rely on your comrades. Take no prisoners and don't leave your wounded behind. This is what the Paintball Patrol Experience is going to teach you. You will come out of this as a T E A M.' And the clients cheer and go off to shoot at each other.

Now he is looking through the highlighted quotation of von Clausewitz for inspiration. And he finds the very quotation he needs:

Kind hearted people might think that there was some ingenious way to defeat
the enemy without too much bloodshed. Pleasant as that sounds, it is a feeling
that must be exposed.

So that's it, then, he thinks – *total Krieg*. When you think about it, the Germans certainly knew a thing or two about waging war. And war is what he is going to wage on Paul Hartley. How dare a bloody peasant farmer presume to take on the might of the British Army, in the person of Major Farleigh Wallop (retired, late Catering Corps).

He suspects that he ought to go and see if the marketing executives are all right. He slaps his swagger stick smartly under his arm and heads off for his mock Afghan village, blowing his whistle to warn of his approach; it would not do to fall victim to blue on blue. He intends to fight another day.

Oh yes!

44

Jed Smith is awakened by a banging on his back door. He hauls himself out of bed, sticks his feet into a pair of trainers and picks up the cricket bat he has taken to keeping next to the door. He opens the door and peers out into the night. He can see two figures retreating slowly. He thinks he can identify them as the two girls, certainly no match for an enraged man armed with a cricket bat. He starts out of the door but his arms are pinioned by Mirko and Vukodin who have been hiding either side of the door. He tries to struggle but the girls return and wrest the cricket bat out of his hands.

'Good evening, Mr Smith,' says Mirko, sounding like a Bond villain of the old school. All that is missing is the cat. And the lair inside a volcano.

'Let me go,' shouts Smith. 'I'll have the police on you!'

'Do they know you employ illegal immigrants, Mr Smith?'

'And pay less than the minimum wage?' says Nervena, who is all for breaking his legs at the start of negotiations to show they are serious; she has been talked out of it by the others who think it might be useful to play good cop/ bad cop first rather than go straight for psychotic cop.

'Whaddayawant?' says Smith.

'What we have always wanted; our passports and our back pay. We think one thousand pounds each is fair.'

'Awright,' Smith knows when he is trapped. 'I'll give you your passports. They're in the safe in the house.'

'And our money?'

'Ah. Now there we have a problem,' says Smith. 'I might have a few quid from the takings but nowhere near a thousand.'

'Each,' prompts Mirko. 'Let us go inside and look in your safe, Mr Smith.'

Keeping a tight hold of his arms the two students march Smith back into his house.

'Show us where the safe is,' demands Nervena, still hoping the use of torture might be necessary.

'It's there,' Smith points to it. Now it has come to a confrontation he is strangely relieved; it was the war of nerves that he was losing.

'Well. Open it!'

'Turn your backs,' says Smith, not wanting them to see the combination.

'Don't be stupid. We are not thieves. We want what is ours, that's all. Get on with it.'

'Shall we cut off a finger?' Nervena suggests.

'Not yet,' Jagoda tells her.

Christ, thinks Smith. She is bloody serious. They are mad bloody Bosnians, after all. He decides never to employ any casual labour from the Balkans again; there are plenty of sub Saharan Africans creeping ashore every day who would jump at the chance at a bit of honest work. Well, he corrects himself: work.

He opens the safe. Inside are their passports, £97 in cash (the day's takings from the garden centre are always collected by an armoured van at the end of the day, so

Smith was telling a little porky there) and some legal documents related to the house and business premises. All the day to day paperwork relating to the business is kept in the office on site.

'Here,' he hands Nervena the passports.

'You are forgetting something, I think,' says Jagoda.

'I haven't got any bloody money. You can see for yourselves.'

'I will fetch axe. And wire.' Nervena announces, handing out the passports.

'Why wire?' asks Vukodin. Smith does *not* want to know.

'For tourniquet. When we cut off foot.'

Smith faints. When he comes round the she-devil is missing – gone to find a sharp instrument, no doubt.

'I haven't got any money. You can see. Take what's in there. Don't cut my foot off. I need it.' Tears are rolling down his face; he has never felt so sorry for himself in his whole life.

The two men and the woman speak together in Serbo-Croat. Nervena comes back. She is carrying a saw. Smith sobs audibly.

'Cannot find axe,' she says in English, for Smith's benefit.

'I haven't got any bloody money in the house,' says Jed Smith slowly, between sobs, in case he is not making himself clear enough to these foreign maniacs.

'OK, we come back,' says Mirko. Jagoda speaks to him rapidly in Serbo-Croat again and he pauses to think. 'OK. You have three days to find money. We will contact you to say where you leave it. Otherwise I let Nervena cut off leg.'

'Perhaps I could cut off his dick. To show we not make joke.'

A dark stain appears on the crotch of Smith's pyjamas.

'I think you've frightened him enough, Nervena,' Vukodin tell her in Serbo-Croat. 'He's pissed himself.'

'I've got an idea,' says Jagoda, wrinkling her nose against the hot smell of urine. 'Tie him up.'

The two young men lift the trembling Jed Smith onto a chair and tie him up with his pyjama cord.

'Right,' says Jagoda brightly. 'We take it in turn to have a hot shower while the others watch this piece of shit.

45

'Crux, I'm expecting a couple of deliveries,' Gwendolyn announces. She is dressed for her morning ride on Prince of Darkness so Crux is safe for the time being. 'They will be addressed to G. Abbas.'

'Oh yes?' says Crux, who is waiting for a delivery of his own.

'They are going to be delivered here at the stable,' says Gwendolyn patiently.

'Why not at the Hall?'

'It's a surprise for Mr St John. I don't want anyone to know it's from me.'

'The postman knows you used to be called Abbas,' Crux points out reasonably.

'They are coming by special delivery.' Really, if it weren't for his fine physique and stamina and the fact that he is *de facto* enslaved to her, she'd get rid of this halfwit in the blink of an eye.

'Oh aye. Fair enough. Do you want me to sign for anything?'

'Yes, if needs be. Sign the name Abbas.'

This could be awkward, as he is expecting a delivery in his own name.

'Now be a good boy and get Prince of Darkness ready for me. I'll be back in ten minutes. I should be out for an hour or so. Back in time for lunch. Always gives me a good appetite, a good ride in the morning. Make sure you are around when I get back, there's a good boy.'

Soon, thinks Crux, soon I'll be free of you, you witch.

'Yes, Gwendolyn,' he says meekly.

46

The basis for a successful military campaign is good intelligence. Major Farleigh Wallop knows this. He has a plan but first he needs detailed reconnaissance. He fires up the ancient Apple Mac in his office and goes on line. Soon he finds what he is seeking and starts to put together the elements of his plan of campaign.

47

Jed Smith is no longer afraid; he is angry. That the Bosnians had used up all the hot water in the tank last night so he couldn't even have a hot shower to wash the wee off was the straw that broke the back of the cowardly camel. A raging tiger emerged from the bathroom in the cold light of day, dripping cold water onto the bathmat.

Pulling on a pair of jogging pants and a tee shirt he goes into his office in the Itchen Prior Horticultural Centre and sits down in front of his computer. His search digs up a name:

Stamford Barholm Security
That will do nicely, he thinks.

48

As the glorious summer slides into July many of the older folk of Itchen Prior are comparing it favourably to the summer of 1976.

The delivery service from Hippolyta.com has arrived at the stables at St John Hall. Two deliveries are for G Abbas and one is for S. Fairfax. Crux Easton signs for all three without any fuss or awkward questions. The delivery driver is not local and doesn't give a hoot as long as he has a signature on his machine. Crux actually signs Gwendolyn St John in his most unintelligible scribble.

He takes his own delivery, unwraps it and slips it in the back pocket of his jeans. The packaging, such as it is, he takes out to the back of the stable and burns.

At ten o'clock Gwendolyn arrives to collect her horse for her morning ride. Today she chooses a bay mare called Molly, an average sized horse of fifteen hands (Prince of Darkness stands at sixteen hands).

Molly is a beast of normally placid temperament and Gwendolyn is not looking for a fast gallop this morning; a gentle hack round a eight mille circuit will be enough to keep both rider and horse in trim.

As Crux makes the horse ready Gwendolyn asks if her delivery has arrived and Crux confirms it has.

'Keep it for me until I get back, will you. Don't mention it to anyone, especially not Mr St John. It's a surprise for him,' she tells Crux.

'Not a word,' he promises.

The horse ready, she mounts and sets off at a sedate trot for her morning exercise. Crux waits twenty minutes and then slips out of the stable after her. He knows her routine and the route she will follow, for Gwendolyn is a creature of habit.

By cutting across the fields and the edge of the woods he reaches a sunken track bounded on each side by an old hazel hedge. He makes sure that he is unseen and pushes his way into the hedge. The day is warm and drowsy with a buzzing of insects and the tumbling aerobatics of butterflies. In the distance is the sound of farm machinery working the fields around the estate, but there is no sign of human life nearby.

Crux settles down to wait. He contemplates lighting up a small spliff but decides against it; he wants to keep his wits sharp.

He hears faint singing coming towards him and then the gentle clop of hooves. It is Gwendolyn approaching on Alice. He has never heard her sing before in all the time and in all the situations he has known her (or she has known him, in the Biblical sense). Gradually he makes out the words. She is singing Abba's *Dancing Queen*: 'Only seventeen.'

For a moment he almost feels something for her. Here she is riding all alone (as she thinks) and singing to herself a song perhaps as she imagines herself to be, or would like herself to be. Young again and innocent, although Gwendolyn Abbas ceased to be innocent long before she ceased to be young.

Crux Easton reaches into his back pocket and pulls out the laser pen he bought from Hippolita.com and aims it at the horse's eye. He has no wish to hurt the animal and knows that she is unlikely to suffer any permanent harm. He switches the pen on. A beam of infrared light hits the animal's eye.

Molly rears on her hind legs and skitters to the side and then takes off down the lane at a rate of knots.

Gwendolyn St John, for all her nasty qualities, is a superb horsewoman. Somehow she manages to stay in the saddle and keep hold of the reins. She fights Molly to a trot and then calms the shivering and sweating animal, dismounting and patting her neck. Gwendolyn is unaware of why Molly was suddenly spooked and will never know.

As soon as Molly reared, Crux took off back the way he came, unseen by the preoccupied Gwendolyn. He does not know if his plan for Gwendolyn to break her neck has been successful or not and is sweeping up in the stables in a fever of anticipation when Gwendolyn rides Molly back into the yard. He tries desperately not to let his disappointment show as Gwendolyn slides off the horse's back.

'Extraordinary thing, Crux. Something frightened Molly. I nearly went arse over tit and broke my bloody neck. I'm glad to be alive and I'm horny as hell. Leave the bloody tack on the horse and take me upstairs and shag me senseless.'

Bugger! thinks Crux.

148

49

The old fashioned bell over the door of the village shop tinkles as Farleigh Wallop enters.

'Mornin' Major,' says Natalie Somerfield, 'you awrigh'?'

'No, Natalie, I am most assuredly not.'

'I'm sorry to hear that, Major. What's the problem, then?'

'Delhi Belly, my dear,' says Wallop.

'What's that, then?'

'The Trots, the Squits, Montezuma's Revenge, the Toilet Tango, the Kabul Shuffle,' says Wallop.

Natalie still has no idea what he is talking about.

'What are they when they're at home?'

Wallop realises he is dealing with a simpleton and that frankness rather than euphemism is the key here.

'I'm suffering from a dose of the shits, my dear,' he explains slowly.

'Well why didn't you say?'

'Never mind. What have you got for it?'

'I got toilet paper.'

'Ah. I was thinking of something more in the curative line,' Wallop explains again, patiently.

Natalie Somerfield has never heard of imodium but does have an impressive line of patent remedies. This is what Wallop is counting on.

She turns to a dusty shelf of equally dusty green bottles with faded yellow labels.

'Let's see. I got *Dr Graham Young's Universal Pills; Genene Jones's CureAll Syrup.* Ah, this might do you *Dr Collis Brown's Linctus.*'

'That sounds promising,' says Farleigh Wallop. 'May I have a look?'

She passes him the bottle and he examines the label. Sadly, it dates from a less exacting age when detailed lists of the components of the contents were not meticulously given on the label, but he decides to take a chance. He has a hunch that all 19th and early 20th century patent medicines were basically tincture of opium.

'That should do the trick nicely. What do I owe you?'

Natalie takes back the bottle and wipes the dust off. She peers closely at the label.

'It says 1/6d. That's old money, that is.'

'We'll call it 10p then, shall we? To allow for inflation.'

'I suppose so,' Natalie agrees dubiously. 'Can I get you anything else.'

'No. Thank you, Natatie, my dear. That will be all. I bid you good day.'

50

A Range Rover draws up in the public car park of Itchen Prior Horticultural Centre that same afternoon. Two large men with shaven heads and wearing well cut suits climb out and march purposefully into the garden centre shop.

'We're here to see a Mr Jed Smith,' one of them announces to the woman behind the checkout counter. She immediately suspects that they are bailiffs and panics.

'I don't know if he is in today,' she says, casting a nervous glance in the direction of the office.

'He's expecting us,' says the other man. 'On business.'

'Miss Twyford,' she calls to a young woman who is fussing around the garden clothing section, 'Could you see if Mr Smith is in his office, please?'

'Right away, Mrs Kingston.'

A few moments later Smith follows her out. He is looking both shifty and worried, an expression that his staff have noticed a lot of late.

'Mr Smith?' asks one of the men.

'Yes,' admits Smith reluctantly. Oh God, he thinks. Are these heavies from HM Revenue and Customs? His stomach lurches and he feels the bile rising. The carefully doctored accounts he gives to his compliant accountant might not bear the minute scrutiny of trained hit men from the tax office.

'Can we go into your office?' asks the second man.

' I'm screwed, thinks Smith, as he leads the way.

'My name is Mullen and this is Mr Regis,' explains Peter Mullen once they are safe from prying eyes in Smith's office. 'We are from Stamford Barholm Security.'

A wave of relief sweeps through Jed Smith like the relief of a pee after six pints of beer.

'I believe you have a problem we can help you with,' adds Bear Regis.

'Oh yes indeed,' smiles Smith, happy for the first time since the Bosnians decamped.

'Take a seat, gentlemen and I'll tell you all about it.'

51

'Hartley,' says Farleigh Wallop into the telephone, back from his trip to the village shop, 'Wallop here.'

'Is it about the lease?' asks Hartley, dispensing with small talk.

'In a way, yes. I think we've got off on the wrong foot.'

'Really? It's clear enough from where I stand. If you want to keep using my land, then you are going to have to cough up an extra thou a month to keep your lease. Otherwise all bets are off.'

'Hartley, I know we've had our differences but I'd like to buy you a drink in the St John's and talk it over. To see if we can come to some kind of accommodation to suit us both?'

'You know my terms. Wallop. What's to discuss?'

'Please, let me buy you a drink and try and thrash this out like civilised men, can we?'

Paul Hartley is never averse to a free drink. What has he got to lose? As far as he can see he has got Wallop over a barrel; the good old capitalist maxim of supply and demand applies strongly in his favour.

'All right. Around eight-ish? I'm still in the middle of harvesting. The combine is working South Field and I need to keep a regular eye on it. I can spare you forty minutes at best.' Should be good for at least three pints of the old fart's money, he thinks. No skin off my nose.

'Eight o'clock in the St John's then it is,' says Wallop in a voice redolent of good fellowship and reasonableness.

He rings off and leans back in his chair, his arms clasped behind his head

I love it when a plan comes together, he thinks.

52

Gwendolyn St John certainly does not love her husband but she does not actually hate him. He has taken her out of what might have been the life of the village scrubber and given her a certain status and wealth she could not have dreamed of. She supposes that she might owe him *something*. That is why she has decided to kill him with kindness. But kill him she has most certainly decided to do.

53

'So that's the story,' Smith is saying, 'basically the four of them planned to rip me off and then blackmail me into giving them a wodge of money to buy them off. I'd always treated them well. You only have to ask my previous summer employees.' Who long ago returned home and are by now untraceable and very unlikely to want to rekindle memories of being exploited by one Jed Smith any way.

'So it's blackmail and threats of violence?'

'Yes. One mad bitch wanted to cut my dick off. And saw off my leg. She meant it, too.' He shudders at the memory of Nervena hovering over him, dirty and rank from the woods, a fanatic gleam in her eyes.

'That's not nice, Mr Smith. Not nice at all,' Peter Mullen says sympathetically. Both Mullen and Regis have worked for obvious lowlifes like Smith before. The two men served together in Royal Marine special forces and have learned not to judge their employers, be they the likes of Jed Smith or HM Government.

'So what exactly would you like us to do, Mr Smith?' asks Regis. Let us cut to the chase here, is what he means.

'Make them stop?' says Smith, vaguely. As long as he does not actually articulate what he wants he cannot later be held responsible for the actions of his minders.

'How *exactly* do you want us to make them stop?' asks Regis again.

'Make them go away?'

'Go *where*? Exactly?' Mullen asks heavily.

'I don't care! Away. Back home. Anywhere.' Smith feels the potential menace of these two men and wonders if he might not have got in too deep.

'Where can we find them?' asks Regis.

'I think they must be living in St John's Wood,' says Smith.

The two enforcers exchange a puzzled look.

'What, in north London?' says Mullen incredulously. He is beginning to think Smith might be a fantasist. But as long as he stumps up their fee plus expenses, what do they care. And stump up Smith most certainly will, of that there is no doubt.

Smith is also confused.

'What has north London got to do with it? St John's Wood. Here in Itchen Prior. It's part of the St John estate.'

'Ah, OK. You had us confused for a moment there. So they're camped out in a local wood. Shouldn't be too hard to find,' says Mullen, glad to have cleared up that bit of confusion. The sort of work they do is much better done in open spaces rather than a smart urban environment.

Both men have undergone jungle training in Belize and Brunei and are as at home in forest as they are in the pleasant modern housing estate where they live lives of upright citizens with their partners and children. They don't shit in their own backyards.

'We'll go and have a looksee, then, shall we?' says Mullen.

'There is just the small matter of the fee,' Regis reminds his partner.

'Oh yes. I think we agreed five thousand,' says Mullen.

'Plus expenses,' says Regis.

Smith begins to wish he had just paid the Bosnians off; it would have been cheaper after all, but he is an angry man and thirsts for revenge. He will show those ingrates he is not a man to be crossed lightly.

Somehow he will find the money.

'I'll write you a cheque,' he says.

'Cash only,' Mullen chides. 'Up front.'

Bugger, thinks Smith as he racks his brains as to where he can raise the cash.

'Tomorrow?' he asks.

'No later than that,' says Regis who gives off the air of a man who is not to be trifled with.

54

Paul Hartley is standing in his South Field watching the progress of the harvest. His phone rings and he sees it is Jed Smith calling.

'Hello Jed,' he says.

'Paul, you're my best and oldest mate,' Smith gushes. Hartley immediately knows that Smith wants something.

'What are you after?' he asks.

'Paul. I'm in a bit of a pickle.'

'I guessed as much. What have you done? Got that lovely Miss Twyford up the duff?'

'No.' Smith protests. 'I need some ready cash.'

Hartley is instantly on his guard. He is a man who is careful with his money but also a man who is an astute businessman.

'Why?'

'That doesn't matter. The thing is I need a short term loan.'

'How much?' asks Hartley bluntly.

'About five grand.'

'Ouch!'

'Just until the end of the summer season.'

'Can't you get a bank overdraft?'

'Not easily,' Smith admits.

Aha, Hartley thinks. His business is stretched. The bank won't touch him.

'You got any collateral?' he asks casually .

'Collateral?' says Smith as if he is unaware of the meaning of the word.

'Yeah. You want five K, what can you put up against it?'

'Paul! You're my mate. You know I'm good for it. I've been in business here for years.'

'I hear there's a new garden centre going to open over Westleigh way.' Hartley has no idea if this is in fact true but a bit of pressure doesn't hurt.

'Wheredya hear that?'

'Don't matter. So, how soon do you need the money?'

'Tomorrow.'

'Tomorrow! That's a bit short notice.'

'I wouldn't ask if it weren't urgent. Paul, you're my best mate.'

'So you keep saying.'

'Can you do it?' Smith is pleading now.

'What's in it for me?' asks Hartley brutally.

'Paul! You're my best mate. I know you can do it.'

'Maybe I can,' says Hartley, dangling his bait, 'but what's in it for me. I'm a businessman not a philanthropist.'

'*Paul! Please!*'

'How about a slice of the garden centre. I'll be a silent partner.'

'*What!*'

'Sounds reasonable to me. If you want the money that badly. I can have it for you tomorrow morning.'

You utter bastard, thinks Smith. You are supposed to be my mate. The thought that if the shoes were on the other foot he would drive precisely the same bargain never occurs to him.

'Say a thirty-seventy split. I'm not unreasonable. Seventy to you, of course,' Hartley adds generously.

Smith contemplates what Regis and Mullen might do to him if he is unable to meet their fee. He does not like where the thought leads him.

'Jed? You still there?'

What choice does he have? Four thousand to the students would have been the cheap option but he has dug himself in too deep now.

'Yeah, I'm still here.' You bloodsucking swine!

'What about it, then?'

'All right, I'll do it.'

'Excellent,' says Hartley, sounding just like Montgomery Burns. 'I'll get on to my solicitor right away and have him draw up the papers. I'll be round to see you tomorrow morning in *our* office.'

Just when Jed Smith thought his life could not get any worse, it suddenly has.

55

Sherborne St John likes to dine formally. Not for him a microwaved meal eaten on his lap in front of the telly. He expects Mrs Wellow to produce and serve a silver service meal that is partaken of by soft candlelight. The correct array of antique (it's been in the family for generations and the St John's have never been ones for replacing anything that is still functional) flatware flanks the place settings and the wine is sipped out of crystal glasses dating from the time of the Regent.

He feels it is incumbent upon him to maintain a certain set of standards.

The evening meal is often eaten in silence as Gwendolyn is not a great conversationalist unless she wants something, so Sherborne is surprised at her animated mood tonight.

'Molly was spooked when I was out riding this morning. I nearly came off. Could have broken my neck.'

'Well I'm very glad you didn't, old girl. What would I do without you?'

'Oh, you'd soon find another to take my place!'

'What a terrible thing to say! I'd miss you terribly. You know that.'

Not enough to sell this dump and go somewhere glamorous, she thinks.

'And I'd miss you, darling!'

'Oh. I'm not going anywhere,' he chuckles.

Don't be too sure about that, she thinks.

'I've made you a surprise. You always drink a sherry before dinner but look, I've mixed you a cocktail for a change. I found the recipe on the computer.'

This is almost true. She has typed *Viagra* into her search engine and found that grapefruit exacerbates the effects of an overdose. Sherborne has issues with high blood pressure and the family has a history of cardiac problems. One of her online purchases was a plentiful supply of the little purple pills. These she has ground up and mixed into the cocktail.

'It's called a Grapefruit Whammy. It's grapefruit, angostura bitters, scotch and rum.' That should disguise the taste of the pills, she thinks.

'I don't usually drink cocktails, you know.'

'Well it's about time you tried something new, you old fuddy-duddy.'

'Are you not having one?'

'I'll stick to my G and T, thank you. Low in calories.'

'Bottom's up!' he says and takes a sip. 'Mmm. Not bad. I could get to like these. What did you say it was called?'

'Grapefruit Whammy,' she replies. *But I don't think you'll be trying many more.*

56

Farleigh Wallop sits in the St John Arms at six o'clock waiting for Paul Hartley to come. He is not really sure Hartley will come but is ready with Plan A if he does.

The door opens and Wallop looks up but it is only the Itchen Prior bell-ringers seeking refreshment after bell-ringing practice. He notices that the couple from London are amongst the group, talking animatedly and enthusing about their new hobby. Tristram Clatford beams in a paternalistic fashion as he ushers the group in. They take over a large round table and Mitchell Dever and his wife go up to the bar to see about drinks.

Other members of the village community drift in and soon Natalie Somerfield is rushed off her feet, but there is still no sign of Paul Hartley. Farleigh Wallop sips at his pint and ruminates over Plan A one more time. He decides to give Hartley another half an hour before abandoning his plan for the time being.

At 8.45 Paul Hartley swaggers into the St John's Arms. He has had a good day, one thing and another considered and hopes to top it off by humiliating Farleigh Wallop. He has no intention of making Wallop any concessions and really just wants the pleasure of making Wallop squirm and beg. He joins Wallop at his table.

'How is the toy soldier business going?' he says by way of a greeting. Wallop grits his teeth and forces a smile.

'What'll you have, Hartley?'

'The usual, a pint of Bishop's.'

Wallop makes his way to the bar and elbows his way through the small knot of drinkers propping it up and orders the drink. Unseen by Hartley and unnoticed by the other drinkers he takes a swig of the pint and tips some of the contents of his bottle of *Dr Collis Brown's Linctus* into the glass. He gives the glass a shake. Old Bishop's is, by its nature, a cloudy pint, not made any better by Gordon Turgis'a neglect of his cellar. Wallop does not think Hartley will notice.

But he is wrong. Hartley takes a long pull at his pint and smacks his lips.

'Old Turgis must be doing summat right. Best pint I've had in here in a long time' he says.

'Look, Hartley, about this lease. Can we discuss it like civilised men.'

'Never said I was civilised,' Hartley replies. A sentiment Wallop wholly agrees with.

'Well, can we pretend. Just for this once?'

'It's like this,' Hartley explains, 'I've got summat *you* want and you haven't got anything *I* want. That's supply and demand,' he points out for the second time today. He really is on a roll. He takes another long draught of his pint. 'This really is good.'

'I'll get you another when you've finished,' Wallop promises. 'But listen. Hartley, another law of economics is this: it is better to have a part of something than all of nothing. If you insist on hiking up the cost of my lease, well, to be frank, I might go out of business. Then you will get nothing. That piece of land is no good to your farm. I know for a fact that you get a grant for it as set aside. You're already winning.'

It is true that Hartley is in receipt of a handsome wodge of DEFRA dosh and that he has somehow overlooked to mention to HMRC that he is also making a bit on the side from Paintball Patrol but that is nobody's business but his own.

He mulls this over while he finishes his pint and hold the empty glass out to Wallop to replenish.

'I dunno,' he says when Farleigh returns with another doctored pint. 'Tell you what, we both know this is about Alice, not money,' he laughs out loud at his witticism; he *really* is feeling good. 'You give her up completely and let her work for me full time an' I'll jes' raise the lease by five hunner'. Deal?'

'What's Alice got to do with this?' asks Wallop, feigning ignorance.

'I love her,' says Hartley, suddenly maudlin. His pupils are shrinking to the size of pinholes despite the dim lighting in the pub.

'That's as it may be,' says Wallop, 'but I don't think I can even stretch that far. I might be able to run to an extra thousand a *year.*'

'Thaz not 'nuff, says Hartley. His speech is getting very slurred.

'I'll get you another pint while you think it over,' says Wallop. When he returns his bottle of *Dr Collis Brown's Linctus* is empty. He will take good care to dispose of it safely.

Hartley lapses into silence as he sups his third pint. Farleigh Wallop watches him closely. Plan A is coming to fruition nicely.

57

Gwendolyn St John hovers outside her husband's bedroom door. She is clad in her second purchase from Hippolyta. com; a split crotch latex cat suit with holes cut out for her breasts. She has allowed ample time for the Viagra to work its magic and is poised to deliver the coup de grace.

She intends to induce a heart attack in Sherborne but feels she at least owed him a happy ending to his life. After all, he is going to leave her a wealthy widow. A farewell bonk to see him on his way and a tearful phone call to the emergency services – 'We were making love. We were so happy. His poor heart just gave out. It must have been the strain. I think he might have taken something, you know, to help him perform' – a respectful period of mourning, say a month and then St John's Hall is on the market. 'I couldn't bear to stay here alone. Without Sherborne. Too many memories!'

She listens at the door and thinks she can hear faint sounds of snoring. Strange, he should be wide awake, dealing with a throbbing member. She opens the door and goes in.

'Darling,' she coos, 'here's the second part of your surprise. I want you to take me. Take me now. Take me as you have never taken me before!' She gets her idea of romantic dialogue from romantic fiction of the Miles and Boon kind: Gwendolyn St John is not a great reader.

Sherborne snores on. She shakes him gently and when that produces no result, quite vigorously.

Nothing.

'WAKE UP!' she shouts.

Nothing. Sherborne sleeps on.

Slowly it dawns on Gwendolyn that she has been conned. The Viagra was nothing of the sort; she has been sold sleeping pills.

'Bugger,' she says and stamps her foot. Tears of anger spill down her cheeks.

She decides to go and wake up Crux Easton and slake her rage on him.

She goes to find her riding crop.

58

The evening is in full swing in the St John Arms. Paul Hartley is in a state of glazed somnambulism. Farleigh Wallop guides him to his feet and links his arm around Hartley's waist. He leads him to the door and manoeuvres him into the Paintball Patrol Land Rover. He drives to the South Field where he sees the lights of the combine methodically combing the field. There is still a section of the field unharvested and this is what Wallop has been counting on.

He drags Hartley out of the vehicle and over to a patch where the barley is tall. He drops him to the ground where he is masked by the high grain. The thresher should be there before he wakes up.

'I always said you deserved a good threshing, you bastard,' Farleigh Wallop says as he goes back to his car.

59

'The weird thing is, I can't remember drinking that much,' says Paul Hartley to his new and very reluctant business partner. 'I was there to shaft it to that old fart Wallop and then I woke up in the South Field. I was having some pretty strange dreams.'

'So what happened?' asks Jed Smith, richer by five thousand pounds but poorer by the loss of thirty percent of his business, which he has just signed away.

'Fortunately the GPS on the combine went on the fritz. It took off across the fields and nearly demolished the Old Barn. Contractor managed to stop the bloody thing and packed up for the night. He's getting it fixed this morning.'

'You had a lucky escape,' Smith sympathises. Shame it didn't happen tomorrow, he thinks, I'd have been quids in and off scot free of you, you leech.

60

Crux Easton is on the phone to Sally Fairfax.

'I've had it with that mad bitch. I really have. She woke me up in the middle of last night. Nearly bloody killed me. She was in a terrible state. Kept yelling "Die, you bastard, die!". She's off her trolley.'

'I said you had to do something about her,' says Sally.

'I tried, Sally. I really did,' but Crux will not elaborate on his attempt at murder. Some secrets are best kept secret, even from the one he loves. 'I'm out of here!'

'What do you mean?' asks Sally.

'I'm packing my kit up and legging it to the woods. I'll camp out 'till I can sort out somewhere to kip. I'll try me mates in Westleigh. Someone will have a floor or a sofa. Or your mum might take me in?' he says, hopefully.

'You know she hates you and won't let you in the house. Says you are a bad influence.' She thinks for a moment. 'We could get a flat,' Sally suggests brightly, visions of a life of blissful domesticity suddenly filling her head.

'Where would we get the money? You're on benefits and I haven't got any. Gwendolyn was never big on paying my wages.'

'We could get jobs,' says Sally, not yet ready to let go of her dream.

'In Westleigh?' Crux laughs bitterly. 'No chance!'

'There must be something we can do. We'll think of something. But I'm so glad you're getting away from that woman. We can make a fresh start. Together!'

'Yeah,' says Crux, a trifle dubiously.

61

Sherborne St John wakes up late. When he comes down for breakfast he finds Gwendolyn already seated at the table.

'Good morning, old girl,' he says cheerily. 'I must say, that's the best night's sleep I've had for years. It must have been that Grapefruit Whotsit. You must make it again.'

'Harumph,' says Gwendolyn, stabbing slice of banana in her bowl of muesli.

'D'ya know, I'm in such a good mood and all is well in the world. Perhaps we *can* afford one of those hot tubbie things you wanted. In fact, I'm sure we can. You can see about as soon as you like.'

'Oh, Sherborne,' says Gwendolyn, not believing her luck. 'You are such a dear.' Sherborne in an expansive and generous mood is the next best thing to Sherborne in the morgue.

But only just.

'And I've been thinking about that Wallop chappie. He's been badgering me to let him use the Wood for his military malarkey. Long Sutton is dead set against it but I don't see the harm. As long as he stays away from the birds. The Wood is plenty big enough. And he'll pay. Nice bit of year round income, I shouldn't be surprised.'

This is a Sherborne that Gwendolyn has not seen for years. She resolves to go back to Hippolyta.com for more supplies of fake Viagra. Grapefruit Wammies might take the place of hot chocolate as the bedtime drink of choice at St John's Hall.

62

Farleigh Wallop has been on tenterhooks all morning waiting to hear of a tragic accident in Paul Hartley's South Field. When the phone rings he grabs it.

'Major Wallop? St John here. I've decided to let you use the Wood for your war games. I've spoken to Long Sutton about it and he'll be in touch to let you know which bits you can use. We can discuss terms later. No need for anything formal. A gentleman's agreement do you? Good.'

Wallop cannot believe his luck. It will mean dismantling the Afghan village on (the late?) Paul Hartley's land but if St John is in agreement he can easily have it re-erected as a 'Cong strongpoint. A bit of living history, he thinks and starts to redesign his publicity broachers in his mind's eye. Re-enact America's Unmentionable War. Can British Pluck win where the Yanks were Defeated? Oh yes. Got to be a winner.

The only thing that could make today better would be the 'sad' news that Paul Hartley has been threshed.

63

'We've a job on evicting some travellers from an unauthorised site,' says Bear Regis, 'but we'll be back in a couple of days to sort out your problem. Mr Smith.'

'But I've paid you,' Jed Smith complains. 'What if they come back tonight?'

'I suggest you lock everything up tight. Maybe ask your local bobby to pass by,' says Peter Mullen.

Getting Barton Stacy involved is the last thing Smith is going to do. He harbours the suspicion that Stacy might have his own doubts about the caravan fires. A friend Stacy might be, he is still first foremost a policeman with a conduit to all manner of official bodies that Smith would rather not trouble.

'How long?'

'I told you, a couple of days,' says Regis, a nasty gleam in his eyes, 'that is, if they kick up rough. If they've got any sense they'll move on peacefully.'

Smith can tell that this is not the preferred outcome. These men exude an air of repressed violence; that is why he has hired them.

'Make it as quick as you can, then.'

'You can count on us, Mr Smith,' Mullen promises.

64

In the woods the four Bosnians are holding a council of war.

'I've had enough,' Jagoda Doboj is saying. 'Living in these woods like animals. I want to go home.'

'We all do, Jagoda,' says Mirko Knin 'but we need money.'

'So let us get it from Smith,' says Nervena Stolac. 'We have given him plenty of time.'

'I agree,' says Vukodin Punta. 'I too am fed up living this life. Besides, I need to be back at university soon. We must visit Smith again.'

'Or leave him a message where to deliver the money. I do not trust that man,' Mirko suggests.

'No, he can't be trusted in any way. That man is a snake,' says Nervena.

'So, we leave him a message,' says Jagoda. 'I can take it in tonight. Push it under his door.'

'Sounds good,' Mirko agrees.

'But where should he leave the money?' asks Nervena. 'It has to be somewhere open where we can watch for a trap.'

'The money will have to be in a bag,' says Vukodin.

'This is just like a kidnapping scenario in a movie,' Jagoda laughs.

'Yeah. But in movies the kidnapper has a motorbike and the money is dropped off a bridge over the motorway,' Nervena points out.

'There is a dead tree with a hollow trunk near the edge of the wood,' Mirko suggests.

'Too obvious?' says Nervena.

'We could just walk into the garden centre and he can give it to us,' says Jagoda.

'Are you crazy? He'll have the police waiting,' says Vukodin.

'*We* are not criminals,' Jagoda protests. 'We just want what is owed to us.'

'The police might see it as demanding money with menaces,' Mirko explains.

'We haven't menaced him,' Jagoda says.

'Nervena threatened to saw his dick off!' Vukodin tells her.

She laughs: 'Yes, I forgot about that.'

'So, that brings us back to the problem. Where does he leave the money?' asks Mirko.

'There is that big standing stone to the west side of the wood,' says Vukodin, who has ranged far and wide. 'It's in a field. I think the field is used for pasture. There are no crops on it. I don't know who it belongs to. Maybe it is part of the big estate.'

'And it's open, you say?' says Mirko.

'Yes. It's a big field, maybe a hectare. Just to the west of the woods.'

'Show me,' says Mirko, aware to the possibilities of a safe drop.

'Show us all,' says Nervena.

'OK. Let's go,' Vukodan says.

65

'Have you seen Crux anywhere?' Gwendolyn asks Sherborne St John later that morning on her phone.

'Isn't he in the stables? That's where he normally is,' he replies.

'That's where I am,' says Gwendolyn. 'The horses have been fed, by the look of it but the stalls haven't been mucked out.'

'Have you tried his room. Maybe he's not feeling well.'

Gwendolyn considers this; perhaps she had been a *little* rough with him last night.

'I don't usually like to bother him in his room,' she lies, 'but I'll go and check.'

She has already done this and found the room suspiciously empty. Crux does not have many possessions but those he has are conspicuous by their absence.

She has never really considered Crux as a person in his own right, rather as a tool to serve her purposes, be they lust or the care of her horses. She knows he has a smart phone that he is never without but has no idea of the number; Crux has always just been there on tap when she wants him.

How dare he just up and go without a by your leave from her.

She will *most certainly* have something to say to him when he comes creeping back.

66

Crux Easton, his worldly goods in his backpack with his sleeping bag rolled neatly on top, is marching through St John's Wood, trying to feel like a tramp in a fairy tale. But what he's really feeling is sorry for himself, cast adrift in the world by the machinations of the wicked queen, who at this moment is no doubt talking to her mirror.

He puts nothing past her.

On the other hand, he has finally made the break. He is free of her. Perhaps, he muses, it was just as well that he didn't manage to kill her. In the cold light of another day his conscience is clear.

Petty criminal he may have been, murderer he is not.

'Heigh-ho, a life on the open road for me,' he sings.

But he is not as cheerful as he sounds. The future looms bleakly ahead. He has no money, no food and no prospects. And this far out in the woods phone reception is pretty lousy.

67

The Bosnians are back in their camp after their scouting trip. They agree the location is suitable. It can be safely monitored from the cover of the trees and offers no chance of concealment in the site itself. It has been decided that Jagoda will deliver instructions to Jed Smith tonight with the two men as backup but discretely out of sight. The mood in the camp is buoyant; at last there is an end to their ordeal in sight. They have no doubt that Smith will cough up the money to get rid of them and then it is up to London and Victoria coach station and home. Their experience as seasonal workers in Britain has been bitter but salutary and they will spread the word once they are safely home.

They have let their guard down and are chatting excitedly about their plans when Crux Easton stumbles upon the camp.

Mirko Knin jumps up and makes a grab for his bow, nocking an arrow onto the bowstring.

'Whoa, whoa,' Crux says, holding out his hands.

'Who are you?' Vukodin demands. 'What do you want?'

'I'm just having a stroll in the woods,' Crux replies. 'Ain't no law against it.'

'Did Jed Smith send you?' asks Nervena suspiciously.

'Smith? From the garden centre? No. Why would he?'

'Are you lying?' Mirko asks. A stupid question; if he were lying he'd hardly admit it.

'Who are you guys?' Crux Easton asks in return.

'It does not matter,' Jagoda says quickly.

'Wait a minute,' says Crux, realisation dawning, 'are you his seasonal workers? From Rumania or wherever?'

'Bosnia,' Nervena blurts in patriotic pride.

'Nervena,' Mirko says in Serbo-Croat. 'Shut up. We do not know who this man is.'

'I think he might be from St John's Hall,' Vukodin says in the same language. 'I have seen him in the village.'

'What are you saying?' Crux asks, not liking this at all.

'Are you from the big house in the village?' Mirko asks switching back to English.

'Not any more,' says Crux.

'What do you mean?' Vukodin asks.

'I've slung me hook,' Crux explains.

This is one English idiom too far for the Bosnians' limited grasp of the English vernacular.

'What hook?' asks a puzzled Jagoda.

'I've scarpered. Done a runner. Had it away on me toes,' Crux tries to explain. Don't these bloody foreigners understand simple English? They ought to be made to takes lessons before coming over here and taking people's jobs.

'I am sorry, I do not understand,' says Vukodin.

'I have left my job at the stables,' Crux explains with exaggerated slowness.

'Ah, you have terminated your employment,' says Jagoda, also no slouch in the linguistic department.

'Well, yeah,' Crux admits.

'And now you are "having a stroll in the woods"' observes Mirko. 'With a rucksack and a sleeping bag?'

'Summat like that. Ain't no law against it,' Crux protests again.

'You are homeless?' Mirko realises.

'Well, sort of,' Crux admits. 'Anyway, what are you guys doing out here?'

The four Bosnians revert to Serbo-Croat for a hurried conference. Mirko lowers his bow but keeps the arrow loosely nocked.

'We, too, have left our employ. We "slung our hook"' says Nervena.

'What are you doing out here, then? Why haven't you gone home? Old Long Sutton won't like you camping out in his woods. He can be a regular terror, can Long.

'We have been careful,' says Jagoda.

'You weren't so careful just now,' Crux points out.

'No,' Mirko acknowledges, 'we were stupid.'

'So why haven't you gone back to Bulgaria?'

'Bosnia,' Nervena hisses.

'Whatever,' says Crux.

'We have no money. Jed Smith would not pay us,' Vukodin explains.

'Yeah, that sounds like Smith. He's known as a tight bastard.'

'But why have you left your employment?' asks Jagoda.

To the increasing incredulity of the Bosnians, Crux gives an edited outline of his life and duties as Gwendolyn St John's stable boy.

'So you were a sex slave?' asks Mirko, with just a touch of envy in his voice.

'Yeah. Summat like that,' Crux confesses.

'You poor man,' says Nervena, genuinely sympathetic.

184

'Yes' says Vukodin, but less so.

'She likes it rough,' Crux says. 'But I was on the receiving end. Bloody near killed me, she did.'

The four Bosnians converse again in Serbo-Croat and reach a decision.

'You can stay here with us. For a couple of days. If you wish?'

'Ace!' says Crux, dropping his pack and sleeping bag at his new home.

68

Paul Hartley is celebrating his new business venture with his new partner in the St John's Arms. He is buying, so Jed Smith, who is not exactly ecstatic about this new business arrangement, has gone along to drown his sorrows at Hartley's expense.

'Bishop's tastes a bit different tonight, Gordon,' Hartley calls over to the publican.

'Well, I ain't changed the barrel,' comes the reply. 'That's Natalie's job an' tonight's her night off. Don't know how I'll manage.'

Apart from Hartley, Smith and Ragged Appleshaw, who counts as a part of the fixtures and fittings, the pub is empty.

'Funny thing,' says Hartley to Smith.

'What is?'

'I'm usually regular as clockwork. Eight o'clock sharp. Every morning.'

'What are you talking about?' says Smith, whose mind is on the return of Regis and Mullen and the revenge he will wreck on his tormentors who have cost him control of his business. Dark thoughts of broken limbs and cracked heads flit through his mind.

'Me bowels,' says Hartley.

'Yer what?'

'Me bowels. Not a twinge.'

'Well, if you will go passing out in a field, what can you expect. Shock to the system, shouldn't wonder,'

'Still. Mustn't dwell on it. Let's talk about Itchen Prior Horticultural. Going Forward, like.'

'Whatd'yer mean? Going forward. It ain't going anywhere.'

'That's *just* what I mean. How are we going to develop it? Make it more dynamic? Maximize profit margins.'

'Have you bin reading them management books?' asks Smith, now very wary about the direction this conversation is taking. He wonders if there is any more mileage in Hartley's bowel movements, or lack of them.

'Stands to reason. New blood an' all. Fresh pair of eyes. I'll need to have a look at the books.'

Oh no you won't, thinks Smith. At least, not the genuine ones. You can have a shuffty at the ones I keep for the tax man. Hardly any profit margin there.

'No hurry, Paul. Let's get the summer over first.'

'Can't agree with you there, Jed me old mate. Soonest sorted the better.'

Before Smith can reply the door to the pub opens and Farleigh Wallop comes in. He sees Hartley and a faint ghost of disappointment flickers across his face.

'What did I drink last night?' Hartley says to him. 'Buggered if I can remember going home.'

'You were drunk,' Wallop says curtly. Behaviour unbefitting an officer and a gentleman, his tone implies.

'Still, Captain Mainwaring, as long as you were buying! Thought any more about our lease?'

'I have actually,' says Farleigh Wallop, 'and I'm afraid I must respectfully decline your terms.'

'You what?'

'I must decline your terms,' Wallop informs him, triumph heavy in his voice. A battle won is sweet and a battle lost by your enemy is even sweeter. 'I have come to a very suitable arrangement with Mr St John. I will be decamping from your land in the next week, as soon as I can facilitate the move. The workmen will be arriving tomorrow. I bid you good night.'

Hartley is struck dumb.

'Bad news?' asks Jed Smith, suddenly cheering up.

'Bugger!' says Paul Hartley. 'That jammy old sod!'

69

Jed Smith's mood of glee at Hartley's defeat by Farleigh Wallop turns to ashes in his mouth when he gets home. Pushed under his door is a note that reads:

Leave the money in a bag by the big rock to the west side of the woods. Come alone.

Tomorrow night at ten o'clock.

Farleigh Wallop has lost no time in trialling his *1960s Nam Jungle Fighter Experience Adventure* (the exact name is still a work in progress). He has sold it as a half-price 'taster' to a regular group of clients, all members of a mid-life crisis motorbike club, men in their late forties and early fifties who want to re-create the wild youth they missed out on.

His agreement with Sherborne St John has only been in place for a couple of days and so there has not been time to erect any buildings yet but Long Sutton is resentfully on board as per the instructions of Sherborne and has allocated Farleigh Wallop a section of St John's Wood 'to play his silly games' in with a stern warning not to transgress his boundaries.

Tonight's exercise will consist of one group 'going to ground' in the woods with the other group charged with a 'seek, make contact and eliminate' mission.

The first group have already disappeared into the wood and the second group are busy pulling on their masks and chatting excitedly whilst hefting their paintball markers; they all wear camouflage uniforms. Unfortunately, Wallop has not yet sourced jungle kit, so the uniforms are the sandy yellow of an Afghan deployment. No-one seems to question the authenticity of the clothing or has realised that they stand out like sore thumbs in the late summer night.

Adrenalin is pumping as they crash off through the woods in search of 'Charlie'.

Seek and destroy!

The four young Bosnians, accompanied by Crux Easton, who has gone along for the laugh, are in position on the fringes of the wood overlooking the field with the standing stone. Crux, the local boy, has informed them that the standing stone is known locally as The Devil's Tooth.

It is nine thirty.

72

Jed Smith has no intension whatsoever in parting with any more cash than this whole sorry business has already cost him. He will not be venturing out in the woods tonight.

But Bear Regis and Peter Mullen will.

They had returned to Itchen Prior Horticultural late in the afternoon wearing boots, dark jeans and long sleeved black tee shirts tightly stretched over muscled chests and firm biceps. They frightened the life out of Smith but attracted admiring glances from his female staff.

'Welcome back,' Smith greets them. 'All go well with the eviction?'

'Oh yes,' says Peter Mullen, a look on his face that reminded Smith of a hungry wolf he had seen on a nature documentary about the Canadian north woods.

'Very tasty,' Bear Regis agrees, 'Good little workout, that one.'

'Keeps yer fit,' says Mullen.

Smith gets down to business. He feels very uncomfortable in the presence of these two men and wants to get them out of his life as quickly as possible.

'They expect me to drop off a bag in a field to the west of St John's Wood at ten o'clock. There is a big standing stone in the middle of the field, The Devil's Tooth it's called. I need you to put the frighteners on them. Scare 'em off for good.'

'Are they armed?' asks Regis.

'Armed?' asks Smith in alarm, 'I shouldn't think so.'

'And they are two men and two women?'

'Yes.'

'Why couldn't you handle them?' Mullen asks with genuine curiosity.

'There are *four* of them,' Smith protests.

'Piece of piss,' Regis mutters to his partner.

'Maybe for you,' Smith retorts. 'I'm not a violent man. That's why I hired you.'

'Oh, we can be violent men, all right,' growls Mullen. 'Love a bit of a ruck, we do.'

'How badly do you want us to do them over. Broken legs, arms? Cracked heads? More?' asks Regis.

'Just frighten them off,' Smith says in desperation, frightened of coming out and actually saying what he would really like, which is 'terminate with extreme prejudice'. But at the end of the day, he does not want to condone murder. Not if it can be traced back to him!

'So, let's get this clear. Is it a baseball bat job?'

'They have to be able to walk so they can go away. That's all I want. For them to just go away.' Smith is almost wailing.

'So, just a good talking to.' Regis confirms. 'Maybe a smack for good measure.'

'To make the point clear,' Mullen adds helpfully, in case Smith does not understand.

'Yes, yes. That's all I want. So they understand that they have to leave and go home.'

'How are they going to do that without any dosh?' asks Mullen practically.

'That's not my problem,' says the Jed Smith of old. 'They should have made provision for that out of their wages.'

'That you didn't pay 'em,' Regis points out.

'Look, that's not my problem,' says Smith. 'If you feel so sorry for them, go and give them some of the money I paid you!'

'We can't do that, my son,' Regis explains, 'we've got mortgages to pay.'

'Wives and nippers to feed.' Mullen adds.

'Well, go and earn it then,' Smith snaps.

'Calm down, sunshine. We're here to do a job an' we'll do it.'

Smith has a sudden thought: 'Do you need plastic bags?'

'What for?' asks Mullen, truly mystified.

'To shit in. I thought all you special forces guys shat in plastic bags and buried it.'

'Not if we don't have to,' Regis laughs.

'I think we'll be all right for tonight. We'll go before we go,' says Mullen. What a wanker, he thinks. Neither of the men are warming to their employer, a coward who employs others to do his dirty work.

73

Long Sutton *really* does not like the idea of Farleigh Wallop and a group of townies mucking about in his woods. But Sherborne St John has given them leave to do so and the Suttons are loyal retainers of the St Johns. However, Sherborne has told him to 'just keep an eye open in case anything goes amiss' and that he will do to the best of his ability. He has business himself later on tonight, but for the moment he is prowling the woods on guard in the vicinity where Wallop is staging his daft war games.

He hears a group of men moving with what they belief is stealth. They are wearing what looks like black pyjamas and are talking in what they imagine to be whispers. Sutton slips behind the cover of a tree and watches them spread out and try to hide in bushes. One of them takes out a vape pipe and blows a cloud of fragrant smoke that hangs in the still night air. Sutton hears the pop of a drink can being opened and the sound of beer being poured down a thirsty throat. After a few minutes on of the men crawls out of hiding to urinate noisily against a tree and then a loud curse when another man discovers he is hiding on top an an ants' nest. In the distance he can hear another group approaching but this first group seem to unaware of it.

He decides that, far from being any kind of threat to the ecosystem of the woods, it might well prove a source of amusing entertainment after all. Bloody townies playing at soldiers in the woods.

What a bunch of twats! he thinks

He does not hear a sound from the two men in black who are moving through the wood guided by a compass.

74

It is twenty minutes past ten o'clock and there is no sign of Jed Smith. Clouds cover the moon but the standing stone is clearly visible, a white sentinel in the middle of the field.

'He's not going to come,' says Nervena.

'Give him a bit more time,' Jagoda urges. She really wants this to happen. She has had enough of living out in nature and longs for the comforts of home; a warm bed, hot water, her family. This trip to England, so full of promise as turned into a nightmare from which there seems to be no escape.

'Let's spread out a bit more,' says Mirko. 'Put some space between us and cover more ground. I agree we should give him a bit more time.'

'What choice do we have?' says Vukodin.

Crux Easton is losing patience.

'Bollocks to this,' he says. 'I'm going to go back to the camp, if I can find it in the dark. I'll have a brew waiting.'

'A brew?' asks Jagoda.

'A cup of tea.' Bloody foreigners.

He stands up and stretches, yawns and sets off to try and find his way back to the camp and his sleeping bag.

He has gone about three hundred metres when two shadows detach themselves from the trees and pinion his arms to his sides. A sudden punch to his stomach makes him double up and retch.

'Time to go home, my son,' one of the shadows hisses at him.

Crux is gasping and trying to catch his breath.

'Did yer hear me?' the voice demands.'

Crux sucks air back into his lungs, tears in his eyes.

'Did that mad bitch send you?' he says.

There is a silence.

'I'm not going back to those stables. I don't care!' he says defiantly.

'What stables?' asks Regis.

'Wait a minute, you sound English,' says Mullen.

'Course I sound English. I was bloody born here in Itchen Prior.'

'Ah,' says Mullen,

'What you doing poncing around in the woods?' Regis demands.

Crux Easton is getting fed up with his right to innocently walk in the woods being questioned.

'Who are you, anyway?' he says.

'Don't ask,' Mullen warns.

'You seen a gang of foreigners lurking in the woods?' Regis asks.

'What kind of foreigners?' asks Crux, a nasty suspicion beginning to dawn on him.

'Foreign foreigners. Kids like yourself. Foreign kids,' Regis explains.

'Could be terrorists,' Mullen says darkly.

'Are you Old Bill, then?'

'Never mind who we are, answer the question,' Mullen says.

'No,' says Crux, who wants no part of this kind of trouble.

'Should we give 'im another little slap, make sure he's not bullshitting us?' Regis says to Mullen.

'I'm not,' Crux says quickly. 'I don't know any foreigners. Honest.'

Suddenly there is a burst of noise, of man shouting and crashing through the undergrowth. Mullen and Regis let go of Easton's arms and melt back into the night.

Easton runs back the way he came and stumbles over Mirko Knin.

'Get away,' Crux tells him. 'It's a trap. There are two heavies after you.'

Without waiting for a reply Crux heads back into the woods in the direction of the commotion. He reasons he will be safe amongst a group of people, regardless of what they are doing.

And what they are doing is running around shooting balls of paint at each other and screaming war cries. The *Jungle Fighter Experience Adventure* has turned out to be a rousing success.

Farleigh Wallop is a happy man.

75

On the edge of the field the four Bosnians, alerted by Crux Easton, make a break for it, running in the open where they can see clearly. There is no sign of pursuit but they run hard, re-entering the wood six hundred metres further down. Cautiously, they sneak back to the camp. There is no sign of Crux Easton and his backpack and sleeping bag have gone.

In the woods themselves the two professional soldiers are trying to dodge the free for all paintball fight that has erupted around them. Mullen is hit by a stray round and a large yellow splodge of paint spreads on his chest.

'Bloody hell,' he says. 'I've been hit.'

'Lucky they're only playing cowboys and Indians,' Regis tells him.

'Do you reckon those kids will still be there?' Mullen asks, angry at the state of his tee shirt.

'Buggered if I know; I wouldn't be,' says Regis.

'Me neither. Call it a day?'

'Yeah. Let's get out of this madhouse.'

'Can I help you gentlemen?' asks a quiet voice.

Trained to survive and fight in the jungle though they are, they were unaware of Long Sutton's approach. He is behind them. They spin round and see the gamekeeper cradling his shotgun, a finger curled around the trigger.

'Are you with Major Wallop's friends?' Sutton asks.

'Who?' asks Regis. It is obviously a night for confused identities.

'I'll take that as a no, then, shall I? Might I ask what you are doing here in the middle of the night?'

Both men are thinking about taking *him* out with extreme prejudice, risking a shot before they can disable him. As if reading their thoughts, Sutton takes a step back and raises the gun slightly: not exactly threatening them but showing he is not to be trifled with.

'We were having a stroll when we ran into these loonies.' Mullen indicates the retreating sounds of the paint ballers with his thumb.

'We'll be on our way,' says Regis. 'If that's OK with you?'

'I'll bid you goodnight, then' says 'Long' Sutton, melting away into the darkness.

'He's good,' admits Mullen.

'Very good, my friend. An' he's watching us,' says Bear Regis softly.

'Home it is, then,' says Mullen.

76

Jed Smith sits drinking whiskey in his lounge and waiting for news. He jumps when he hears the soft knock on his door. Mullen and Regis stand outside.

'Well?' Smith demands.

'It's a bloody madhouse out there,' Mullen tells him. 'Look at my tee shirt.'

Smith sees the yellow stain on Mullen's chest but can make no sense of it,

'Geezers running round shooting at each other with paint ball guns. Pack of bloody cowboys,' Regis explains.

'Never mind that, did you find them?' Smith asks with some urgency.

'Nah. We found an English kid waltzing around in the woods.'

'Had six fingers on his left hand.'

'Oh,' says Smith, 'he'll be a local.'

Mullen and Regis exchange a glance.

'And there was this tall guy with a shotgun. Good woodsman,' Regis adds grudgingly.

'That'll be Long Sutton,' Smith informs them. 'Anyway, what about these blackmailers?'

'Not a sight of them an' then that Sutton bloke sort of warned us off. We didn't think we should hurt him. Not what you paid us for.'

'No,' says Smith, the whiskey giving him courage, "I paid you to see off my problem. And you haven't!'

'Early days yet,' says Regis.

'It's not good enough! It's not difficult to beat up a few kids. You're supposed to be professionals.'

'Why didn't you do it?' asks Regis in a low voice.

'I've got better things to do than chase around after a pack of no-good, work-shy, greedy foreign students.'

'He hasn't got the bottle,' says Mullen to his partner.

'How much do you owe them?' asks Regis shrewdly.

'No of your business,' Smith snaps at him.

'You didn't pay up their wages, did you?'

'Is that it? You were swindling them outta their wages?' says Mullen, contempt in his voice.

'It isn't like that. I can't have my workers making demands. What if the others found out?'

'Working on the black, were they? No tax, no stamp?'

'How dare you!' Smith has foolishly lost all fear of these two men who have the temerity to question him.

'We dare,' says Peter Mullen. 'We *are* professionals.' He takes a step forward until his face is very close to Smith's. 'Be a big mistake for you to forget it.'

Smith suddenly feels his knees go weak; he realises he might have pushed these men too far.

'I paid you to do a job,' he whines.

'We are not usually picky who we work for,' says Bear Regis. 'but you really are a piece of shit.'

He leaves the house.

Mullen raises a fist to Smith, who cowers in terror. Mullen laughs and follows his partner out the door.

He slams it shut after him.

'What a gobshite,' he says.

The paint ballers have gone happily back to their motor-bikes and roared off into the night, waking everyone in Itchen Prior in the process after a fun-filled night of mock mayhem with promises that they will be back. Farleigh Wallop is a happy and somewhat richer man.

A group of figures are winding widdershins around The Devil's Tooth. They are carrying flaming torches and chanting, casting distorted shadows on the ground but there is nobody around to see or hear them.

The moon is setting, silver.

The Bosnians have returned to their camp; they have nowhere else to go. Their mood is despondent. They had not expected Jed Smith to resort to bringing in thugs from outside to attack them, for they are sure this is what he has done.

Their food has run out and they have very little water. Between them they have just £87.45 in cash, not enough to do anything.

They are listlessly debating what to do.

'We can give ourselves up to the police. Maybe they will deport us?' Jagoda suggests.

'Smith will accuse us of criminal damage. We could go to prison,' Mirko points out.

'At the very least we will have to pay a fine and we have no money,' Nervena says.

'I just know I can't live like a hunted animal any longer,' says Jagoda as she starts to cry.

Nervena puts her arm around her friend and hugs her.

'I wish we had never met that swine,' she says.

As if by magic, a large man with a shaven head materialises out of the trees. Mirko makes a grab for his bow.

'Put it down, son,' says a voice from behind him. 'You don't want to do something you may regret.'

'Are you the men from Smith?' asks Vukodin. In many ways he is happy that it has come to a confrontation. Maybe this will resolve things.

'In a way,' says Bear Regis. 'Why don't you make a cup of tea and tell us your side of the story?'

The tension eases as they brew up the last of their tea and they start to tell their tale.

'And all we want to do is to go home,' Mirko sighs. 'We are students. We must go back to our studies.'

'But how can we? All we really wanted from Jed Smith was the money he cheated us out of,' says Vukodin Punta.

'He paid us very well to duff you up,' says Peter Mullen.

The idiom is strange to the Bosnians but they can make a shrewd guess at its meaning.

'And are you going to 'duff us up'?' asks Jagoda Doboj, not really caring any more.

'Nah,' says Mullen. 'Me and me mate here talked it over last night. We are going to give you some of the dosh Smith paid us to put the fear of God into you.'

'We've got kids ourselves,' says Regis. 'A grand get you home?'

'A what?' asks Nervena.

'A thousand quid.'

Jagoda cannot believe what is happening and starts to cry again.

'You mean you will give us a thousand pounds?' asks Vukodin. 'Just like that?'

'It's Smith's money and we are not going to give you *all* he paid us. We've got wives and kids to support.'

'Tell you what, pack up your kit and we'll give you a lift to the nearest station,' says Mullen.

'Is this a trick?' It seems too good to be true to Mirko.

'If it was, we'd hardly tell you, now would we? Let's just say we agree that Jed Smith is a slimeball. Way I see it, you've got nothing to lose.'

'Here,' says Bear Regis, pulling a bundle of £20 notes from his pocket and tossing them to Jagoda. 'Stop crying and start packing.'

Twenty minutes later they walk out of the forest and head for home at last.

Long Sutton watches them go; there is nothing that goes on in his woods that he is unaware of. He has been listening to their conversation with Mullen and Regis, two gentlemen he has his eye on, and can only wish them God Speed. He has no love for Jed Smith either.

Perhaps now his woods will settle back to normal.

Then he remembers the paint ballers and gives a groan.

What *was* Sherborne St John thinking!

Gwendolyn sits in her boudoir, brooding and plotting.

Of Crux Easton there has been no sign for over a week and Sherborne has approached Henry Grey to use his connections with Shearwater Agricultural College to find a replacement for Crux.

When Sherborne questioned Gwendolyn as to whether she had any idea why Crux has decamped she played the mystified innocent and admitted herself as puzzled as her husband why Crux would abandon a secure job.

'Perhaps he decided to go travelling?' she said. 'He's got a girlfriend. A bit of a bad influence, I think. You remember, we had her helping out at the garden party.'

'Funny thing, though, old girl. I thought we'd straightened him out. What with that brush with the law and his mother throwing him out.'

'I agree. It's the ingratitude that I can't understand. Just leaving like that and not saying a word.'

'Well, anyway, Henry Grey thinks he might have someone for us. Someone from the College's Equine Studies course.'

'We don't need a vet, darling.'

'I think it's a made up name for stable-handing. Like all those university courses in Drama and Fast Food Science. There seem to be an awful lot of made-up courses nowadays.' Sherborne had gone to Balliol College, Oxford and studied Anglo-Saxon, a fact of which he is immensely proud, though he has not spoken a word of the language since graduating, or at least only the occasional four-letter words.

'Oh,' Gwendolyn said, then left a decent pause before adding, as if on a whim: 'Is Henry looking for a male or female?'

'No idea. Does it make a difference?'

'Oh, of course not,' Gwendolyn said, then quickly added, 'just curious. We've always had male stable hands.'

'Might be time for a change, then,' said Sherborne. 'Move with the times. Equality and all that.'

Not if I can help it, Gwendolyn thinks. *A girl might have trouble performing her extra-curricula duties*. But then again, she reflects, *I'll try anything once*.

'How soon will you know, darling? We need a replacement soon. I'm looking after things for the moment but I can't go on doing it. It's not proper.'

'I thought about getting young Hatch Warren in for the moment. What do you think?'

Gwendolyn thinks that if she made a move on Hatch, Hare would take a Stanley knife to her face.

'He might be a short-term solution,' she says in a dubious tone. 'Does he know anything about keeping horses?'

'He's good country stock,' Sherborne tells her, 'he should be fine. You can teach him the ropes, can't you, old girl?'

Gwendolyn thinks about Hare Warren again and shudders inwardly. She knows that Hare Warren is what the term 'feral psychopath' was invented for.

'I can try,' she says bravely.

'Well, that's settled then. I'll have a word with Seth and Ashley. Can't have you getting your pretty little hands dirty now, can we.'

'You're so thoughtful,' Gwendolyn purrs.

And starts thinking about Plan B.

81

Tristram Clatford is on the telephone to Mitchell Dever.

'Mitchell, I've just come off the phone from talking to a woman from the BBC. Radio Four. They want to record us for *Bells on Sunday*. Ringing a Triple Bob Major. Can you imagine? Us! On the radio?'

'That's fantastic news, Tristram,' says Mitchell. 'I'll tell Jocasta. She'll be thrilled.'

'It'll be a feather in the cap for St Bride's and Itchen Prior. Put us right on the map.'

St Bride's-in-the-Bath is the early thirteenth century church that is the architectural pride of Itchen Prior. It stands on the site of a very early shrine sacred to the goddess Brigit and her holy spring (the Bath) that has morphed into the village duck pond by the Green.

The carving of the Green Man over the door to the vestry is accounted amongst the finest in the land.

'I say,' says Tristram. 'Jocasta works for the Beeb. Did she perhaps put in a word?'

'Wrong department, I'm afraid.'

'I see, well, look, here's the thing, they want to come down in a couple of weeks to record us, some time in early August, so we need to practice every night. Are you and Jocasta available?'

'I've got to go up to London for some meetings and I won't be back until late but I'll check with Jocasta to see if she's free. I can't see any problems. She basically works from home now. God bless the internet.'

'Amen,' says Tristram automatically. 'Try and make it if you can.'

'Will do.'

Dever rings off and goes to tell Jocasta the news.

82

Sherborne stands at the doorway of the Warren's cottage and knocks. The sound of thrash metal booms out of an open window; Hare is generously sharing her music with the neighbours.

In the Dever house all doors and windows are tightly closed against the racket and Mitchell is playing his new *Mumford and Sons* album on his iPad. Jocasta is listening to bells being rung on YouTube through her headphones. They are becoming used to Hare Warren and her taste in music.

Hatch opens the door and bellows: 'Dad, it's the Squire!'

'Actually, it's you I've come to see, Hatch,' Sherborne says.

From somewhere inside the house Seth shouts: "Turn it down, Hare. The Squire's here.'

And miraculously the music is turned down and the window frames stop shaking.

'Me, Squire?' asks Hatch. Adding swiftly, 'I ain't done nothing.'

'Nobody said you have. I'm here to offer you a temporary job, if you want it?'

Hatch Warren is a stranger to the world of legitimate employment and looks puzzled, as if struggling to come to terms with the concept.

Seth has joined his son in the doorway. 'Afternoon, Squire,' he says.

Sherborne only visits the Warrens when something is amiss. Seth can't think of anything that can be proved against them to warrant this visit. He shuffles his feet as Ashley Warren joins them in the doorway.

'Ah, Seth. Ashley, I'm here to see if your lad would like a bit of temporary work. We've lost our stable lad and we need someone to step up and fill the gap until we can find a replacement.'

The Warrens take a collective step back into the hallway and hold a quick muttered conference. In this they are joined by Hare, who has intuited that something is going on and has left her lair and her music to investigate.

In the gloom of the hallway four pairs of eyes glint like foxes caught in the headlights of a vehicle.

As the matriarch and de facto head of the family, Ashley Warren steps forward.

'You want our Hatch as a stable lad, is that right?' she asks.

'Yes, until we get a full time replacement. We wouldn't expect him to live in. And we'd pay him over the minimum wage.'

'How much is that, then?' asks Hatch eagerly.

'Never you mind, my lad,' says his mother, 'it'll come straight to me to pay for yer keep.'

'Aw, Ma! That's not right,' Hatch protests.

'It's not for me to say,' says Sherborne, 'but the lad should get something in his pocket for his hard work.'

The mention of hard work brings a frown to Hatch's face.

'What would I have to do like, Squire?'

'Mucking out, feeding, keeping the tack neat, getting the horses ready for Mrs St John when she wants to go riding,'

'I'll do it!' Hare Warren shouts.

'I was asked first,' Hatch insists.

'Perhaps you could both do it? It's called "job sharing", I believe,' suggests Sherborne.

'Can we, Ma?'

'Yeah, can we?'

'When do you want them to start?' asks Ashley, giving implied consent.

'I'll take them over now and Gwendolyn can show them the ropes, if you like?'

The Warrens retreat into the gloom one more time and huddle together, muttering.

A decision has been reached.

'You tek 'em, Squire,' says Ashley.

'An' mind you behave,' Seth warns them.

'Jump in the Range Rover, then, and I'll run you over to the house. Mrs St John will be so glad to see you. You can start right away.'

83

Marjory Hinton Daubrey and Jocasta Dever are fast becoming best friends forever.

The idea to move to the country was mainly Mitchell's dream; Jocasta misses London and all that it has to offer and the friends she has there. Her work does take her back to London but she is usually back in Itchen Prior by nightfall and for the first few weeks she felt cut off and lonely. Marjory has proved to be a rock for Jocasta to cling on in the restricted social world of the village.

Jocasta's former best friend, Rachel Highbury, seems to hold her (most unfairly, Jocasta thinks) in some way responsible for the bust up of her marriage to the exiled Toby - perhaps because Mitchell gave Toby shelter after the housewarming party. But that was *hardly* Jocasta's fault. And *she* wasn't the one who was playing away, now, was she?

The Cuthbertsons, too, have maintained a frosty silence, claiming their children are having to have expensive counselling after being traumatised by the Warren twins.

Again, *not* Jocasta's fault.

Her one consolation is her brand spanking new bright yellow VW Beetle; Jocasta did not have a car in London. The extensive transport system made two-car ownership an unnecessary luxury and parking would have been a nightmare, but here in the country, with its one bus an hour policy, a car is essential. At least, that is what she told

Mitchell. And there is some truth in that, after all said and done.

Jocasta and Marjory have been out on a girly-day-out to the bright lights of the county town and the boot of the Beetle is loaded with shopping bags. Marjory is enjoying the summer school holidays and enjoying the company of her sophisticated chum.

'Why aren't you married?' Jocasta asks her.

'Never found the right man,' Marjory laughs, 'and the gene pool around Itchen Prior is hardly worth diving into.'

'How about Tristram Clatford? You seem close.'

Marjory smiles a wistful little smile.

'He *is* a lovely man. But not the marrying type. Not for me, anyway. A bit too old.'

'You must have had boyfriends?'

'Oh, there were a couple at university when I was doing my teacher training. But nothing serious.'

She smiles again at the memory; in her first year she had slept with most of the male fresher intake before moving on to the male faculty in her second year and moving on again to an eclectic mix in her third. In her PGCE year she added a number of teachers to her score. The demure little school marm is a persona she has adopted for the benefit of Itchen Prior. But she is determined her past promiscuity will forever be a locked secret, that not even her new best friend forever will become privy to after a careless bottle of Chardonnay.

'Anyway,' Marjory asks, 'when are you and Mitchell going to have children?'

'He doesn't want them. He's had the snip.'

'What about you?

'Bit late for me and Mitchell now,' says Jocasta with a tinge of sadness.

'But you would have liked to?'

'I might have done. If things were different.'

They drive on in silence, each preoccupied with their own thoughts.

They arrive back at Yew Tree Cottage where Mitchell is waiting to greet them. He is bubbling over with news.

'We're going to be on Radio Four,' he says as he fusses them into the living room. '*Bells on Sunday*. In a fortnight!'

Marjory claps her hands and gives a little squeak of excitement.

'Wow!' says Jocasta.

'Tristram phoned me earlier,' says Mitchell with a feeling of superiority that he should be the bearer of such important news.

'Good for St Bride's,' says Marjory.

'And good for us,' adds Jocasta.

'It'll mean lots of rehearsals and I've got to be up in Town quite a bit,' Mitchell says ruefully. "I hope I make the cut.'

'I'm sure we'll manage, darling,' Jocasta says, just a little spitefully. 'You can always be in the reserve team.'

'Oh, I don't think we've got a reserve team,' says Marjory. 'You'll just have to manage as best you can. Cheer up. You've done ever so well and picked it up ever so quickly. You must be a natural.'

Mitchell grins and preens. 'Do you think so?'

'Oh yes. It took me simply *ages* to get it right.'

Mitchell cannot contain himself and bounces on the balls of his feet.

'Well, ladies,' he booms, 'you must be exhausted after all that shopping. Can I get you a drink? Marjory? What'll you have? White wine? G and T? Jocasta?'

They settle on a glass (or two) of chilled Prosecco.

I can still turn a man's head, Marjory thinks.

And didn't Mitchell jump when I goosed him in the hot tub!

84

'You've done *what*?' Gwendolyn shrieks.

'I've solved the problem with the stables. Until we get someone in permanently.' Sherborne is surprised at his wife's reaction; he had honestly thought she would be pleased at the news.

'Those two little hooligans! I wouldn't put it past them to be horse slashers!'

'Hush, old girl. They'll hear you!'

The twins have their faces pressed to the window of the Range Rover looking for all the world like cherubs. Gwendolyn's shriek is slightly muffled but they heard what she said.

'She sounds pleased,' Hatch says to his twin.

'Nasty old bat. I'd like to slash *her*.'

'Don't knock it, Hare. We could be onto summat good here. Don't mess it up.'

'I'll mess her up.'

'Cool it! Ma'll skin you if upset Squire.'

Somehow Hare manages to suppress the rage that is constantly boiling up inside her like a volcano on a fault line and has done ever since she can remember. She cannot fully understand the world of other people, cannot empathise with their complex feelings and emotions. Apart from Hatch, she has always been alone, isolated even from her parents. She hides herself in death metal music and retreats from the alien outside.

'Give them a try, old girl. Fair crack of the whip!' Sherborne is saying to Gwendolyn.

But not the sort of whip she liked to crack with Crux, she thinks.

'What do they know about horses?' she demands, dropping her voice so the twins can't hear her.

'*You* know about horses, my dear. Teach them. All they really need to know is how to muck out and keep things in good order. When to feed the animals and what and how much. That sort of thing,'

'I don't trust them an inch. They are *never ever* to come into the house. Not without an armed guard.'

'You're being a trifle hard, old girl.'

'With Hare and Hatch Warren? Impossible!'

'Shall I send them away? It'd mean you have to keep on doing the hard work.'

Gwendolyn loves, or at least, is very fond of, her horses but she has not dragged herself up the social ladder of Itchen Prior to shovel horse shit. Whereas that is *exactly* the kind of work suited to the skills of a member of the Warren family; the Warrens and the Abbas's go back a long, long way in Itchen Prior and each has the measure of the other. As indeed she once had the measure of Seth Warren, without Ashley finding out.

'All right,' she agrees reluctantly, 'we'll give them a try out. But the first sign of anything, back they go! Ashley Warren will not be too chuffed with them. God help 'em.'

Sherborne open the door of the Range Rover and the twins bound out like a pair of demented red setters.

'Mrs St John will show you the ropes. You can start immediately. The stables have been a bit neglected since Crux Easton vanished.

'Bet she killed him,' Hare says *sotto voce* to her brother.

'Shut up,' he hisses through closed teeth. 'Remember what I said.'

'Come on, then. And don't touch anything until I tell you.' Gwendolyn strides to the stables and throws open the double doors.

The ripe smell of horses and befouled straw hits them in the face.

'Bloody hell!' says Hare, retching.

'You'll get used to it,' Gwendolyn smirks.

One up for the Abbases!

85

Jed Smith is having a refreshing evening drink in the St John's Arms with his new partner. The Bosnians are out of his life for good and he has resolved to only employ illegals from sub-Saharan Africa in future summer seasons. He is feeling almost at one with the world, especially after Hartley has confided that he still has not had a bowel movement and is in considerable discomfort. Hartley's defeat in the Alice Lacey War by Farleigh Wallop is an added bonus for Smith.

With Hartley on the back foot, now is the time for Smith to start extricating himself from the partnership agreement he has been forced into. He raises his glass to Hartley in feigned sympathy whilst pondering if Bear Regis and Peter Mullen might be employed to solve the Hartley Problem with extreme prejudice, as they say in the CIA. Regretfully, he doubts that they would be up for a little bit of murdering. What they got up to in foreign parts in the service of Her Majesty and the full blessing of the State they might baulk at here at home. And broken arms and legs, whilst gratifying, would not solve the dilemma.

He must think of a solution himself.

The bells of St Bride's start to ring out.

'Bloody racket,' Gordon Turgis moans from behind the bar and Smith realises that Ragged Appleshaw is missing from his usual perch.

'Ol' Appleshaw tells me the BBC want to record 'em ringin' the bells for some programme about bells,' Turgis adds. 'Goin' to be practisin' every day. It'll kill trade.'

'Yeah, Gordon, but they always come in here for a drink after practise, don't they?'

'Well, there is that,' Gordon admits gloomily.

He is very much a glass-completely-empty-and-dropped-onto-the-floor-where-it-shatters type of pessimist. If there is a bright side of things, the light has yet to shine on Gordon Turgis.

'Have you considered the Christmas stock for the gift shop?' Hartley asks Smith. The bells have put him in mind of the festive season only scant months away. 'I've got some ideas along those lines.'

Smith stifles a groan: a solution to the Hartley Problem must be found.

And quickly.

Gwendolyn sits in her boudoir brooding and plotting.

Her day has not been all bad. The Warren twins have mucked out the stables without traumatising the horses; Sherborne has been packed off to bed with a Grapefruit Whammy (she has invested in more of the fake Viagra – if it's no good for one job, then it's good for another!) and there is the prospect that Henry Grey will soon come up with a replacement for Crux Easton. Whom she finds she actually misses; a good workout would set her up nicely for bed.

She has come up with Plan B with regard to Sherborne.

She switches on her laptop and goes online to Hippolyta. com.

Hatch Warren has been ferreting around behind the stables. He rushes back in to where his sister is sitting, having a staring match with Prince of Darkness. Gwendolyn has been out on him this morning and he is feeling good after the exercise. Hare is trying to project an air of menace in revenge for the horse nipping at her when she went to rub him down. She has made an enemy here but dare not extract physical revenge for fear of what Gwendolyn might do if she finds out. Psychological warfare leaves no visible marks.

'Sis! Guess what!'

'What?' says Hare, not taking her eyes off the horse's. Is the Prince of Darkness beginning to shuffle uncomfortably? Ha!

'I reckon I've found Crux Easton's stash!'

'What stash?'

'Round the back. Hidden.'

'What you talking about, Hatch. You gone daft?'

'Crux. He were up to his tricks. Growin' weed!'

'Weed?'

'Yeah. Couple o' plants. I picked off a few leaves an' that. We just need to dry 'em out.'

'Wicked!'

Gwendolyn has launched Plan B.

She goes online and buys several box sets of *Midsomer Murders*, this time in her own name. Where is the harm in watching a prime-time TV show? However, she has her own agenda researching tips on rural based murder. So far John Nettles and Gus Dudgeon have outsmarted the villains but Gwendolyn is sure she can spot an opportunity, a twist she can employ to kill her husband and, most importantly, get away with it.

The murderers in Midsomer can never just *leave it* at one killing but have to go on a spree. The Barnabys *never* catch on to the first in what, inevitably, becomes a slaughter fest. This is the lesson she has learnt: just do Sherborne and don't try to overextend. There are any number of people she would like to off but that would just be *greedy*.

Careful and cautious does it.

'Hello, Sherborne?' Henry Grey says into his mobile the next morning.

'Speaking.'

'I think I've got you a replacement for young Easton.'

'Excellent!'

'She's just qualified with her BTech Extended Diploma in Equine Studies from Shearwater College.'

'Sounds most impressive,' says Sherborne with approval.

'I had a long chat with her course tutor and he spoke highly of her. She's keen as mustard. Loves anything horsey. And a hard worker, by all accounts.'

'Again, she sounds right up our street. When can we see her, vet her, so to speak. We've got the Warren twins filling in but Gwendolyn's not happy with the arrangement.'

'I'll give the college another ring. See what I can set up.'

90

The Warren twins are at that moment sprawled on the floor of the stables enjoying the fruits of Crux Easton's labours and listening to death metal on Hare's smart phone.

'Bugger me, that's good,' Hare says, passing the joint to her brother.

'He knows 'is stuff, does Crux,' Hatch agrees, taking a long toke into his lungs and releasing a stream of smoke in the direction of the horse stalls.

'Chills the horses, too,' says Hare, taking the joint from her brother and inhaling deeply. 'Whoa, I'm blattered.'

'Yeah,' murmurs Hatch, beginning to drift off to the music. 'Pass the spliff.'

She goes to pass the joint to her brother but fumbles and drops it onto the floor. She is too stoned to notice and Hatch is away with the fairies and has forgotten all about the joint.

'Whoa!' she says again and becomes engrossed in a long guitar solo.

The smouldering joint comes into contact with the loose straw strewn on the floor of the stables and ignites it. Hatch is lying back with his eyes closed vaguely drumming his fingers to the music that is seesawing around in his head, while Hare is lost in the synaesthetic display in her own.

Gwendolyn chooses that moment to visit her horses and is confronted by the sight of the twins crashed out on the floor and a pall of smoke rising from a rapidly spreading fire.

'WHAT THE HELL ARE YOU DOING!' she screams, rushing in to grab a bucket of water standing by the stalls, waiting to be given to the horses.

She flings the water onto the flames and runs out to get the water hose that serves the stables. She plays the jet of water onto the straw and manages to douse the flames. Then she turns the hose onto the twins who are still oblivious.

The cold water hits them like a brick chucked in a riot, shocking them into a semblance of consciousness.

Hare stumbles to her feet, fumbles for her Stanley knife but can't locate it in the pocket of her overalls.

'Wha' choo do that for?' says a dripping Hatch Warren.

'GET OUT!' Gwendolyn thunders at them. "JUST GET OUT OF MY STABLE!'

'Chill, Missus!' Hatch admonishes her. 'What's yer problem?'

'You set my stables on fire!' Gwendolyn's voice has dropped to a sibilant hiss. She reaches for the mucking out shovel and grips it in both hands.

'Wha'?' Hatch still has not grasped the nature of the problem.

'Oi,' says Hare, 'you soaked my phone. It's knackered.'

'You'll be next if you're not off my land in the next twenty seconds,' Gwendolyn warns them, hefting the shovel to show she means business. How DARE they endanger her horses; the only creatures she has any vestige of love for. Like a mother lioness protecting her cubs she is ready to kill and to hell with the consequences.

Hare recognises a savagery to match her own and prudently grabs her brother by the hand and drags him out of the stables, closely followed by Gwendolyn, who is panting with rage.

They run.

'Your mother will hear about this,' Gwendolyn shouts after them.

And that *really* puts the fear of God into the twins.

91

Henry Grey draws up outside St John Hall in his old Vauxhall Astra. Sherborne is expecting him and waits in the doorway.

Grey gets out of the car and a young woman emerges from the passenger side. She is slightly plump, of medium height, wearing tight jeans, a green sleeveless gilet over a tee shirt with the logo of Shearwater College and riding boots. She has the rosy completion of someone who spends a lot of time outdoors and likes it, a bright, fresh–faced, wholesome look that she does not spoil with make-up. She wears her long dark brown hair in a pony-tail.

Henry introduces her: 'This is Penny Taylor,' he says to Sherborne. 'From Shearwater College.'

'I've just graduated,' Penny explains, proudly

'How do you do?' says Sherborne formally, 'Henry tells me you come highly recommended'

'Thank you,' she says and makes a small curtsey.

'And you know your way around a stable?'

'I've always loved horses,' Penny says. That's why I did the course in Equine Studies. I want to work with horses for the rest of my life,' she gushes. 'Do you want to see my certificate?' She brandishes an impressive-looking document covered in embossed writing at him.

'No, I don't think that will be necessary,' Sherborne says, but with a smile.

She looks crestfallen and so he relents and takes the paper from her and studies it closely.

'Yes, I see,' he says. 'Very impressive.'

She looks like a puppy that has just been stroked. If she dared to jump up at him, she would.

'Well,' says Sherborne, 'the final decision will be down to Gwendolyn, my wife. The stables are her prerogative. But I don't see a problem.'

And here comes Gwendolyn, still clutching her shovel and still apoplectic.

'Those bloody Warren twins. I'll swing for them. Little buggers!' She does not appear to notice Penny or Henry.

'Ah, Gwendolyn. I'd like you to meet Miss Taylor,' says Sherborne.

'What?' Gwendolyn comes back to the real world with a start.

Penny Taylor's expression is now like the same puppy that has been smacked with a rolled up newspaper. Henry Grey retreats to the safety of his car, a quick getaway might be in order here.

'The replacement for Crux,' Sherborne prompts.

Gwendolyn's red mist fades.

'Oh, sorry. I'm a bit upset. The twins nearly set fire to the stables,' she explains to Sherborne.

'Oh no!' Penny cries. 'How could they? How awful!'

'I've sent them packing,' Gwendolyn explains. 'You've arrived just in time. Know anything about horses?'

'She's got a certificate.' Sherborne says, leaping to her defence.

'From Shearwater College,' adds Henry, seeking his share of the kudos.

234

'When can you start?'

'Whenever you want me to,' says Penny in a small voice. She is having second thoughts: Gwendolyn in a rage is not a reassuring spectacle.

'Married?'

'No.'

'Got a boyfriend?'

'No.'

'You a lesbian?'

'*No!*'

'Is this important, old girl?' asks Sherborne a little quizzically.

'Crux was always thinking about sex,' says Gwendolyn, the hypocrite. 'Couldn't keep his mind out of his trousers.'

'I didn't know that,' says Sherborne.

'*You* didn't have to deal with him. Randy little sod!'

'Er, I'm only interested in horses,' says Penny timidly. 'Perhaps...'

'Maybe a trial period, Gwendolyn?' Sherborne suggests.

'Well, you can't be any worse than those Warrens,' Gwendolyn grudges. 'We'll give you a go. It's live-in. Could you start right away? The horses haven't been properly cared for in days and I'm at my wit's end.'

'I've got a suitcase in the car,' Penny volunteers. 'I can start right away.'

'Well, that's great. Follow me. There's plenty of work to do.'

And so Penny Taylor moves into her new home.

92

The passing of the year in an English village is marked by certain fixed events. In the case of Itchen Prior there are the four Quarter Days when Sherborne's tenants pay their rent to him up at St John Hall.

At Christmas there is the am-dram panto in the village hall, usually organised by Marjory Hinton Daubrey and Tristram Clatford. And with a cast of village children who nag their parents to cough up the admission to come and see their darlings perform and which pays the running costs of the hall for the rest of the year.

Spring is celebrated with the same pool of youthful talent dancing around the maypole on the village green with the same doting parents in attendance and the beginning of summer is marked by the select of the area with the St John Garden Party.

Autumn is marked by the Harvest Festival in St Brides-in-the-Bath (again, principally organised by Marjory and Tristram and featuring the stalwarts of the village school and their ever-loving mummies and daddies).

But the high point of the summer is the village fete that incorporates all that is best and most eccentric of English village life. In Itchen Prior it is held on the first weekend in August, come sun or rain.

The fete itself follows a time hallowed tradition of stalls, competitions, entertainments and an excess of food and drink and a good time is had by all.

At least, that is the theory.

The reality is seething rivalries over the various competitive events. Competition for the jam making prize is cut-throat; ancient feuds are fought out over the flower and vegetable judging with accusations of bias and corruption bitterly hurled; strong drink taken has led to fist fights and unwanted pregnancies that have long term repercussions in the social dynamics of the village.

Yet ask anyone in the village of Itchen Prior and they will defend the Annual Fete as the high point of the year.

The Fete Committee sits in the village hall at the end of July to discuss final arrangements. In the Chair is Sherborne. Unsurprisingly the Committee members are Tristram Clatford, Marjory Hinton Daubrey, Ragged Appleshaw, Henry Grey (the Secretary) and, perhaps surprisingly, Ashley Warren. A new member has been co-opted this year on Marjory's recommendation: Jocasta Dever.

Henry Grey is called upon to report on progress so far,

'I've been in touch with Cagliostro Entertainments to book the usual stalls and they will be arriving next week. Everything should be in place on the Friday for the Grand Opening on the Saturday. And the long-range weather forecast looks very promising indeed.'

'Excellent,' says Sherborne.

'The Morris Side from Netherborne Parvis are booked and raring to go,' says Clatford. 'And this year, of course, we will have the BBC here to record the bell-ringers.'

'What are you giving us?' Sherborne asks Appleshaw.

'Bob Triples,' Appleshaw tells him.

'Amongst my favourites,' Sherborne approves.

'What are the stalls?' asks Jocasta, the newcomer.

She feels that the Devers are really integrating into their new life in the country and are becoming a genuine part of the community. Life in West London was never so *involved*. Where she was at first a little wary of Mitchell's plan to re-locate she is now a fervent convert to all things rural. Except, of course, for the lack of decent shops within walking distance. But she now has her new little yellow Volkswagen 'runabout' to compensate her.

'Much as you would expect,' Grey tells her. 'There is the Flower and Produce stall. We have Jed Smith to judge the winners this year after the unpleasantness with Mrs Easton last year.'

'Don't ask,' Marjory whispers to her.

'And naturally Ashley will be Gypsy Rosie Lee in the Fortune Teller tent.'

Ashley Warren has a good dollop of Old Mother Cando-ver's mitochondrial DNA sloshing about in her gene pool and so is a natural as a fortune-teller. Many of her readings have an unsettling habit of being true. For a serious reading the client is expected to cross her palm with folding money which goes into her pocket rather than the cupronickel 50ps that go towards the proceeds of the fete.

'And there is the ever popular Duck The Vicar,' Clatford beams. 'My high point. We collected over sixty pounds last year!'

'Nice to be so well loved, eh Vicar?' says Marjory with twinkle.

'I live for my parishioners,' says Clatford.

'And they live to plunge you in the duck pond,' Sherborne observes.

'Too true, too true. But all for a good cause.'

'There is a bouncy castle for the kids,' says Marjory, trying to get back to the point.

'And a shooting gallery. We hope to rope Major Wallop in for that. Cagliostro supply the air guns and the prizes but the Major will give it a bit of military credibility. Especially if he wears his uniform.'

'There are races for the children. Egg and spoon. Three-legged race. Hopping with a balloon. The children love it and the parents get very competitive.'

'Yes,' says Sherborne slowly, 'but we don't want a repeat of last year's outbreak of fighting. Those mothers got completely out of hand. Mrs Titherly had to have treatment in the first aid tent for that nasty wound.'

'I've asked Sergeant Stacy to come this year,' says Gray. 'He's bringing his police car and is going to demonstrate his 'blues and twos'. I'm not exactly sure what that means. That should help to keep law and order.'

'Don't you be so sure,' Ragged Appleshaw mutters. 'A lot of people gets very nasty with a bit o' drink inside them.'

'And that reminds me, Gordon Turgis and Natalie will run the beer tent as per usual

'And this year Alice Lacey will organise and run the Hog Roast.'

'I can see that making a lot of money from Major Wallop and Paul Hartley,' says the vicar: the love triangle is an open secret to the folk of Itchen Prior.

'I was wondering if we could get your Mitchell onside to run the White Elephant stall,' says Marjory to Jocasta.

'What does that involve? I'm sure Mitchell would be glad to help.' Jocasta says.

'People bringing along any old rubbish they can't be bothered to take to the tip.' Appleshaw says before Marjory can reply.

'*Mr Appleshaw*! No, we don't have a charity shop here in the village so this is a chance for people to donate items they no longer want.'

'Just what I said,' says Appleshaw.

'Don't forget the Treasure Hunt,' says Clatford, heading Appleshaw off.

'How does that work?' asks Jocasta

'People pay a pound to enter and then they get a set of clues leading them from one place to the next and at the end there is a buried treasure,' Grey explains. 'It takes them all around the village and the country round about. It's very popular.'

'What's the treasure?' Jocasta asks.

'Usually a bottle of something from the St John's Arms.'

'Is Mrs Wellow judging the cake stall again this year?' asks Sherborne. 'Only I'll have to arrange for her to leave out something cold for Gwendolyn and myself.'

'Yes. If that's all right?'

'Fine, fine, we'll manage.'

'So will you ask Mitchell about the White Elephant?' Marjory urges.

'I'm sure he'll do it,' says Jocasta with the conviction of a woman who knows what is best for her man if he wants a quiet life.

'So,' says Henry Grey, 'any other business? No? Shall we reconvene in a week's time? Ok for everyone? A week it is then.'

240

93

The St Bride's bell-ringers are honed to the peak of preparedness and fitness. No athlete training for the triathlon could be more mentally and physically ready to meet the challenge. Two hours a night of enthusiastic practice under the harsh regime of Ragged Appleshaw is about to pay off.

Those members of the Itchen Prior village community who were not exactly aficionados of the noble art of bell-ringing were at their wits' end to make the racket stop so they could watch their evening soaps in the comfort of their own homes whilst being able to actually follow the twists and turns of the dialogue.

There has been dark talk in the St John's Arms and plots against the continued well being of the ringers: the best kind of ringer, some said, was a dead ringer.

And the great day is here at last.

The BBC sound recording team, a brisk middle-aged woman called Imogen Marsh who is the producer and a willowy young man named Hugo Courtney, who is fresh off his degree course in Media and Sound and is earnestly ambitious, handles the technical equipment, have arrived in Itchen Prior.

The St Bride's Bell-ringers are gathered in a small knot outside the West door of the church, talking together in subdued voices. This is their time and they will not be found wanting.

Imogen Marsh introduces herself and as an afterthought introduces Hugo Courtney.

'He will look after the actual recording,' she explains with a dismissive wave of her hand.

'Shall we have a run-through,' he asks, 'to check the acoustics and sound levels?'

YES! YES! Jocasta says to herself. *We've cracked it. We are part of the village.* Mitchell, however, who has missed some of the rehearsals because of work commitments, is in a bit of a sulk. He has been nominated First Reserve and, unless there is a serious mishap, will not be ringing today. He is trying to show a brave face to the world but Jocasta can tell he is not a happy bunny.

Ragged Appleshaw leads his troops in to the church and they climb the steep spiral stairs to the ringing chamber.

'When you are ready,' says Courtney, fiddling with his kit.

'And one. And two. And three!' Appleshaw gives the command.

The ringers pull the sallees to get the bells into the perpendicular set position and then they re released. The ringers gradually increase the strength of their tugs on the ropes and the bells start to swing.

94

The pantechnicon from Cagliostro Entertainments arrives at the village green while the bell-ringing is in progress and start to unload the stalls for the fete. They are a crew of skilled professionals and by mid day the stalls are up and ready for action. A crowd of local children watch their progress with surging excitement while their parents mooch about feigning a lack of interest and complain about the bells and breaches of public order.

Sherborne drives up in his Ranger Rover to supervise. Stalls such as the shooting gallery, the hoopla and the coconut shy contain prizes such as assorted stuffed animals (made in China), boxes of chocolates (well past their sell-by dates), and the prize items of tee shirts proclaiming the names of rock bands long defunct and have to be locked up to prevent premature temptation and downright looting and Sherborne, in his capacity of Chairman of the Fete Committee takes charge of the keys.

The workmen slope off to the St John's Arms for richly deserved refreshment. Gordon Turgis is working so hard pulling pints his wrist is aching. Natalie is busy in the village shop catering to demand for sweets and ice creams as the village children load up on sugar.

The triumphant bell-ringers, with Imogen Marsh and Hugo Courtney in tow, come into the pub to celebrate.

'I think that went very well,' Tristram Clatford is saying.

'Yes,' Imogen Marsh says noncommittally.

'When will it be broadcast?' asks Henry Grey.

'Oh, not for some time yet. We like to build up a bank of recordings. Plenty in reserve, so to speak.'

'But you *will* let us know?' says Jocasta. 'I'm a researcher for the BBC, you know.'

'Oh, really,' says Imogen, drily. 'We are a very big organisation, of course.'

That's Jocasta firmly put in her place. Imogen is a *producer* and aware of being far more important than a mere researcher.

'I'll send you an email,' says Hugo Courtney kindly.

'Thank you *so much*. You're very kind,' says Marjory Hinton Daubrey and lays her hand on his arm.

'You're welcome,' says Courtney, blushing. He is a shy sort of a lad whose main recreation is twenty-four-hours internet gaming when he is not working. He does not have a girlfriend.

Sherborne is standing at the bar watching Gordon Turgus's exertions with mild amusement.

'Go well, did it?' he calls to the bell-ringers.

'Aye, Squire, it did that,' says Ragged Appleshaw proudly.

'I'd better buy you all a drink, then,' says Sherborne. 'And then, perhaps, we need to finalise arrangements for the fete tomorrow?'

'I'll have a pint o' Bishops', Squire, if you be so kind,' says Appleshaw hastily before Sherborne can change his mind. 'A pint, when you're ready, Gordon.'

'I'll be ready in me own time, Ragged Appleshaw,' pants Gordon Turgis. 'Run off me feet, I am. Can't you see.'

Although as far as anyone can see Gordon Turgis is simply resting against the bar trying to catch his breath.

'Beer'll be off by the time you're ready,' Appleshaw mutters darkly.

And then Turgis's day gets even more hectic when the rest of the bell-ringers place their orders.

'That bloody skiving Natalie Somerfield. Never here when she's needed. How's a man expected to cope with all this rush?'

He wipes a fevered brow and sighs a little sigh and has a wallow in self pity.

On Saturday morning, Gwendolyn, in her guise as Lady of the Manor, is all set to open the Itchen Prior Annual Village Fete. She is feeling cranky as she has been up half the night watching back episodes of *Midsomer Murders* but she thinks she might just have hit upon an idea. She coughs to clear her throat and mutters 'onetwo, onetwo' in the approved style to check that the PA system is working. It is.

The crowds are restive, waiting for the fun to start, but no-one can make a dash for the amusement of their choice until Gwendolyn gives them the official word.

'When you are ready, old girl,' says Sherborne, who is standing next to her and beaming at the assembled multitude. The Itchen Prior Annual Village Fete is renowned throughout the district and always attracts an enthusiastic following.

This is Gwendolyn's big moment. From the daughter of a shepherd of dodgy repute to Lady of the Manor who dreams of more, oh, so *much* more. Sherborne, who raised her up, is the stumbling block to greater things. She smiles the smile of the devoted wife at him and raises the microphone to her lips.

'It gives me great pleasure,' she simpers, 'to officially declare the Itchen Prior Annual Village Fete officially open.'

A round of cheers, whistles and whoas greet her words and a moment later the rush to spend money is underway.

Itchen Prior cherishes its traditions and the old tried and tested ways of rural life. The old has not been swept away with the changes of the centuries. Perched on the edge of the village pond is The Ducking Chair, first erected during the time of the Civil War and used to curb the excesses of nagging wives and scolds. Old Mother Candover had seen it as an improvement on the practice of witch floating as it gave the accused a half decent chance of surviving the ordeal with her dignity, and more importantly, her life, intact. As the rest of the village were terrified of crossing her, they happily went along with the idea.

The Ducking Chair is now rigged up with a square metal target attached to a series of levers. Tristram Clatford will sit in the chair and for a pound punters can hurl wooden balls at the target. Hit the target hard enough and the vicar gets a soaking. Clatford takes his annual dunkings in good part and the money raised goes towards whatever part of St Brides-in-the-Bath needs a bit of upkeep.

A queue has already formed. Fortunately, the day is warm and the pond water is mild in its sting. Clatford wears a pair of Bermuda shorts of alarming dayglo hue. His chest is covered in a fine mat of hair and his upper body is surprisingly toned, attracting an admiring elderly female following.

The Flower and Produce tent is closely guarded by Long Sutton. Rivalry over the prize for largest vegetable (leeks, carrots, marrows, onions, tomatoes) is intense and last minute sabotage cannot be ruled out. Likewise, the competition for cakes, jams and chutneys. As for the bitter feuding over the floral entrants, the princes of Renaissance Italy were a band of loving and fraternal chums by comparison. Families have been rent asunder; neighbours have not spoken for generations; elderly ladies have indulged in no-holds-barred, eye gauging fights over who has grown the most impressive rose, sweet pea or dahlia. Accusations of bribery, both monetary and sexual have been levelled at past judges.

Into this bear pit steps this year's adjudicator: Jed Smith.

98

Farleigh Wallop, resplendent in full battle dress and wearing an impressive array of medals and honours gained from a long and distinguished military career supervising the mess halls of the hell holes into which the British Army have been pitched over the years, is in command of the shooting gallery and the archery butts.

Here, for the price of a pound sterling, the wannabe marksmen can step up and prove his prowess with a wonky air rifle to his admiring female companion. Prizes include teddy bears and other stuffed toys. Goldfish in little plastic bags are a thing of the past, thanks to enlightened laws governing animal cruelty.

The archery butts (three arrows for a pound) are a new innovation and a chance for the ladies to participate. Prizes ditto.

99

Ashley Warren, in her incarnation as Gypsy Rose Lee, sits in a small round tent with a scrying ball and a pack of greasy Tarot cards as props. She will read your palm for 50p. For considerably more she will provide you with a bottle of something to pep up your love life, dampen down excessive ardour or a little charm or poppet to blight the life and prosperity of an enemy.

She usually does a roaring trade.

100

Marjory is in charge of the bouncy castle. As the village school marm she has the required authority to keep the children in some kind of order and curb their enthusiasm for playing The Sack of Jerusalem as they squabble over space.

Later she will organise the heats and finals of the three-legged race and the egg and spoon race for the under sevens. The fathers will then compete in the Fifty Yard Dash, an event that brings to mind the friendly rivalry between the German and Russian armies at Stalingrad. Prizes are awarded to all runners in the children's races in the new spirit of equality of opportunity where there are no winners and losers and it is the taking part that matters.

But everyone knows who the winners are and bragging rights are essential to grind the faces of the losers into the dust. This is especially true of the dads.

101

Alice Lacey, 48, buxom and jolly as a barmaid and the disputed love object of Farleigh Wallop and Paul Hartley, is in charge of selling choice cuts of roast pork in a bun from the Hog Roast stand. Hartley is in close attendance. Jed Smith is proving somewhat intransigent over his suggestions for changes to Itchen Prior Horticultural but he is confident that he can pull his reluctant partner round to is way of thinking. With Wallop engaged in the shooting gallery he has Alice Lacey to himself and he intends a day of intensive wooing This might go better if it were not for the hungry of Itchen Prior and surrounding district constantly demanding to be fed. He thinks he might well take himself off to Gordon Turgis' Beer Tent round about lunch time

102

Mitchell Dever is manning the White Elephant Stall. He is in the grip of mixed emotions. On the one hand he is feeling slightly resentful of Jocasta for lumbering him with this unwanted chore and on the other he is feeling a *real* member of the village community, which, after all, is why he undertook this move to the country in the first place.

Piled high on the counter of the White Elephant Stall is the detritus of another year of people clearing out their garages and attics of junk that they can't sell on eBay or that the Charity shops of Westleigh turn their nose up at.

Chipped plates and jugs (might be some valuable antiques in that lot, Henry Grey suggests – but there isn't. People watch Antiques Roadshow, Flog It and Bargain Hunt and scrutinise everything that Granny might have squirrelled away); books with pages missing; broken toys and board games lacking a full complement of parts; canteens of cutlery with wonky handles; incomplete jigsaws of the stately homes of England; terrifying dolls with amputated limbs ('GI Joe – he were in Iraq, weren't 'e? Authentic that is! A war hero!'); pots and pans that have outlived their hygienic life.

Many have come and rummaged: none have purchased. Mitchell is bored rigid but manages to smile encouragement as each prospective customer approaches. He has honed his costermonger skills and shouts out his wares, suitably sexed up but all to no avail.

Jocasta, who is helping Marjory keep order at the bouncy castle, wanders over holding a warm pint of Bishop's in a plastic glass.

'I thought you might need this, darling. How's it going?'

He growls at her and downs half the pint in one go.

'That bad?'

'Worse!'

'But isn't it fun to be part of village life?' she says.

'I'm not convinced. Are you going to take over from me?'

'Darling, I'd love to but I'm busy with Marjory. Bye.'

'Don't leave me,' he wails.

But she is gone.

A bright red fire appliance with its crew of fire fighters in full gear is parked next to a police car by the St John's Ambulance first aid tent. Both vehicles have their blue flashing lights on and a small group of children are watching wide eyed as the fire fighters demonstrate their art.

Clifton Maybank, the fire chief, is chatting to Sergeant Barton Stacy of the Rural Policing team.

'Did you ever follow up on that fire in the garden centre?' Maybank asks. 'It was as clear a case of arson as I've ever seen.'

'He says it was probably travellers,' Stacy tells him.

'Why would they do that?'

'Dunno.'

'That's what he told me, an' all. Funny thing is, I did some checking around and there weren't no travellers around at the time.'

'Really?' says Stacy, aware that his friendship with Smith might have made him a little remiss in his investigations.

'Could maybe take a bit of looking into,' Maybank suggests. 'Arson is a serious business. Wouldn't want people to think they can get away with burning stuff down. I don't care about the insurance, that's not my job, but it's my lads that have to deal with it. Fires can be dangerous things.'

'No argument there,' Stacy agrees.

'So you'll give it another look?'

'I suppose I should,' Stacy agrees.

Crux Eaton has been dossing down on a mate's floor in Westleigh but a vestige of filial piety has brought him back to Itchen Prior to support his mother's entry in the flower show – an event that caused all the trouble in the first place with her unfortunate entry of his prize Jamaican Funnybush. He is accompanied by a much happier Sally Fairfax who announces her sole proprietorship of his affections by linking her arm through his and leaning her head on his shoulder.

The Warren twins are lurking on the periphery of the fete with a knot of Itchen Prior teenagers who are affecting total boredom with the proceedings and having a lovely time sneering at all those enjoying the simple pleasures on offer. They all have earphones thrust into their ears and check their social media every few minutes. Sometimes they text each other with witty comments about how uncool this all is.

Hatch catches sight of Crux and Sally and makes a beeline for them, closely followed by Hare.

'You awrigh' Crux?'

Crux Eaton is a local hero to the outcast and misunderstood youth of Itchen Prior. He dared to confront the forces of reaction and was martyred for his pains; he has *served time*!

'Awrigh' Hatch, Hare? How's it going?' Sally says nothing; she does not really approve of the Warren twins, whom she has known and been wary of, all their lives.

'We had a job in the Squires stables,' says Hare. 'Didn't last. That cow Gwendolyn.'

Crux feels a frisson of fear at the mention of the name of the woman he tried to murder; Sally increases the pressure on his arm.

'We found your stash,' Hatch blurts out.

'Weren't mine,' Crux denies automatically.

'We got baked, proper!' says Hare in admiration.

'Had a bit of an accident and nearly set the place on fire,' Hatch adds.

'If I hadn't been so wasted I'd of had her,' says Hare.

'You set the stables on fire?' asks Crux in amazed horror. Although he hated his enforced sexual slavery (most of the time – it had its moments) to Gwendolyn, he did love working with the horses. The thought that they might have come to harm upsets him.

'It were an accident,' says Hatch, the picture of wounded innocence.

'She threatened us with a shovel,' says Hare indignantly. No-one has dared to threaten Hare Warren since she was old enough to wield a Stanley knife and her defeat rankles.

'Yeah, well, nice to see you. I've got to go and find me Ma,' says Crux, edging away.

'They got a young girl in now. To look after the horses,' Hatch informs him.

I bet Gwendolyn is royally pissed off about *that*, Crux thinks as he heads for the Flower and Produce tent. Can't see it lasting.

He makes a note to try and avoid seeing Gwendolyn if at all possible.

The meeting could turn nasty.

Poor Tristram Clatford has been ducked so many times his skin is turning pruney and blue. By tradition, Sherborne will take over the lunchtime slot. Although, also by tradition, none of his tenants in the village will put much of an effort into their pitch at the target. It is the thought of *noblesse oblige* that counts. Once a year he offers up his body as a sacrifice to lesser mortals to shy at.

Gwendolyn has exhausted the fun of the fair in the first twenty minutes and has taken herself back to St John Hall for her morning ride and to check up on Penny Taylor, who has not been given time off to fritter away at the fete. Crux Eaton's departure and the lacklustre performance of the Warren twins have left much work to do.

Besides, she has plans for Sherborne's Range Rover, which she has driven home in.

Paul Hartley ambles over to the shooting gallery to wind up Farleigh Wallop on his way to the Beer Tent.

'Howdy, Mainwaring. Shot any nasty terrorists?' he greets his rival.

'Go away, Hartley. You'll scare off the punters,' Wallop replies. He knows full well that Hartley is hanging around Alice Lacey, pushing his suite while he, Wallop, is marooned here.

'Free country,' observes Hartley, 'I can go where I like.'

'Well, dig into your pocket and pay up for a go. All for a good cause.'

'You must be joking! You couldn't hit a barn door with those clapped-out air guns of yours.'

This is a challenge to the honour of the Wallops and Farleigh rises to the occasion.

'I'll take you on,' he says. 'Best of six!'

Farleigh Wallop might not have fired a shot in anger but on the range he proved himself to be a fair marksman and is confident he can beat a mere civilian like Hartley.

'Go on then,' says Hartley and adds cannily 'but I get to have a test shot to get my eye in. My choice of airgun.'

'That'll be two pounds.'

'An' you cough up too.'

'Of course,' says Wallop, an officer and a gentleman to the core.

A small crowd has witnessed the exchange and side bets are being taken. Word spreads and the crowd grows. The animosity between these two men is widely known in the village and this might well be the start of a diverting confrontation; so far there has been no violence to speak of and the fete is already two hours old.

Hartley picks up one of the weapons that are chained to the counter, sights it and takes a shot. He hits the rim of the target.

'Just as I thought,' he announces to the crowd. 'Bent.'

'Then I will take that one and you have the other,' says Wallop gallantly.

'Won't be any better,' mutters Hartley.

He shoots off six pellets and scores a bull, two inners and three outers. He flings the gun down in disgust.

Wallop neatly places four shots in the bull and nicks two inners.

'Not *that* bent, then,' he observes.

Hartley stalks off in disgust, followed by the jeers of Wallop's supporters, who have just won their bets.

The consensus is that blows will be exchanged before the day is done.

And nobody would want to miss that.

107

It is early afternoon and the Netherborne Parvis Morris Side are performing a set in a clatter of staves and a jingling of bells and a waving of handkerchiefs. Music is provided by a concertina player and the hobby horse weaves in and out of the crowd frightening the children.

The White Elephant Stall has been temporarily shut down for lack of interest and Mitchell is taking a break with Jocasta to watch the dancing. He has lived a sheltered life in the metropolis and Morris dancing strikes him as about as incomprehensible as cricket is to a French person.

'Do you have *any* idea what this is about?' he asks his wife.

'It's Morris dancing, darling,' she says brightly with a show of knowledge that she does not possess.

'It's bloody weird, that's what it is,' says Mitchell.

'Actually,' says Henry Grey, who has crept up behind them, 'it's very ancient.'

Mitchell jumps.

'Sorry to startle you,' Grey apologises. 'Morris dancing is first recorded in the Fourteenth century but it is actually far, far older. There are variations all over the country but they all follow a basic pattern.'

'Really?' says Jocasta.

'Oh yes,' says Grey with confidence. This is his field and he feels very comfortable lecturing about it. 'I would confidently assert that the ancient people danced something very like the Morris dance along the cursus ways between the henge sites.'

'What?' asks Mitchell, way out of his own comfort zone.

'The whole area around Stonehenge was a massive complex of religious sites. Long before Stonehenge itself was built. They were linked by processional ways called a cursus. There is evidence of thousands of people gathering at these sites. All 'primitive' societies express themselves in dance; why would the old people of Britain be any different?'

'That is just *so* interesting,' says Jocasta.

'There is still an awful lot of the old customs about.' Grey tells her. 'You just need to know how and where to look. I'd love to tell you all about them.'

'I'd love to hear about them,' says Jocasta with genuine enthusiasm.

Mitchell is not so sure and can't make the connection with a lot of cavemen dancing around stone circles with these Twenty First century folk weaving in and out of each other and striking staves and waving hankies.

108

The Reverend Tristram Clatford is making an announcement over the public address system. He has changed back into dry clothes and has done his duty on the ducking stool for this year.

'Would all those intending to take part in the Treasure Hunt make their way to the Village Hall to pick up their pack of clues. Roll up, roll up. Only a pound to enter. Lots of fun for the whole family. Fabulous prizes.'

A man of the cloth should not lie but on this occasion Clatford excuses himself. The chance of a free bottle out of Gordon Turgis is certainly a rarity to be treasured. And there are sweets from the village shop for the kids.

The Treasure Hunt is a popular feature of the fete; the Committee have had great fun devising cryptic clues to lead the prospective Indiana Jones's on a merry chase that will, eventually, bring them back to the Village Hall. Everyone in Itchen Prior knows that this is the final destination but the fun is in going through the motions to get there. And it *is* a firm favourite with the children.

Up to a certain age.

As the crowd drifts off to get their packs, the Warren twins are plotting with their peers.

'So,' says Hatch, 'you up for a laugh or what?'

Hatch and Hare Warren are the warlords of the teenagers of Itchen Prior, a village that does not hold a whole lot of prospects for entertainment for the young adult; where they lead others will willingly follow.

'I got an idea. Come with me,' says Hatch mysteriously.

109

With the lunchtime rush over Paul Hartley no longer has an excuse to help out at the Hog Roast and anyway feels he deserves a refreshing pint or two in the Beer Tent. It is difficult to tell whether he has advanced his suit with Alice Lacey as the lady is as enigmatic as the Sybil.

The lady is enjoying the rivalry between Hartley and Wallop and has no intention whatsoever of opting for one or the other; she is having an affair with a married man from Westleigh called Tarrant Rawston and is very, very discrete about it. No-one in Itchen Prior has the slightest inkling and she plans to keep it that way for as long as it lasts. Perhaps if the affaire implodes she might review her options but for the moment all is ticketyboo, thank you very much!

Jed Smith sits in the Beer Tent fortifying himself for the coming ordeal of judging the fruit and produce, which is the grand finale of the fete. He has already had a couple of pints and is thinking about a third when Hartley comes over to join him.

'Bloody women!' says Hartley by way of a greeting.

'Alice Lacey playing hard to get?' guesses Smith.

'I don't know where I am with her. You'd think she'd jump at the chance of a chap like me.'

'Maybe she's more up for the Dashing Major,' Smith teases.

'That bastard!'

'I heard he thrashed you at the Shooting Gallery.' says Smith, rubbing it in. He is enjoying this.

'Bloody gun were wonkey.'

'I heard he let you choose your weapon.'

'Let's just forget it, shall we?' Hartley snaps. 'Do you want a drink or not?'

'Thought you'd never ask. A pint of Bishop's.'

Hartley goes to the bar and orders the drinks from Turgis.

You really are a git, Smith thinks. I really must get shot of you.

'Here you go, then,' says Hartley, setting the full glasses down. 'Cheers!'

'Cheers!' Smith takes a pull at his pint.

Sherborne, spruce and dapper in the tweed suit he has changed into after his stint in the ducking stool, enters the Beer Tent like a man on a mission. Which is exactly what he is. He scans the assembled drinkers and fixes his eye on Hartley and Smith.

'Paul! Jed! I'm looking for a volunteer.'

Both of these men slavishly follow the rule 'Never volunteer for anything'. They shuffle their feet under the trestle table and try to avoid his gaze. St John is having none of it.

'Gentlemen,' he says. 'it's for a good cause.'

Hartley holds his tenancy from the St John estate and in the semi-feudal tradition that still exists in Itchen Prior is on shaky ground; Jed Smith less so.

'We need a volunteer to sit in the ducking stool for the last hour of the fete. The Treasure Hunt will be over soon and people will be coming back.'

Jed Smith gives a sigh of relief.

'I'd love to, Squire,' he says with mock unctuousness, 'but I've got the produce judging to do.'

'Oh, yes, of course,' says St John and shifts the full force of his gaze upon Hartley, who wriggles like a maggot on a fishing hook.

'Well respected member of the local community like yourself, Hartley. You'd be the perfect chap for the job.'

'I'd like to, Squire,' Hartley lies, 'but I ain't got me swimming trunks.'

'Not to worry, the vicar can fix you up with something. So that's settled, then. Say in twenty minutes?'

What Hartley says under his breath is 'bugger!'

Smith resolves to invest in a good number of balls to pitch at his partner.

110

Ashley Warren packs up her tent and counts her unofficial takings; she had made more than £200 from her combination of fortune-telling and witchcraft. Her official tally for the day which she will declare to the Fete Committee will be a paltry £42. All in all, a nice little earner for the Warrens. She makes her way to the Village Hall to hand in her £42 to the Committee. On the way she meets Mitchell Dever looking dejected.

'Had a good day, Mitchell?' she asks.

'Nine pounds fifty,' he replies. 'And some of that was Jocasta buying an old jigsaw of The Golden Age of Steam out of pity!'

'Better'n last year, then,' she tells him. 'That stall only made sixty pee.'

'Then why bother?' Mitchell says bitterly.

'Tradition, innit. Got to have a White Elephant stall. Can't have a Fete without a White Elephant stall.'

'What do I do with all the junk?'

'Usually gets fly tipped. Stick it in the back o' that posh car of yorn. Drive out a couple of miles and find a nice hedgerow and chuck the lot. That's what Vicar did last year.'

'You *are* joking?'

'Mebbe,' she says enigmatically and winks at him.

Mitchell is at a loss to know if she is telling him the truth. She lets him sweat for a moment.

'Tell you what,' she says, 'I'll send the twins round to take it off yer hands. For a tenner. Seth'll get rid of it.'

Mitchell considers it and decides that £10 is a small price to rid himself of the detritus of the village. 'OK,' he says and shakes her hand on the deal.

He's a right mug and no mistake, she thinks, pocketing the note.

111

A large crowd has gathered round the ducking stool to witness Paul Hartley take a bath. He is not the most popular figure in village life; Jed Smith is first in the queue. Hartley is wearing an old pair of tracksuit bottoms, which are a little large on him, and a tee shirt that is snug around his paunch. The Itchen Prior Posse have decided to take a surprising interest in the proceedings and are gathered at the periphery of the crowd, shouting encouragement led by Hatch Warren.

Jed Smith, a one-time stalwart of the village Cricket Eleven, takes a short run up and bowls over arm at the target. He hits the centre of the target a mighty thwack and the arm of the ducking stool pitches Hartley into the pond. And keeps going down.

And down.

Hartley disappears under the water in a cloud of bubbles.

There is a collective gasp from the crowd. This is a real unexpected treat with the promise of an actual drowning; something to tell the grandchildren.

Smith is stunned. He didn't think he still had such strength in his bowling arm. He feels a flash of elation and pride and when Hartley does not emerge, of hope.

The Itchen Prior Posse are rolling on the ground howling with laughter, for it was they who tinkered with the safety mechanism during the Treasure Hunt. The prank has worked beyond their wildest dreams.

There is a thrashing in the water and Paul Hartley emerges spluttering and festooned with weeds.

There is another collective sigh from the crowd, perhaps of disappointment.

'You bastard,' Hartley screams. 'You tried to kill me!'

He struggles to the bank where the weight of water causes his tracksuit bottoms to fall, revealing a pair of boxer shorts adorned with images of teddy bears.

The crowd hoots.

Hartley makes an attempt to lunge at Smith but is tripped by the sodden tracksuit bottoms.

Smith beats a hasty retreat, protesting his innocence and pointing out that he has spent the last hour in the Beer Tent with Hartley himself.

Farleigh Wallop, attracted by the commotion, strolls over from the Shooting Gallery to see what the fuss is about. He sees the pathetic figure of Paul Hartley looking like some kind of monster of the deep and bursts into satisfied laughter.

Hartley becomes aware of his rival gloating over his misfortune and sees red. He rips off the tracksuit bottoms and lunges at him, knocking Wallop to the ground.

The crowd is ecstatic and quickly form a ring around the pair of them. Although Hartley is the younger man, Wallop is the fitter and they are fairly evenly matched. Bets are laid on the outcome as the two combatants exchange blows.

Before the fight can reach a bloody conclusion it is interrupted by the arrival of Sergeant Barton Stacy who is attracted to the melee by the shouting. He pushes his way through the throng and hauls the two fighters apart.

'He tried to kill me,' Hartley accuses, lost to all reason.

On this occasion Wallop is not guilty of the charge and vehemently protests his innocence.

'The man is obviously mad,' he says to Stacy.

'You hate me!' Hartley accuses.

'While there might be an element of truth in that,' Wallop concedes, 'I had nothing to do with you taking a bath. Must be the shock of the unusual event.'

Hartley tries to take another swing at Wallop but is restrained by the policemen.

Upon the arrival of the law, the Itchen Prior Posse have taken themselves off to enjoy the fruits of Crux Easton's horticultural labours in triumph. Crux has fallen back into bad ways to eke out his benefit payments and has hurriedly made himself scarce when he sees Stacy.

'Go and get dried off and changed. And calm down,' Stacy tells Hartley. 'Otherwise I'll charge you with affray.'

Hartley squelches off to the Village Hall, muttering threats and imprecations.

The crowd, urged by Stacy, disperse in search of further diversions, agreeing that this fete is among the top ten of recent years.

But the fun is not over yet.

112

The fete is drawing to a close. Barton Stacy is enjoying a well deserved half in the Beer Tent and chatting to an almost comatose Gordon Turgis, who has made a very handsome profit this day; some of which he will declare to the Fete Committee and none of which he will declare to HMRC.

Marjory Hinton Daubrey, very agitated, bursts in to the Beer Tent.

'Sergeant! Come quickly. There's been an Incident! At the Flower and Produce!'

A policemen's work is never done, thinks Stacy as he follows her out to the scene of the crime.

Jed Smith lies on the ground, semi-conscious, surround by the smashed remains of a large marrow.

'What happened?' asks Stacy, wearily pulling out his note book.

'A dispute over the judging,' Marjory explains. 'I'm afraid Ragged Appleshaw took offense at only being awarded second prize for largest marrow in the show and hit Mr Smith over the head with it,'

'Where's Appleshaw now?'

'I think he took himself off somewhere.'

Smith groans and shakes his head. 'I'm never doing this again,' he promises.

'Last year it was Mrs Eaton with her roses. Kicked me in the goolies. Not my fault they had greenfly.'

'Do you want to press charges?' asked Stacy.

'What's the point? Let some other poor bugger do it next year. I've had it.' Smith sits up, brushing bits of marrow out of his hair. This is not turning out to be Jed Smith's year.

And then it gets worse.

'By the way,' Stacy says, 'I've got to have a word with you about that fire. I'll come round sometime over the next few days.'

Bugger! thinks Smith, why me?

113

On the weekend following the Fete, Jocasta and Mitchell Dever are hosting a dinner party for the three people who have become their closest friends since moving to Itchen Prior: Tristram Clatfield, Marjory Hinton Daubrey and Henry Grey. Jocasta has discovered a cookbook of authentic and somewhat obscure Chinese dishes and has produced a menu of rock sugar pork hock; Hunan red-braised spare-ribs; twice fried cumin beef; cat's ears noodles (no *actual* cats harmed) with an accompaniment of hot and sour cabbage and a boiled rice washed down with tiny cups of Pu'er tea. She has spent the afternoon chopping and dicing, marinating and braising, bent over a smoking wok and having a lovely time.

For her guests, more accustomed to ordering number 47: Sweet and Sour Pork Balls or number 52: Kung Po Chicken with mixed fried rice (Number 67 from the Westleigh Chinese Takeaway, 'The Golden Pagoda') this meal has been a revelation.

Jocasta had driven up to London with Marjory to source her ingredients from a Chinese wholesaler and to touch base with her colleagues at the BBC and give Marjory a chance at celebrity spotting. Altogether a productive day which has led to closer bonding between the two women.

Mitchell draws the cork from a bottle of Rioja and glugs wine into their glasses.

'Ashley Warren took all the rubbish off the White Elephant stall and offered to get rid of it. She told me you usually take it out into the country and dump it.' He tells Tristram.

'Ah, Ashley,' says Tristram fondly. 'Not a word of truth in it, of course. I expect Seth will be flogging it off in a car boot sale somewhere.'

'I paid her a tenner to get rid of it.'

'An enterprising family, the Warrens,' Grey comments. 'Been around these parts forever.'

'They *are* a classic example of the continuity of the life of a close knit rural community,' says Tristram.

'Close knit!' Mitchell snorts, 'they are bloody in-bred!'

'That's the thing with these small villages,' Tristram explains. 'People were tied to the land, the communities were basically self-sufficient. People didn't travel much further than the local market town and the gene pools didn't spread very far from the well.'

'That's why we are so glad to welcome you to the village,' says Marjory brightly. 'New life and all that.'

'Well,' says Mitchell, 'I'm sorry to disappoint you on that score but we are not planning to procreate and add our drop to the pool.'

'But you are still young. Never say never,' says Henry Grey.

'Mitchell had the chop.' Jocasta tells him, with perhaps a touch of wistfulness in her voice. If Mitchell notices, he does not comment.

'We both had such busy lives in London,' he explains.

'Anyway, here we are now in this lovely village with lovely new friends in this lovely countryside. Our new life,' says Jocasta, trying to move away from what seems to be an uncomfortable subject.

'Yes, indeed,' Mitchell agrees.

'Well,' says Marjory, diplomatically supporting her friend, 'you survived your first Village Fete.'

'Is it always so eventful?' Mitchell asks.

'Oh yes,' says Clatford, laughing, 'they're a lively bunch.'

'Bunch of bloodthirsty nutters,' Mitchell mutters.

'They don't *often* come to blows,' says Clatford, by way of an apology for his flock.

'I loved the Morris dancers,' says Jocasta to Henry Grey. 'You were telling us all about the tradition.'

Mitchell uncorks another bottle of wine.

'Anybody driving?' he asks.

'No,' says Grey. 'It's a fine night. We walked over so I imagine we can stagger back. This is excellent wine.'

'Glad you like it,' says Mitchell with a proprietary air as if he had picked and pressed and bottled the grapes himself.

'Have you got any more stories about country traditions?' Jocasta asks Grey. 'If we are to be country folk we need to know all there is to know.'

A barely perceptible look passes between the three guests as if everything has been leading up to this moment.

'Well,' says Grey, adopting lecturer mode, 'where should I begin?'

He pauses as if reviewing his notes before a group of eager students, although in his experience students tended to leave a recording device at the front of the room and spend the lecture checking up on the doings of their hundred of 'friends' on social media. Either that or playing games on their laptops with the sound muted.

'It's all to do with the rotation of the seasons,' he says. 'Vitally important, of course, to a farming community. When to sew, when to harvest. The changing of the old year to the new; mid summer when the year starts to wane. When to lay in supplies for the barren months of the winter. Times to celebrate a slackening of work in the fields. Time to put the rams to the ewes, the bull to the heifers. A time for births. A time for death when the pigs are slaughtered and salted or smoked for the lean months. This is a pattern that has not changed in thousands of years and still holds true today despite modern farming methods and food imported from around the globe. The land and the seasons do not change much, despite global warming. Even the warming of the seasons and the cooling of the seasons go in cycles. It's just that we, human beings, are tilting Mother Nature's balance. But, essentially, it's all part of a pattern.'

He pauses to take a mouthful of wine.

'So what you are saying is that even in the Twenty-first century people are still bound by these archetypal rhythms?' says Mitchell.

'Oh yes. We think of ourselves as above and beyond these things but the lives of billions of people on this planet still revolve around the changing of the seasons. Obviously, if you work year round in an office or a factory life does not seem to be affected by Mother Nature but think of people affected by Seasonal Affective Disorder, of the depression caused by commuting to work for months in the dark. Country people come to terms with the seasons and are comfortable with them.'

'I know. I hated the winter months and the dark,' says Jocasta, 'stuck in an office under artificial light in the winter in the rain and the cold.'

'That's just it,' Clatford says. 'For the country people winter was, is, a time of ease. OK, perhaps it was also a time of tightening the belt to get through to the next harvest but the hard work of spring and summer, of harvest, was over. It was a time to gather their strength for the coming year.'

'The Celtic people marked the new year at Samhain, the onset of winter. We now celebrate it as Hallow'een and we light bonfires on the fifth of November, a few days later but originally they were lit on the evening of October the thirty-first itself.'

'Samhain?' Mitchell queries. 'I've never heard of it.'

'There are four great festivals in the Celtic world to mark the passage of the year,' Grey explains. 'Samhain marked the beginning of the new year after the toil of the old; Imbolc falls at the beginning of February and is a time of procreation, when the ewes are put to the tups, as I said.'

'The Church took it over as the feast of St Bride, after who our church is named. Bride is the name the church gave to the goddess Bridget, who is the goddess of fertility,' Tristram interjects.

'Beltane is May Day and the last of the four, Lughnasa, after the god Lugh, is on August the first. In the old days this was the beginning of the harvest, although we harvest earlier now,' Grey continues.

'But surely no one still goes in for these old festivals?' says a sceptical Mitchell.

'Oh, they still exist,' says Grey. 'Folk might not call them by the old names but May Day is a Bank Holiday and Harvest Festival is celebrated even in churches in the cities.'

'And by kids in school,' says Marjory.

'We light bonfires to mark important national occasions, like the royal Jubilees, don't forget,' Grey points out.

'And don't forget the Quarter Days when rents are paid to the landlord.'

'Surely people pay by standing orders,' Mitchell objects.

'Not in Itchen Prior,' Marjory tells him, 'and many of the villages around here.'

'This is living in the past,' Mitchell scoffs. 'More wine?'

'I find all this really fascinating,' says Jocasta, her eyes shining. 'I had no idea, had you, Mitchell?'

'Stuff and nonsense in this day and age.' Mitchell pauses for a moment, thinking back to something Clatford said earlier. 'Tristram, you said Bridget *is* the goddess of fertility. Not *was*.'

'She still is,' says Clatford, staring directly into Mitchell's eyes.

'But you are a Christian vicar,' Mitchell protests.

'I am a man of religion,' says Tristram simply and holds out his glass for a refill.

'Are you seriously telling me that people still believe in these old Celtic gods? You having a laugh!' Mitchell shakes his head in disbelief.

'Call them what you will. These are the primeval deities of the countryside. They have had many names over the millennia. The church simply took them over and made them saints, like Bride, for example.'

'I can't believe you are serious.'

'Oh, I'm serious enough,' Clatford tells him

'And do people here in Itchen Prior believe in the old gods?' ask Jocasta.

'Some do,' says Marjory. 'The belief is old and ingrained.'

'This is getting silly,' says Mitchell. 'Old gods and paganism! Bollocks. It's like something out of that film, *The Wicker Man.*'

'Why do you think they could make it?' Grey asks him.

'You're having us on,' Mitchell says. 'Winding up the city folk.'

'You asked about country traditions,' Grey says. 'These are the oldest. Like the Green Man.'

'The who?' says Mitchell.

'The Green Man. You saw the carving in the church.'

'Oh yes,' Jocasta remembers, 'over the vestry door.'

'That's the fellow,' Grey confirms. 'He is the spirit of the woods and the wild places.'

'There aren't any wild places left,' Mitchell objects.

'St John's Wood is still a wild place. OK, it's no longer part of a great forest full of wolves and wild boar and bears and such. But is it still on the boundaries of civilisation and cultivation. It was a place where Man ventured at his peril. Think of the Grimm Brothers' tales. Dark deeds in dark places.'

'I've heard all about Farleigh Wallop and his wars in the woods,' says Mitchell sarcastically.

'Shut up, Mitchell,' Jocasta admonished him. 'Go on, Henry. This is really interesting.'

'Oh, really, Jocasta. Come on. Green Men! From Mars! They'll be kidding you about UFOs next.'

'Not those, I do NOT believe in them,' says Grey, trying to lighten the mood.

'But you *do* go along with this other stuff?' says Mitchell.

'It's been around a long, long time.'

'So has the Yeti!'

'Possibly,' says Grey drily

'Go back to the Green Man,' says Jocasta. 'This is fun, Mitchell. Don't be a wet blanket. Get another bottle out and shut up.'

'For you, my dear, anything.' He gives her a mock bow and goes to get the drink.

'Please forgive my husband,' she says. 'Sometimes he takes things too seriously.'

'Nothing to forgive. As I said, the Green Man represents the wild, untamed places. He is at one with Nature. The Greeks called him Pan.'

'You've met Long Sutton?' Marjory asks quietly. 'He is totally at home in the woods.'

'*He's* the Green Man?'

'He is *a* Green Man, yes.'

'Still at the Fairies and Goblins?' says Mitchell, returning with another bottle.

'I think we have finished,' says Tristram, decisively. 'Time to talk of other things, don't you think? And enjoy this fine vintage.'

And so the evening draws slowly to a close with good company and fine wine.

Marjory, Upton and Clatford thank their hostess for a delicious meal and their host for his cellar (a rack in the kitchen) and take their leave.

'What a load of old bollocks that was! Green Men and old gods,' says Mitchell after they have departed.

'Let's leave it and go to bed. I really enjoyed the evening.'

'We could worship old Bridget with a bit of procreation, if you're in the mood,' says Mitchell hopefully.

'We could that,' says his wife, kissing him.

114

Tristram Clatford, Marjory Hinton Daubrey and Henry Grey walk back to the centre of the village along the lane. The night is soft and redolent with the small night noises of the countryside.

'That was a fabulous meal,' says Grey.

'I think it went well altogether,' says Clatford.

'She was more receptive than he was,' says Marjory.

'That's not a problem,' replies Clatford. 'It's her we are most interested in, after all.'

'True,' Grey agrees.

'Keep in with her, Marjory,' Clatford tells her.

'I will. I genuinely like her, so that's not a problem.'

'I will speak with Cernunnos, then,' says Clatford.

They walk on for a few minutes in silence until they reach the church and the Vicarage.

'Good night to you both and walk in peace,' Clatford bids them as he goes to his door.

'Walk in peace,' they reply softly.

115

Penny Taylor has settled in to her duties at St John Hall nicely. She does not find the work onerous and has fallen in love with the horses, particularly Prince of Darkness. She has not found Gwendolyn an easy employer to work with but she has managed a *modus vivendi*, a sort of uneasy truce with the two women circling around each other like two tom cats on the prowl. When they have occasion to speak to each other, Gwendolyn is coldly civil and Penny is at a loss as to how to break the ice. She does not know why Gwendolyn is stand-offish, where Sherborne is affability itself. She hopes, in time, that Gwendolyn will unbend; after all, they have a love of all things equestrian in common. She does not. of course, know about Gwendolyn's previous extra curricula arrangements with her predecessors and how much she is missing them.

To make matters worse, Penny has not had much chance to make any friends in the village as there are few people of her age in the village. She has tried going to the St John's Arms but finds that establishment unconducive, presided over, as it is, by Gordon Turgis, surely a front runner for Surliest Landlord of the Year, and old barflies like Ragged Appleshaw. Not really her scene. She is beginning to miss the lively student life of Shearwater College but is determined to see this, her first job, through.

Of her predecessor, Crux Eaton, Gwendolyn will only say: 'He was an idle little bastard who left me in the lurch.'

Penny wonders what their history was, if only to avoid giving the same offence.

In the meantime, Gwendolyn has been working on Plan B.

116

A handwritten letter has arrived on Barton Stacy's desk addressed to:

The Police,
  Itchen Prior,
  England

It bears a stamp from the Federal Republic of Bosnia and Herzegovina and was postmarked a week ago. It reads:

Dear Sir,

Mr Jed Smith, the owner of the Itchen Prior Horticultural Centre is a criminal who breaks many of the laws of your country. He employs workers without the necessary work permits for your country and he does not pay a lawful wage. He has done this for many years and must not be permitted to do this in the future. He does not treat his workers well. Please make an investigation of this man.

The letter is unsigned.

Stacy taps the letter against his desk and thinks: Oh Jed, you bloody fool, what *have* you been up to?

117

It is two o'clock in the morning of a moonless Thursday night towards the end of August. Gwendolyn cautiously opens the front door of St John Hall and slips out. She is dressed entirely in black with a black knitted cap covering her hair. She is wearing a thin pair of gloves and carries a lug wrench that she sneaked out of the tool shed earlier in the day. Sherborne's Range Rover is parked outside on the drive. She creeps over to it and applies the lug wrench to the wheel nuts on the front offside wheel. Twenty minutes of hard graft sees her loosen the wheel nuts so they will fall off when the car is in motion.

Next, she eases open the driver's side door and drops a tiny glass vial into the socket of the seat belt. The vial contains a small amount of superglue that will shatter when the seatbelt is locked into place. Within minutes of this happening the seatbelt will be glued closed, trapping the driver in the vehicle when the wheel comes off. With a bit of luck, if Sherborne is not killed outright, the car will catch fire and toast him. She wonders about secreting an oily rag in the engine to expedite a fire but has only a vague knowledge of the workings of an engine. Best not, she decides. Leave it to chance.

With an untroubled conscience she goes back to her warm bed.

118

The next morning Jed Smith is up early going over the books, the real ones, not the set of accounts he keeps for HMRC and the ones he has shown to Paul Hartley.

The Gift Shop is going well and it is time to order in the Christmas stock which will go on sale in early October. Profits from the sale of the garden plants and small trees, which is the core business of the Itchen Prior Horticultural Centre, have held steady as the summer season draws to an end but he could do with more help in the growing tunnels; he contemplates getting in help through a gang master he has dealt with in the past but dismisses the thought with a shudder. Never again. His experience with those wretched, ungrateful Bosnians has put him off for life being an employer of Eastern Europeans: they are the cause of all the woes that blighted his summer, made his life a living hell and ultimately saddled him with a partner he loathes. Not to mention making a large hole in his bank balance which will take some making up.

That leaves the prospect of local labour and he hits upon the idea of local school leavers. The school year has ended and there is bound to be a crop of local children who failed miserably to gain the English and Maths GCSEs needed to be employable elsewhere, even stacking shelves in the discounters or selling fries in a fast food restaurant. There is, of course, the added bonus that even employed legally they are on the minimum of minimum wages. He ponders putting an ad in the local paper until he realises that the sort of person he wishes to employ would be highly unlikely to be able to read, much less want to. Word of mouth, then, or perhaps an ad in the window of the Itchen Prior store for a parent to see.

He finds a card and a black marker pen and writes:

Job Opportunity
Help Wanted
At
Itchen Prior Horticultural Centre
Young Persons
Willing to Work and Learn
Excellent Prospects
In the Garden Trade
Apply in Person
To
Mr Jed Smith
(Itchen Prior Horticultural Centre)

That should do the trick, he thinks. No need to bother the Jobseekers office with unnecessary paperwork (and national Insurance or PAYE complications). A zero hours, self-employed contract seems to be the going scam. He resolves to pop down to the shop later in the morning a post the notice.

119

At ten o'clock that same morning, Gwendolyn, attired for her morning ride, walks to the stables and find Penny Taylor hard at work scrubbing the floor with a bucket of hot soapy water and a large hand brush.

'Good morning, Penny,' she says. She is in a good mood for today her fortunes will change immeasurably for the better.

'Good morning, Mrs St John,' says Penny, looking up at her and wondering why she is being pleasant.

'Horses all present and correct and raring to go?'

'Yes,' says Penny, a trifle warily.

'I'll take Prince of Darkness. I feel like a good gallop today. Get him ready for me, please.'

Please! That's a first, thinks Penny as she goes to get the tack and saddle the horse.

Gwendolyn leans against the stable door, humming a tune and tapping her leg with the riding crop, watching the girl.

'Oh, Mrs St John, we need to stock up on a few things. The alfalfa is getting low and we could do with more meadow grass and a stable lick.'

'Talk to my husband. He deals with all that sort of thing.' Gwendolyn says.

But not for much longer, she thinks. *I wonder if I'll keep the horses when I get shot of this dump. I'll keep Prince, of course, but I'll get rid of Molly. Damn near killed me, spooking like that. The knacker's yard for her. That'll teach her!*

Penny leads Prince of Darkness out and hands the reins to Gwendolyn who mounts and clatters off, still humming to herself.

120

Jed Smith is also humming to himself as he strolls to the village shop, advertisement in hand. The sun is shining and he feels at one with the world. He pushes open the door and the bell chimes to announce his arrival.

'Mornin' Natalie,' he calls out.

'Mornin' Mr Smith,' she replies. 'What can I do for you?'

'Will you post this notice in the window for me?' he says.

She takes it from him and gives it a cursory glance; reading does not play a large role in Natalie Somerfield's world.

'Wassit for then?' she asks.

'I'm on a recruiting drive,' he explains. 'Providing work experience for the young people of the village.' He feels a wash of pride at the civic duty he is about to perform. It sounds *so* much better than saying he is after cheap, minimum wage labourers.

'That'll be five pounds a week, then.'

'What?'

'To display your notice.'

'*Five pounds!* You must be joking. I'm doing a public service. You don't charge the post office to stick up notices about pensions.'

'I *am* the post office,' says Natalie and produces a cardboard triangle with the words Post Office written on it in blue crayon which she puts on the shop counter. 'Can't charge meself, can I?'

'That's bloody daylight robbery, that is, Natalie.'

'Tek it or leave it. You can always go down the Job Centre,' she says shrewdly.

Money-grubbing bitch, thinks Smith as he fumbles for money to fling down on the counter.

'Ta much,' says Natalie, sticking a wodge of blue tack to the notice and sticking it in the window along with signs offering dog walking, light gardening duties by retired but active pensioner, a ladies' tea circle and piano lessons by 'a lady', amongst others.

Smith is about to leave when Barton Stacy comes in to buy his copy of *The Daily Express*.

'Jed!' he exclaims. 'You and I need to have a little chat.'

Smith's blood freezes in his veins: 'a little chat' with a representative of the Old Bill, albeit a long time chum, bodes no good at all.

The two men leave the shop swiftly to escape Natalie's prying ears. Any juicy gossip repeated in the shop will be round the village like a flash.

'Always a pleasure, Barton, but I'm up to my eyes in it at the moment. Can it wait?'

'Not for long; I've received an anonymous letter. From Bosnia. Something about you employing illegals.'

'Not me,' says Smith in fierce denial. 'Never have; never will. Look, I've just posted a notice up here in the shop advertising work for local youngsters. A step on the ladder for them.' At a bloody fiver a week!

'That's as maybe but we still need to talk. There's that business with the fire, as well.'

'Can it wait, Barton. I really am all out.'

'In the next couple of days, then. But we do need to have a chat. Sort some things out.'

Smith shoots away from the shop like a cork from a champagne bottle and heads swiftly in the direction of his car. Stacy regards his fast disappearing back thoughtfully.

Definitely something to hide, he thinks.

There again, in his experience, most people had.

121

'Oh, Mister St John,' Penny Taylor calls when she sees him strolling back from his morning rounds of the estate, "Miz St John told me to tell you before she went out on Prince of Darkness this morning that we are running out of supplies for the horses.'

'Please, my dear, call me Sherborne. Nearly everyone does.' He smiles at her.

She wonders for a moment if he might be coming on to her but he is not; he is a genuinely friendly man, almost avuncular in his dealings with the world at large, despite the fact that most of the villagers who trace their roots back in Itchen Prior insist on calling him 'Squire' out of ingrained respect for the St John name.

'Thanks, Sherborne,' she says a little uncertainly.

'That's better. Now, what do we need?'

'It's mainly everyday stuff: alfalfa, meadow grass, salt lick. That sort of thing.'

'Well, I've nothing pressing on for the rest of the morning. Why don't I run you over to the suppliers and sort it out?'

'Could you?'

'Pleased to do it. We can have a chat about how you are settling in. Any problems, that sort of thing. I'll go and get the motor.'

St John returns with the Range Rover and Penny hops in the front next to him and off they go.

Sherborne has been driving the lanes around Itchen Prior since he used to steal his mother's Mini Clubman at the age of sixteen and illegally hare round the countryside at improbable speed with the firm immortality of youth and total disregard of other motorists.

It was a time when the local representative of law and order took a more relaxed view of the doings of the scion of the local landowner and as long as his mother had third party insurance and Sherborne was not actually involved in an accident, tended to turn a blind eye to his boy racer antics. He has mellowed with age and responsibility but knows these lanes with their high hedges and blind corners with a comfortable intimacy. He is a confident driver, still a little aggressive and tends to drive just a *little* over the limit.

Penny Taylor is beginning to unburden herself to him about her feelings of isolation and he is listening sympathetically to her.

Suddenly the car starts to shake and rattle. He applies his foot to the brake peddle to slow his speed but the car lurches and the bonnet drops on the driver's side. It swerves to the right and crashes into the small ditch on the edge of the lane. Driver and passenger are thrown forward towards the windscreen as the airbags deploy. The vehicle comes to a stop at an angle with St John's door rammed against the bank. Penny's door looms over her but she manages to disengage her seatbelt and climb out. She leans against the car feeling shaken and sick but otherwise unhurt.

St John tries to disengage his seatbelt but for some reason it refuses to open. The engine is making a ticking noise as it cools and he can hear a drip from the ruptured fuel line. He has a moment of panic and pulls desperately at the seatbelt that is restraining his escape.

'I'm stuck,' he shouts.

Penny pulls herself together as she sees a spreading puddle of petrol. She is a practical girl, an ex Girl Guide with badges to her credit. In the pocket of her overalls she carries a very impressive Swiss Army knife, complete with a gadget for removing stones from horses' hooves.

She climbs back into the car and starts to saw at St John's seatbelt. She cuts through it and helps him to climb over to the passenger side and drop down into the lane. He sinks down with his back to the car, panting.

'What happened?' she asks him.

'No idea,' he replies. He is feeling dazed and cannot quite take in what went wrong.

Penny walks around the front of the car to inspect the damage.

'The front wheel has come off,' she reports.

'What?'

'It's come off.'

'The front wheel?' Sherborne is a little dazed and having trouble understanding what she is saying.

'Yes. Right off. It's in the ditch. Oh God, we could have been killed.' The realisation and the delayed shock start to kick in and she begins to tremble. Soon she is sobbing great gulping sobs.

St John pulls himself to his feet, goes to her and puts his arm around her shoulders, hugging her to him. In trying to comfort her he can deal with his own shock and this is how Paul Hartley finds them when he arrives along the lane in his tractor and trailer.

298

122

Paul Hartley sits at his usual table in the St John's Arms relishing the taste of a large single malt, and the gossip.

'He was all over her like a rash,' he tells Jed Smith. 'Disgustin'. An old bloke like that and a young girl.'

The presence, however fleeting, of Penny Taylor in the village has been noticed with appreciation by many of the men of Itchen Prior, Smith amongst them. Smith entertains a moment of fantasy of being all over Penny himself. Ahhh. Yes!

'You said Squire had a crash. They must have been shocked.'

'An excuse.' Hartley takes a sip of his whisky, rolling it around his mouth, enjoying the moment.

'Go on! Gwenny Abbas would kill him.'

'If she found out,' Hartley says darkly.

'Are *you* going to tell her?'

'No chance.'

'Anyway, what happened?'

'Squire says the wheel just came off and they ended up in the ditch. They were bloody lucky, if you ask me. Could have been real nasty.'

'Lucky you came along, then.'

'It were all over by the time I came along. He were copping a feel by then.'

'Go on!' Smith says again, less than convinced.

'So I got on the blower to the AA and stayed with Squire until they turned up. I didn't have any kit with me to pull 'em out.'

'What were you doing, then?'

Hartley suddenly turns shifty. 'I'd been doing a bit 'o business with a pal over Westleigh way. I was just on my way back to the farm.'

With three barrels of illegal neonicotinoid pesticide at a knock-off price loaded in the trailer. No need to worry the Health and Safety Executive unnecessarily, thinks Hartley.

Hartley has a nice little deal going with chemicals produced in the Far East and shipped to North West Europe with a fake MAPP number and product description. From there an obliging distributor (and fellow carouser with Hartley of the delights of Amsterdam's red light entertainment district from way back) ships batches of dodgy chemicals to another contact of Hartley's who runs a smallholding near the town of Westleigh; nothing is shipped bearing Hartley's name or address. He is confident that he has plausible deniability all along the line and everyone takes a cut.

Perfect.

'So no-one was actually hurt, then?' asks Smith.

'What?' says Hartley, lost in his train of thought.

'The Squire an' that new crumpet.'

'Nah. Funny, though, his wheel coming off like that. Posh car an' all.'

'You never know what to expect,' Smith agrees philosophically. ''Nother drink?'

'Can't hurt. Large single malt. Splash of water. Don't drown it.'

123

'Oh you poor darling,' says Gwendolyn. She has come back from her ride hoping to break out the mourning clothes and found an alive but shaken Sherborne collapsed on the sofa in the lounge. She listens to his story and hugs Sherborne's head to her chest and kisses the top of his head. 'And you're sure you're not hurt?'

'Jolly lucky, if you ask me,' comes Sherborne's muffled reply.

'How could it have happened?' Gwendolyn asks. *Could they tell it wasn't an accident?* she's thinking.

'No telling. The chap from the AA was at a total loss to explain it,' he says, extricating his head from his wife's bosom to come up for air.

'What a good thing Penny was with you,' says Gwendolyn. *I'll pay that interfering little bitch back for this. I'll make her life a misery.*

'Yes, is she hadn't been able to cut me free I don't know what would have happened.'

I do, thinks Gwendolyn bitterly. *I'd be down to the estate agents and have this place on the market. After a seemly period of mourning, of course. Got to keep up appearances.*

'She's a little treasure,' Gwendolyn coos.

'I say, old girl, is it too early for one of your grapefruit thingies.'

'Not for my poor gallant soldier. And then off with you for a lovely lie down.'

'You're very good to me, old girl. Sometimes I don't know what you see in an old buffer like me.'

An awful lot of money, Gwendolyn thinks.

124

There are ructions going on in the gift shop and till area of Itchen Prior Horticultural Centre. Unsuspecting members of the public are shuffling uncomfortably as the Warren twins are shepherded in by Ashley.

'Don't you little bleeders touch anything.' Ashley warns as Hare picks up a jar of artisan honey and tosses it to Hatch who throws it back, laughing.

Mrs Kingston bustles into action while Miss Twyford looks scared. She knows the twins and wants nothing to do with them.

'Can I help?' Mrs Kingston asks.

'We're here to see Jed,' Ashley announces.

'Is he expecting you?' Mrs Kingston asks, somewhat sceptically.

'Sort of,' replies Ashley, enigmatically. 'Hatch! Leave it!'

Hatch reluctantly replaces the hand axe he has been enthusiastically swinging.

A number of customers are making for the exit, putting their shopping trips on hold for the moment. Shopping trolleys and baskets are left, their contents abandoned. Miss Twyford wrings her hands. Hare is making threatening faces at her, silly cow!

'I'll see if he is in,' says Mrs Kingston and hurries to the office.

Jed Smith is working his way through a pile of paperwork. He looks up as Mrs Kingston enters.

'Mrs Warren wants to see you. With those awful hooligan twins of hers. Says she has an appointment.'

Smith is surprised. 'Not that I know of,' he says. 'What does she want?'

'To see you.'

'What about,' he tries again.

'*I* don't know,' she says.

Before the conversation can go in another fruitless circle Ashley Warren erupts into the office with the twins in tow.

'I've come about the advert,' she explains.

Smith looks blank while Mrs Kingston beats a hasty retreat back to the near empty shop.

'Put the kettle on,' she tells Miss Twyford. 'I need a cuppa!'

'What advert?' asks Smith, his mind a blank.

'In the shop,' Ashley tells him slowly.

'Shop?' Smith really isn't with it this morning. Last night's session with Hartley was a good one.

'About the jobs,' Ashley reminds him.

A terrible realisation dawns on Jed Smith; she wants him to employ her ghastly unemployable and psychotic offspring in *his* business.

'Er,' he says.

'Young persons willing to learn,' she quotes at him. 'My kids are willing to learn, ain't you?' She gives the twins, who are trying to hide behind her back, a shove. They mutter something that Smith does not catch.

'See,' she says triumphantly. 'Willin' ter learn.'

'Do you have any work experience?' Smith asks hopefully.

'Don't need it, do they. Advert says "willing to learn". An' they is.'

Neither Hatch nor Hare Warren seem to share their mother's conviction. They shuffle their feet and scowl at Smith.

'It only pays minimum under eighteen wages,' says Smith, hoping to put them off.

'Don't matter. Gotta start somewhere. They's good workers, they are. When can they start?'

'I've got other candidates for the posts to interview,' Smith tries to bluff.

Ashley Warren fixes her eyes on him and says: 'Not when they find out my kids are first in line.'

'Ah,' says Smith, realising that he can't go against the Warrens. The Bosnians, he reflects, were mere pussycats against a Warren scorned. All they have to do is mount a picket outside and the garden centre will never see another customer. He shudders at the thought.

'It's mainly outside work. It'll be cold in the winter.'

'Ain't winter yet,' Ashley points out.

'Are they any good with plants?'

'They can learn. It says that in the advert,' Ashley reiterates.

Jed Smith sees he is caught between a rock and a hard place. He is about to capitulate when Mrs Kingston pokes her head round the office door.

'Sergeant Stacy to see you,' she says, marvelling how Smith has managed to summon the forces of law and order to the rescue.

A jolt of relief shots through Smith at the look of apprehension that flickers across Ashley Warren's face. But his relief is short lived as he realises what Stacy probably wants.

'We'll come back later to fix things up,' says Ashley, hurriedly shooing her feral children out of the door. 'Mornin', officer,' she says to Barton Stacy as they push past him.

'Ah, Barton,' says Smith with forced bonhomie, 'you saved my life.'

'They taken up a protection racket?' asks Stacy, only half in jest. He closes the door to Smith's office so they are alone and sits down in the chair facing Smith.

'She wants me to give her brats a job,' says Jed, hoping to keep things light.

'Good idea. Keep 'em out of mischief.'

'Easy for you to say. It's not you'd be doing the keeping!'

'Think of it as a public service.'

'I don't want to think about it at all.'

'Anyway, that's not why I'm here.'

'What can I do you for?'

'It's more what I might have to do *you* for,' says Stacy, all trace of humour gone.

'Sound ominous,' says Smith, still trying to keep things light.

'I'm afraid it is. I told you about the anonymous letter I received. The one from abroad.'

'Yes, vaguely' says Smith.

'It made an accusation that you were employing illegals.'

'Which I assure you I have never done,' Smith interjects. Always get your denial in first, is his motto.

'But you *have* employed immigrant workers.'

'Well, yes.' There is no point in denying this; too many people know about them.

'Without work permits?'

'Ah, now, wait a minute. It's true I have employed seasonal workers from abroad but they were all Europeans. Don't need work permits. They come from a reputable gang masters who I pay for his services.'

'Bosnia isn't in the EU!'

'Really!' says Smith, feigning genuine astonishment at this geopolitical revelation. 'I never knew that. And were these workers from there?'

'Apparently.'

'Well I never. The gang master never let on.'

'And what is the name of this gang master?'

Smith racks his brains for a suitably foreign sounding name. From the dim past one comes to him.

'Chowcesco.'

'Who?'

'Chowcesco. He's a Romanian. They're in the EU, aren't they? I think he is a Gypsy or a Roma or whatever. He supplied all my workers.'

'Has he got a first name?' ask Stacy, not at all convinced.

'Stanislav!' says Smith, promptly.

'And where can I find Mr Chowcesco?'

'He goes back to Romania every summer. To look for new recruits.'

'Does he have an address in Romania?' Stacy asks, his patience wearing thin.

'I'm sure he does.' Smith is on a roll and beginning to enjoy himself.

'And what is it?'

'I've no idea. He phones me when he gets back.'

'I don't suppose you have his phone number?'

''Fraid not. Sorry.'

'Tax and National Insurance?'

'Mr Chowcesco pays it.'

Barton Stacy can see he is on a hiding to nothing and changes tack.

'I was talking to Clifton Maybank at the fete,' he says.

'Who's he?' Smith interrupts.

'He's the fire chief. The bloke who came out to your caravan fire.'

'Oh, yeah. I remember.'

'He doesn't think the fire was accidental.'

'I told you, it must have been travellers.'

'Friends of Mr Chowcesco, perhaps?' says Stacy, drily.

'Who knows,' says Smith, pokerfaced.

'Why would they do that?'

'Who knows?'

'So where are you workers now?'

'They left.'

'When?'

A light goes on in Jed Smith's brain; the classic cartoon light bulb moment. He decides to break the careful habit of a lifetime and tell the truth – or at least an edited version thereof.

'Round about the time of the fire,' he says and pauses for thought. A stricken look creeps over his face.

'You don't think….?' He pauses, unable to finish the thought, unable to cope with the unbearable truth that is dawning.

'What?' says Stacy, not yet following Smith.

'That they might have had something to do with the fire?' His expression shows that he is in a state of inner turmoil. Can this be true? After all that he has done for the ingrates?

'You think your illegal immigrant workers might have set fire to your caravans?' asks Stacy.

God, you're slow on the uptake, thinks Smith. No wonder crime figures are at an all time high. Dork!

'It's the only explanation I can think of,' says Jed slowly.

'Why would they do that?'

'Spite! There is no other reason. I treated them fairly. Like a father, almost. They just up and left.'

'And this was the time of the caravan fire?'

How many times do I have to tell you, Smith thinks. And it's the TRUTH!

'Can anyone corroborate this?'

'Well, the fire brigade can,' says Smith, just a little sarcastically.

'I mean about the workers?'

'Obviously no-one saw them *actually* setting fire to the caravans. They might have mentioned it to me, don't you think?'

Stacy concedes the point.

'Do you have their names and addresses?'

'I know their names, obviously. But I've no idea of their home addresses. It was never an issue. They just came recommended from Karadzic.'

'Who is Karadzic?'

'The gang master,' Smith replies.

'I thought his name was Chowcesco?'

Bugger, Smith thinks.

'I think Karadzic is his assistant. They have lots of workers to place. Chowcesco is a busy man. He delegates.'

'Look, Jed, your story is full of inconsistencies.'

'*I'm* the bloody VICTIM here,' Smith shrieks in outraged innocence. 'Those ungrateful bastards walk out on me in the middle of the summer season rush and burn down my property out of pure wickedness and you are questioning me over petty details. I don't know where they live. I didn't know they were illegals. I don't even know where bloody Bosnia *is*. All I know is that from now on I'm going to give good local kids a chance of work. Fully legal. Stamps an' all. Pukka!'

Barton Stacy is unsure what to believe and decides to give his friend the benefit of the doubt, even though he knows Jed Smith to be as crooked as a paperclip. Besides, the amount of paperwork and time he would have to invest is a nightmare.

'Will you come down to the station and make a formal statement?'

'Of course,' says Smith, ever the upright citizen.

'Sooner rather than later,' Stacy warns.

'I'll be right on it,' Jed promises.

'Have fun with the Warrens,' Stacy calls over his shoulder as he leaves the office.

Sod off, thinks Smith.

125

The allure of bell-ringing is beginning to tarnish for Mitchell Dever. He is a man of enthusiastic fads that burn brightly and then die. In the past he has raved about photography, spending a small fortune on cameras and accessories; learning Spanish; astronomy (useless in light-polluted West London); writing the great novel (abandoned on page 47 – 'I just couldn't reconcile the characters' psychological motivations'); and collecting the Provincial coin issues of the Emperor Hadrian. Last Christmas, at his office party, he developed an enthusiasm for Mary Nixon, a new secretary, who wisely fended off his advances. *This* was the underlying incentive for the move to the country after 'a concerned friend' mentioned it to Jocasta. Unknown to their friends, Mitchell is on a final warning!

He is even beginning to regret his rash move to the village of Itchen Prior with its collection of eccentrics and downright lunatics.

So when Jocasta asks him if he is coming to bell-ringing practice he fudges and makes a lame excuse about pressures of work. Since the dinner party with Henry Grey, Tristram Clatford and Marjory Hinton Daubrey, he has ranked them high on the list of Itchen Prior weirdo's that he intends to steer clear of.

'Well, *I'm* going,' Jocasta informs him, giving him a peck on the forehead. 'They're my friends and God knows we need *some* kind of social life.'

'Having regrets about moving down here?' Mitchell says hopefully.

'Not at all. I'm getting quite used to the place. It's a real little community. Not like London where you never really got to know your neighbours.'

'Like the Warrens?'

'They're not so bad. At least, Seth isn't. The twins, maybe. But we don't have anything to do with them.'

'Thank God!' Mitchell, the atheist, almost crosses himself at the thought of the Warren twins – surely the Spawn of Satan if ever there were such a thing. Although, given the theological bent of the vicar, he wouldn't be at all surprised.

'Have fun, darling,' he calls to his wife's back as she heads for the door.

'Misery guts,' she calls back, laughing.

126

Ragged Appleshaw puts the team through their paces for a good hour, disturbing the peace of the rest of the village in the name of tradition; only an incomer would seek an injunction on the grounds of breach of the peace and immediate ostracism would ensue. Besides, the only recent incomers to the ancient settled community of Itchen Prior are Mitchell and Jocasta.

After bell-ringing they adjourn to the St John's Arms and drift apart, almost as if by pre-arranged agreement. Ragged Appleshaw props up the bar and is joined by Seth Warren. Jocasta finds herself seated with her usual cabal of Marjory, Henry and Tristram. By way of a change they order a bottle of wine from the St John's extensive wine list – red or white – causing Gordon Turgis much consternation and muttering under his breath. He brushes the dust off as he brings the bottle to their table.

'Don't get much call for this posh stuff,' he explains as he unscrews the top of the bottle of finest Moroccan red. Jocasta takes a sip and realises why.

'Mistake,' observes Henry Grey.

'Indeed,' Tristram agrees.

'Never mind,' says Marjory, always the optimist.

'I've got an idea,' says Jocasta and orders a large bottle of lemonade. 'I learnt this in Spain when we on holiday in Andalucía. It's called *Tinto de Verano*. It's really quite refreshing.' She pours a generous slug of lemonade into the wine. 'It really needs ice, but it'll kill the taste nicely.'

And indeed it does.

'Have you thought any more about what we discussed at your lovely dinner party?' Henry asks innocently.

'What? About that old pagan stuff?'

'Yes.'

'Not really. It was fascinating and all that but I can't say I've given it much thought since. Mitchell thought it was a load of old baloney.'

'But how about you?' Tristram asks her.

'Well, now that you ask me, I can see how these old traditions survive. Especially in the countryside. The rhythm of the seasons and all that.'

'The land exerts a powerful force,' Grey says in all seriousness. 'The patterns of life and death.'

'You make it sound spooky,' says Jocasta with a little nervous laugh. What is she getting into?

'Some of us still celebrate the old ways,' Marjory confides in a voice little above a whisper.

'Are you serious?' Jocasta does not know what to think. These are her friends, not some bunch of New Age hippies and proto Druids.

'We *are* serious. A group of us meet to greet the rising of the new moon and thank Mother Earth for her gifts.'

'What? Even you, Tristram?'

'I told you I was a man of religion. Religion has taken many, many forms in the history of Humankind. The three Abrahamic religions are just the latest manifestations that worship a male sky god. But the oldest religious images that we have are the Venus figures of the Neolithic people.

The symbol of the Earth Mother. It can be argued that the cult of the Virgin is a disguised form of the Mother.'

'I'm not really a religious type of person,' says Jocasta. She is feeling uncomfortable with this turn of the conversation.

'I'd love you to come along to one of our meetings,' says Marjory. 'Just to see,' she adds and places her hand on her friend's arm to reassure her. 'There is nothing *sinister* about it. You know me. We've become good friends. At least, I hope so.'

'Yes, we have. Of course we have.' Jocasta takes a pull of her drink to give herself time to think. What the hell is going on! Worshipping the moon? Earth Mothers. They must be barking. Perhaps Mitchell is right and they are all inbred nutters. But Henry Grey is an educated man, as is Tristram Clatford and Marjory Hinton Daubrey is a *school teacher* for heaven's sake. If this were coming from a horny handed son of the soil like Ragged Appleshaw she wouldn't be at all surprised. But from these three?

'Just who is in this group?' she asks.

'You have met many of us,' Tristram tells her. 'All the bell-ringers. And some others.'

So Ragged Appleshaw *is* a part of it. She can't say she is surprised. And Seth Warren. No surprise there, either. All the village idiots gathered together to howl at the moon. She starts to laugh at the picture that has formed in her mind of capering madmen in loincloths and, for some reason, shaking sticks and then it hits her.

'The Morris dancers?'

'Oh yes. The dance is very, very old. All so called 'primitive' societies have traditions of ritual dance,' Grey confirms.

'I don't believe this,' says Jocasta, shaking her head.

'You said you wanted to experience true village life,' says Grey softly.

'This is the Twenty-first century! The internet, social media. Humans have *walked* on the moon. It's not some kind of god. For goodness' sake.'

'The moon is a symbol of death and rebirth. Like Orpheus and Osiris and indeed Jesus,' Grey explains. 'Symbols of the infinite.'

'Look, if we are going to go on with this I need something stronger than this horse piss,' says Jocasta.

'Perhaps a brandy. I think Gordon might have something decent. He keeps it for Sherborne.'

'I think I need it,' says Jocasta with relief. 'I can't take this in.'

'Just think about it,' Marjory tells her. 'No pressure.'

'Sounds like my first boyfriend trying to get me into bed,' says Jocasta, laughing.

'And did you give in?' asks Marjory, also laughing.

'In the end. It was the easiest course of action. Bit of a disappointment, actually.'

'I don't think you will be disappointed if you join us,' says Tristram. 'It is an intense spiritual experience. Just the sort of thing that is lacking in the Twenty-first century with its shallowness and self obsession.'

When Grey comes back with the brandies Jocasta knocks hers back in one. What planet are these people on? She thought she knew them.

'Just think about it, will you,' says Marjory as they leave the pub. 'Keep an open mind.'

'I will,' Jocasta promises. But she has no intention of dancing around under the light of the new moon with a bunch of demented pagans.

She resolves not to mention any of this to Mitchell who would make great millage out of the foibles of the yokels. Despite everything, she likes the new life they have forged here and does not want to give him any excuse to move back to London.

Besides, with the way house prices are rising, she is not sure they could afford to move back.

127

'Good night?' Mitchell greets her on her return.

'Yes. It was, quite.'

'What did you get up to after you gave the bells a bashing?'

'Oh, we had a very interesting chat about this and that. And drank some dreadful old plonk.'

'I'd be surprised if Gordon Turgis has even heard of wine. Not really his thing. Not very rustic.'

'No. You're right,' she agrees. 'I'm bushed. I'm going to turn in.'

'I'll be up in a minute,' he says. 'Got a bit of work to finish.'

'Good night,' she says and hopes a decent night's sleep will clear the thoughts swirling in her mind.

128

By late August matters of the heart have come to a head for Alice Lacey. Mrs Rawston has found out (through the information laid by a helpful neighbour) about hubby Tarrant's affair with Alice and has thrown him out of the matrimonial home, a not wholly unwelcome development for Tarrant. He has asked Alice Lacey to move in with him and has made something of an ultimatum of it. Alice herself, is not averse to the idea and has no real regrets to shaking the dust of Itchen Prior off her feet for good. She has requested a meeting with Farleigh Wallop and sits at the table in his well furnished (as befits a Major in the Catering Corps) kitchen.

'What can I do for you?' Wallop asks with a sense of foreboding.

'I want to give notice, Major.'

'Why? Aren't you happy doing for me?'

'It's not that. It's personal.'

A sick feeling hits Wallop in the pit of his stomach.

'Is it Hartley?' The eternal question of the loser in a love triangle.

'Hartley? Oh, goodness me, no,' Alice laughs. 'Not in a million years!'

Relief flows through Wallop; he can stand anything but defeat to his rival. In fact, he feels a sensation almost of glee. If he, Wallop, can't have her, at least Hartley has not won the prize either.

'The truth is, Major, I've been seeing a man in Westleigh for some time. I'm leaving Itchen Prior to move in with him.'

'So you were just stringing us along all the time?' says Farleigh Wallop sadly. No fool like an old fool, he thinks.

'You were both stringing yourselves along,' she says kindly.

'Ah well, when are you leaving?'

'I'll see the week out for you, Major. Give you time to find a replacement. You could put a notice up in the shop. I'm sure you'll find someone. It's not like there are many employment opportunities round here.'

'Have you told Hartley yet?'

'No. I'll do that when I've finished cleaning up here.'

'I'll miss you, Alice,' says Wallop softly.

'You'll get over it,' she says and gives him a peck on the cheek.

129

'I've been bloody dumped,' Paul Hartley announces to Jed Smith over their lunchtime drink in the St John's Arms.

'Whatdaya mean, dumped?'

'Bloody Alice Lacey. She's only gone and given her notice. Can't do for me anymore.'

'Oh,' says Smith with barely suppressed glee, 'has she decided to marry the Galloping Major?'

'Him? No chance. Why would she want to marry that dried up old fart?'

'I thought that was what all the bad blood between you was about. Everyone knows. Whatcha going to do?'

'She suggested I put up a notice in the shop.'

Smith thinks about his own recent efforts at advertising in the village shop with a shudder.

'Could be a good idea,' he says. And the best of bloody luck to you!

'I'll do that,' says Hartley. 'See who I get. Might be a juicy young thing all ripe for a farmer's wife.'

You're living in a fantasy world, you daft git, thinks Smith.

'One for the road?' he suggests.

'Just the one. Some of us have work to do.'

130

Farleigh Wallop is in his sitting room with a large brandy snifter listening to a recording of Sousa marches. He is feeling mellow (it's his third glass) and at peace with the world despite the cruel defection of Alice Lacey. Business is good and the bookings are rolling in. He is thinking about taking on an assistant, someone young and full of getgo. Maybe he can take things a little easier.

He does not register the ring on the doorbell as Sousa is in a rousing mode. He finally hears the pounding on the door, turns the music down a notch or two, puts his glass on the small table next to his chair and goes to answer the summons.

Ashley Warren stands in his doorway.

'Mrs Warren. How can I help you?'

'I've come to help you,' she says.

Wallop is at a loss to know what the woman is talking about.

'I'm sorry,' he says, 'I'm not sure what you mean.'

'The job. I've come about the job.'

For a moment he is confused. Does she mean with the paintballing business? he wonders. But he has only just thought about it. He knows the woman was Gypsy Rose Lee at the fete but is she really psychic?

'Ter do for you,' she explains. 'The advert. In the shop.'

'Ah, the housekeeper.'

'Yeah. Cleaning an' stuff.'

'Oh.'

'Only it didn't mention wages. What are yer offering?'

'I was paying Alice Lacey £10 an hour,' admits Wallop, taken off guard.

'Cash in hand?' Ashley demands.

'Well, yes.'

'Two hours a day. Three days a week. Monday, Wednesday an' Friday.'

Wallop feels he has lost any control of the interview that he might have had. His head is spinning. Does he really want to give any member of the Warren family unfettered access to his home while he is out?

He is on a hiding to nothing with the hurricane that is Ashley Warren.

'I'll start on Monday next. You provide the cleaning stuff. I do vacuuming and light dusting. No heavy lifting and shifting. I don't do cooking. I get enough of that at home.'

'Er,' says Wallop, outflanked and out manoeuvred.

'So that's that. Monday. Say around eleven o'clock. I ain't an early riser.'

'Er,' says Wallop again. And then he has a thought. 'Mr Hartley may be looking for help.' He says. 'Alice Lacey used to do for him as well.' Might as well salvage something from this. If he can inflict Ashley onto Hartley all might not be bad.

'He's next,' says Ashley, disappearing into the night from whence she came.

Wallop closes his door, goes back to his Sousa, gulps down his brandy and pours himself another.

What just happened? he thinks.

Seth Warren sits at the table in the kitchen that serves as the nerve centre for the Warren household. The windows are open to admit the warm night air and to allow the fug from his roll-ups to escape. He is drinking the Warrens home-made cider from a cracked mug and thinking how all is well with the world and with the Warrens in particular and will be even better after another mug. He hears the front door open and Ashley Warren bursts into the kitchen with a smile on her face.

'Sorted!' she says and gives Seth a big sloppy kiss on the lips.

'What's that then, my angel?' asks a happy Seth.

'I got Major Wallop to give us a job, part time like. An' then I got old Farmer Hartley to, as well. Odds and sods of cleaning. Doddle. Reckon on clearing hundred an' twenty a week. Cash in hand.'

'Result!' says Seth, returning his wife's kiss.

'An' with the twins starting for Smith at the garden centre next week the dosh will be rollin' in.'

'Don't forget my Invalidity Benefits an' my bits o' deals here an' there,' Seth points out.

'I know, my chuck. The Warrens are gonna be minted! Pour us a mug o' that cider. We're celebratin'!'

'An' then off to bed to *really* celebrate?'

'Oh yes, definitely,' she says and winks lasciviously.

An Extraordinary Event has gripped the imagination of the curious (and the feckless) of Itchen Prior. The St John's Arms is packed, unprecedented for a Thursday night; Natalie Somerfield has hung a CLOSED sign on the door of the village shop and is helping Gordon Turgis to cope with the rush. Tongues wag. The whole village is agog.

Paul Hartley and Farleigh Wallop are sitting and drinking together!

Trade is so good that Gordon almost offers them a free drink before sanity kicks in and he thinks better of it

'She played us both for a couple of old fools,' says Farleigh Wallop with the benefit of hindsight.

'She did that, the bitch!'

'Still, life goes on.' Farleigh waves philosophically.

'An' she were carryin' on with some bloke from Westleigh?'

'So she said.'

'The bitch!'

'Best we put all that behind us now. What do you say…' Farleigh pauses for a moment as if he is trying to reluctantly shape the word '…Paul?'

'Fallin' out over a piece o' skirt. Yeah. It were daft.'

Hartley is aware of what falling out with Farleigh has cost him. A nice little earner on the side without him lifting a finger.

He will never know how close he came to being murdered by his rival.

The crowd in the bar look on amazed as Farleigh Wallop buys them both a drink.

'Has Ashley Warren been to see you?' he asks innocently.

'Whoooah,' says Hartley and shudders. 'She has.'

'Hard woman to refuse.'

'Them Warrens are the Itchen Prior Mafia. She made me an offer I couldn't refuse. You?'

'Monday, Wednesday and Friday.'

The two men sup their drinks reflectively as the crowd watches and marvels. Each suffers the pangs of rejection while savouring the knowledge that the other was also spurned. A kind of victory in defeat that softens the blow.

They both know that they may be drinking to drown their mutual sorrows now but they can never be friends – if indeed they ever were.

133

Gwendolyn St John is getting desperate. Her resolve to murder her husband is as resolute as ever but she is at a loss as to *how* the deed is to be done. She has abandoned her research of *Midsomer Murders* as the murders are too obvious – she needs subtlety: the murder must go undetected. She has therefore switched her research to box sets of *Silent Witness* and the various *CSI*'s. If she can outwit the forensic scientists she will be home and dry.

It is time for Plan C.

She has tried to induce a heart attack and a fatal motor accident, neither of which worked, so now the gloves are off; no more Mrs Nice Girl!

She fires up her desktop and hits the Internet.

134

Although by early September summer is drawing to a close there is no respite in the activities of the Itchen Prior Horticultural Centre. The Christmas stock for the shop must be on the shelves by October in time for the Christmas shopping frenzy and in the potting and growing sheds all must be made ready for next year's spring offerings. Contrary to Jed Smith's worst fears, the Warren twins are proving to be adequate workers. He does not know that they were dispatched on their first day with their mother's kindly admonitions ringing in their ears:

'Mess this up, yer little bleeders an' I'll skin yer. It's time yer paid yer ways. DON'T FORGET!'

Ashley Warren is the only living being in Itchen Prior that the twins fear and the message has sunk in. They are on their best behaviour. As a further incentive to keep their jobs Hatch has found a corner of a potting shed where he has surreptitiously planted some skank seeds in the best traditions of Crux Easton. He plans to sell the fruits of his labours to the members of the Itchen Prior Posse now that Crux is out of the scene.

Smith and his unwanted partner, Paul Hartley, are meeting in the office behind the shop to discuss the strategy for the year, going forward. Smith has prepared a power point presentation full of spread sheets, graphs and illustrations. It has taken him some time to create but it will be worth the effort if he can dazzle Hartley with data and get him off his back. Smith has run his business for several successful years and deeply resents Hartley's intrusion.

'That's all a load of bollocks,' says Hartley, dismissing Smith's presentation with a wave of his hand. 'Get in the usual load of tat to flog to the punters – kitchen gadgets that no one will ever use more than once, Christmas lights an' flashing Santas for the chavs to hung on their houses, plastic reindeers for their gardens, Santa Stop Here – I've Been Good signs. You know, the usual crap you get in from a bunch of heathens in China.'

Smith is deeply offended, although he does not let it show. He prides himself on his range of Christmas stock and while it is true that most of it *does* come over in containers from Shanghai at least some of it is made in Britain - it tends to be the tackier items, but then, he *is* doing his bit to keep the economy afloat.

'I've got some ideas for some new lines,' he says, 'let me show you some pictures.'

'As long as the mark-up is in excess of 100 per cent I don't give a toss.'

'I've also thought about using the parking area to set up a German Christmas market.'

'So where are the punters going to park, eh?'

'Ah.'

'Exactly.'

'Well, how about on your farm?'

'What, for the parking. Too far away.'

'No, for the Christmas Market.'

Hartley thinks for a moment. The idea appeals to him. It is a slack time of year and another revenue stream never goes amiss.

'Good idea. 80/20'

'What do you mean?'

'I get 80 per cent of the profits; you get 20. Can't say fairer than that.'

'But it's *my* idea!' Smith protests.

'And it's *my* land,' Hartley points out. Not unreasonably, he thinks. 'You're getting money for nothing. All you have to do is organise it, so you'd better get on with it.'

If Smith could grind his teeth, he would.

'Now,' says Hartley, changing the subject, 'about the stock for next year. Where do you source it from?'

'Well, there are a number of growers in this country I use.' Smith tells him.

'How about from abroad?'

'There are all sorts of regulations about the import of plants. You have to comply with the Plant Health and Seed Inspectorate guidelines and the Plant Health Propagation Scheme. It's called importing 'on the book' and involves a load of paper work.'

'I know a bloke in Holland,' says Hartley. 'He might be able to help.'

'Whatdya mean?'

'Let's just say, he can get things done in the way of certification. His prices are always keen. Know what I mean?' He actually winks and taps his nose.

'Tell me more,' says Smith, suddenly very interested.

Mitchell Dever is beginning to think he has made a terrible mistake in moving to the country. It is not the bucolic bliss he fantasied about when crammed on the District Line at 8.47 in the morning. He finds that he misses all of the things he thought he hated about London.

Jocasta, on the other hand, has taken to country living like the proverbial duck to water. She is spending most of her time with Marjory Hinton Daubrey who has had plenty of free time during the long Summer break from her teaching duties. Mitchell regards Marjory and her coterie of Henry Grey and Tristram Clatford and their enthusiastic paganism as being away with the fairies that they seem to believe in. Something of a rift has open between Mitchell and Jocasta as a result. Nothing serious, but they are no longer as close a couple as they were before moving to the sticks.

He no longer rings the bells, preferring to console himself with strong drink on the nights Jocasta is out at practice with the yokels.

136

Gwendolyn St John has taken to driving out and about with a print-out she has downloaded from the internet. She is searching for something that takes her away from the immediate vicinity of Itchen Prior, looking for a plant that does not grow locally. And besides, she does not want prying eyes to see what she is up to. When she finds what she is seeking she will take great care to destroy her document.

Plan C is afoot and this time there is nothing left to chance. She just has to be *very* careful and set the whole thing up properly.

'I thought I might invite that new girl from the St John stables along,' says Marjory Hinton Daubrey into her mobile phone. 'From what I hear she hasn't made many friends in the village.'

'Good idea,' replies Jocasta into her mobile. 'What's her name again?'

'Penny something.'

'Where were you thinking of going?' asks Jocasta. 'Not the St John's Arms?'

'No, I thought we'd go for a drive. See what we can find.'

'The accident with Sherborne St John hasn't put her off cars for life, then?'

'I hope not. She came out of that quite well. Sherborne says she saved his life.'

'Bit dramatic. Does dear Gwendolyn actually give her a day off?'

'Wednesday and Sunday afternoons. So how about next Wednesday? It's my last weekday before school starts up again.'

'Fine. Mitchell is going up to London so I'm at a loose end. Have you asked her?'

'No. I thought I'd better check with you. See if it was OK.'

'Another recruit for the coven?' asks Jocasta mischievously.

'You never know,' Marjory responds leaving Jocasta unsure whether she is joking or not. 'Have you given it any more thought? We have a gathering quite soon.'

Marjory has been putting gentle pressure on Jocasta to attend a 'gathering' for some time. Although Mitchell regards the whole thing as 'a bloody stupid bunch of nutters playing at silly buggers' Jocasta is tempted. The vicar and Henry Grey and Marjory herself are educated people not, in Jocasta's opinion, given to superstition. Perhaps they are celebrating age old rituals of country life in a harmless ceremony. Like Harvest Festival. Or Wassailing. Or Morris dancing. Where's the harm?

She makes a decision.

'OK, Marjory. I'll do it.'

'You'll come along? Oh, Jocasta, I'm so pleased. You'll love it.'

'Like bell-ringing?'

'A bit different. But nonetheless.'

'When?'

'There is a full moon on Saturday. I'll pick you up.'

'What'll I tell Mitchell. He'll think I'm going native.'

'Tell him you're coming over to mine for a girl's night in.'

'Right,' says Jocasta and commits before she can change her mind. 'Let's do it. Do I need to bring anything?'

Marjory laughs and says: 'Just come as you are.'

'OK. Let's do Wednesday even if Penny can't.'

'See you then.'

138

Much to Mrs Wellow's surprise Gwendolyn St John is taking notice of the kitchen at St John Hall. In all the years Mrs Wellow has been doing the cooking Gwendolyn has studiously steered clear of the domestic arrangements on the principal of why keep a dog and bark yourself. In matters culinary Mrs Wellow has enjoyed complete autonomy, save on her day off when Sherborne orders a take away from the Golden Pagoda or a pizza from Giovanni's Neapolitan Oven. Over the years Mrs Wellow has produced a seemingly endless stream of roasts (flesh and fowl), pies (game from the estate), stews, curries, ragouts and suet puddings – a favourite of Sherborne. Hearty meals all with full trimmings. Gwendolyn, it is true, often just pecks at these offerings but Sherborne likes his food and he likes it just the way Mrs Wellow makes it.

Mrs Wellow is caught unawares in the act of rolling out pastry, her forearms streaked with flour when Gwendolyn breezes into her domain and announces she would like to make changes to the menu.

'I'm worried about my husband. All this rich food. I don't think it is good for him.'

'He's never complained about my cooking,' Mrs Wellow protests indignantly, resting her arms on her work surface, her rolling pin clutched in her hand in a gesture of defence.

'Please don't get me wrong, Mrs Wellow. I'm sure your cooking is excellent. It's just that my husband is getting on a bit. He's of an age when all sorts of things start to go wrong.'

'Are you saying my cooking is ….'

'No, no, no,' Gwendolyn interrupts. 'I'm just worried that all this food can lead to things like Type 2 diabetes. Heart attacks. Strokes.'

'Mrs St John,' says Mrs Wellow. 'My food never hurt no-one.'

'Of course not, Mrs Wellow. Not *intentionally*.'

'Then what are you saying?'

'I want to make some changes to his diet. More salads. Less red meat.'

Mrs Wellow cannot imagine a meal that does not revolve around large portions of dead animals. This is the country, after all. It is what animals are for. To be eaten, along with a good helping of carbohydrates. She is at a loss for words. Has the woman gone mad?

'I've found some recipes on the internet,' Gwendolyn explains. 'To reduce cholesterol.'

Mrs Wellow has no idea what cholesterol is when it's at home but is sure she has never served it up to Sherborne St John in her life. Beef, pork, lamb, rabbit, venison, chicken and goose. Gammon. But never cholesterol. From what she has heard, it's probably the sort of thing that that newcomer Jocasta Mitchell might dish up at her dinner parties.

But not Mrs Wellow.

'I've never….' she begins again but is again cut short by Gwendolyn.

'So that's settled. I'm going to start making my husband healthy food a few times a week. For his own good.'

'*You're* going to *cook*?' Mrs Wellow is having trouble believing what she is hearing. Gwendolyn St John is not and never has been, a domestic goddess.

'Not *every* day, Mrs Wellow. Don't you worry. Your position here is quite safe.' Until I can get shot of this place and then you are out without a pension and then see how you like it, you fat witch. 'I'll start tonight. You can have the evening off,' Gwendolyn says sweetly and wafts out of the kitchen, leaving Mrs Wellow stupefied.

139

Penny Taylor is becoming depressed with the isolation of her existence in Itchen Prior. Gwendolyn St John is making her life a misery with constant nit picking over her work in the stables and Penny misses the student social whirl she enjoyed at Shearwater College, where the Autumn term will just be kicking off. So when Marjory Hinton Daubrey turns up at St John's Hall to inviter her out for a girly afternoon with herself and Jocasta Dever she jumps at the chance. Admittedly, Jocasta and Marjory are not *quite* in her age group, but they are better than the nothing she now has and she would welcome a break away from the stables and Gwendolyn St John.

Jocasta has been busy on the internet and found a well recommended gastro pub not too far from Itchen Prior where the three women now sit sharing a platter of mixed anti-pasti and sipping chilled white wine. Penny feels very sophisticated as she nibbles cracked green olives marinated with coriander seeds and slices of salami with fennel. At heart, she is still a simple girl with simple tastes.

Marjory is talking about some kind of nature group that meets once a month, apparently at night for some reason, but Penny is not really listening. She is daydreaming about a different life for herself; one where she is appreciated and spoiled by an adoring man, perhaps a little older than herself. A man who would cherish her and care for her and look after her. A man who would awake her potential as a loving, sensual woman. A handsome man of the world, a man of property.

She realises with a shock she is fantasying about Sherborne St John.

140

Sherborne St John, in the flesh, sits at the head of the dining table in St John's Hall staring aghast at the plate his wife has set before him. Candles flicker in the antique silver candelabra, the light reflecting off the silver flatware and the crystal of the glasses.

'What's this all about, old girl?' he asks in bemusement.

'Can't I spoil the man that I love?' coos Gwendolyn.

'That's lovely, of course, old girl but what's *this*?' He indicates the plate in front of him.

'Kidney bean, red onion and tomato salad.'

'*Why*?' Sherborne St John is not a great fan of salads.

'It's good for you,' replies Gwendolyn.

'Mrs Wellow made *this*?' Has the world gone topsy-turvy?

'No darling, *I* made it for you. I found the recipe online.'

'*Why*?' says Sherborne again.

'It's good for you,' she answers sweetly but firmly. "All that red meat that Mrs Wellow serves up. It's not good for your cholesterol level.'

'But I *like* red meat. There was talk of a steak and kidney pie for tonight.'

'Well, you've got kidney beans instead. So have I.'

'Is it a starter?'

'No. That's it. Eat up.'

Sherborne stifles a moan and gives the salad a tentative poke with his fork. To his great surprise he finds that it is quite tasty. He risks another mouthful.

'Can I at least have some cheese and port.'

'Low fat cream cheese on rye crackers but no port. We don't want you to die, now do we?'

'Might be better than living on this,' he mutters and wonders whether he can sneak down in the night after Gwendolyn has gone to bed and raid the fridge.

Gwendolyn watches him eat the salad and pulling faces. Not only has she found the recipe online, she has also discovered that as few as four raw kidney beans can be mildly poisonous, causing stomach upsets, nausea and diarrhoea. This will not kill Sherborne, she has other plans for the coup de grace, but will establish a medical history that she can exploit later when she administers the fatal poison.

141

Jocasta sits next to Marjory in the front of Marjory's little Renault. Her stomach is churning. Butterflies? she thinks, more like a flock of crows! I can't believe I'm doing this. In a way it feels almost as if she were cheating on Mitchell – a thing she has never done. But she still hasn't entirely forgiven him for his Christmas crush on Mary Nixon. She has told him she and Marjory are having a night out together and that she might stay the night if a second bottle of wine gets opened.

'You're spending more time with that woman than you are with me,' Mitchell grumbles.

'It's only for the summer,' she explains. 'When the school opens again I expect Marjory will be too busy to socialise. Especially on week days. Then you'll have me all to yourself and you'll get sick of me underfoot all the time. She smiles at him and gives him a kiss.

'Go on,' he laughs, 'bugger off to your girls' booze up. I've got work to do, anyway. I'll enjoy the peace.'

And now she sits in Marjory's car heading off for who knows what.

'I'll just run through it,' says Marjory, reading her thoughts. 'We meet up at the Devil's Tooth on the edge of St John's Wood. There will be quite a few of us and you will know most. This is not one of the major festivals of the year like Samhuinn or Imbloc.'

'Yes. I remember what Henry and Tristram said at our dinner party.'

'Good. Just relax.' Marjory pats Jocasta's knee to reassure her.

'What do I do? Do I have to say anything?'

'Just follow the others. I'll be with you most of the time.'

'*Most* of the time.'

'I've got a special role in tonight's ritual. You'll see. Don't *worry*. Just enjoy the spiritual experience.'

Marjory turns the car off the road and bounces along a track on the edge of the wood. Jocasta sees a number of cars already parked up. It looks like Dogging Central, she thinks and wonders for a moment if that is indeed what is going on. Rural Rutting perhaps.

People are clustered around chatting and greeting each other, men and women both. Jocasta is reminded of gatherings before meetings or in the breaks in training courses. Any minute now she expects a coffee trolley to arrive. It is all very civilized, not the wild Dionysian rout she half expected.

Marjory gets out of the car and she follows her to where Tristram Clatford is standing talking to Ragged Appleshaw and Seth Warren and a couple of men that she thinks she recognises from the Morris side that danced at the Fete.

'Jocasta! So glad you made it at last,' Clatford greets her.

'Marjory was very persuasive.'

'We should be starting soon,' says Clatford. 'It's time to get changed. I've got a robe for you.'

'Robe?' says Jocasta, images of Gandalf and Harry Potter flashing through her mind.

'White robes in honour of the Goddess,' Marjory explains. 'You can get changed behind my car if you are shy.'

'We come to the Goddess naked beneath the robe. In purity. We are all children of the Goddess,' Tristram explains.

Oh dear, Mitchell was right, they are a bunch of loonies. Jocasta thinks. But there is no going back now. If she walks away she will have to find her own way home and she has no idea how to get there or how far it is.

There must have been some kind of signal that Jocasta has missed because the groups are breaking up and going to their cars to change. Clatford brings her a long cotton robe that reminds her of a Moroccan hooded cloak.

She follows Marjory back to the car where Marjory starts to undress. In for a penny, Jocasta thinks and pulls off her own clothes. For a moment she feels the night air on her naked skin and shivers. Cold? Excited? Frightened? She is not sure how she feels as she dons the robe. Again she thinks, no going back now.

She hears the sound of what she thinks is a hunting horn and a figure dressed in green hose and a tunic steps out of the wood. She recognises Long Sutton. On his head he wears a wreath of woven oak leaves.

'The Green Man,' Marjory whispers. 'Now it begins.'

142

Sherborne St John pushes his chair back from the dining table. The posh silverware is back in the safe and electric light replaces the candles but the diet regime goes on. Tonight's offering is a low fat chilli con carne made with soya meat substitute and at least one or two beans he found rather chewy.

'D'you know, my dear, I don't think this new diet idea of yours is doing me much good.'

'Why do you say that?' asks Gwendolyn, all solicitous for the welfare of her husband.

'I've got a bit of a gyppy tummy.'

'That's just your system detoxifying.'

'Well, I wish it wouldn't. Can we please go back to Mrs Wellow's regular cooking?'

'It's for your own good, my darling. I worry about you. But if you don't care about your own health…' Gwendolyn leaves the sentence hanging and gives a shrug with a sad face.

'I know you just want what is best for me, old girl.'

'You're not getting any younger, you know.'

'It's just….' He starts and then makes a sudden bolt for the door and a downstairs toilet. Gwendolyn follows and listens at the door. She hears him vomiting and rubs her hands.

Plan C is going according to plan.

143

Marjory takes Jocasta by the hand. 'Follow me,' she says as she joins the procession making for the standing stone. 'Just repeat whatever tonight's Grove Leader says and does.'

'What's a Grove?' asks Jocasta.

'It's what we call a gathering like this. Just watch and copy. I'll answer your questions later, OK?'

'OK,' says Jocasta and determines to go with the flow.

Tristram Clatford with Ragged Appleshaw beside him follow the Green Man to the standing stone and lead the procession anti clockwise around the stone until the Grove have formed a complete circle. Jocasta sees Ashley Warren and a woman she thinks might be the housekeeper at St John's Hall. Even Natalie Somerfield is there, as well as other women she does not know.

A man she thinks is one of the Morris Men steps into the middle of the circle and chants:

'Hail to the Guardians of the North.'

'Hail to the Guardians of the North,' the circle repeats.

Marjory digs her elbow into Jocasta's ribs and feeling very foolish Jocasta joins the chant.

The Grove Leader repeats the salutation to the other points of the compass and Jocasta goes along with the rest of what she can only think of as the congregation.

'Hail to the land, the Earth Mother, Mother of us all' calls the Leader.

The group start to circle the standing stone, the Leader chanting the Invocation and the Grove echoing the chant.

'Hail to the Spirit of the Sky.'

'Hail to the Spirit of the Sea.'

The procession speeds up slightly and breaks into a chant of 'Awen. Awen. Awen.'

'Who or what is 'Awen'?' Jocasta whispers to Marjory.

'Awen is the spiritual force, the poetic nature of life, but I have to leave you now,' Marjory tells Jocasta. 'Don't worry. Nothing bad is happening.'

'Who stands for the Earth Mother; Bridget, Goddess of the Standing Water and of the Spring of Life?' asks the Grove Leader.

'I have that honour,' Marjory announces.

'Step forward, Earth Mother!'

Marjory steps into the centre of the circle. An expectant hush falls over the worshipers.

Now what? Jocasta thinks.

'The Earth Mother is the fertility of the land,' the Grove Leader intones. 'She has sustained us and our ancestors since time out of mind. She is the Origin and the Future and our Present. To Her all hail.'

'To Her all hail,' call the assembly.

'She is the Bride of Cernunnos. Lord of the Hunt and the Wild Places.'

'Cernunnos, Lord of the Hunt and the Wild Place. All hail,' they chant.

'Then let us celebrate the Mystic Union of Cernunnos and Bridget,' calls the Grove Leader, raising his arms into the air.

Marjory Hinton Daubrey shucks off her robe and stands naked in the circle, her skin pale in the moon light.

'Who stands for Cernunnos, Lord of the Hunt?'

'I have that honour,' says Seth Warren, who also steps into the circle and discards his robe.

Jocasta is shocked. She has a terrible suspicion of what is about to happen and does not know how she feels about it. She sneaks a glance at Ashley Warren and is surprised to see her looking perfectly composed. Like everyone in Itchen Prior Jocasta has heard about the exclusivity of the Warren's mating habits.

Marjory has dropped to her knees and elbows, facing the standing stone in what Jocasta can only call 'the doggy position'. Seth, naked, kneels behind her, spreading her legs. The flickering torchlight casts a red glow on their skin.

Marjory! Oh my god, thinks Jocasta. However, prurient curiosity will not let her tear her eyes away and she realises that somehow Seth is not actually tumescent and that the sex is being simulated.

'All Hail the Sacred Union of the Lord and Lady,' the onlookers intone.

The ritual coupling lasts a scant minute before the two protagonists break apart, scoop up their robes, bow to one another and take their places back in the circle, which starts to move again anti clockwise, holding hands and chanting 'Awen! Awen!'

With Marjory's hand in hers, Jocasta is struck dumb. She thought she had come to know this woman over the course of the summer. She is the demure school marm, respected by both her pupils and their parents. What would the school governors say if they knew she was a sexual exhibitionist. The Local Authority? Did she put Naked Earth Goddess on her c.v. when she applied for the job?

Jocasta thought not.

Marjory turns her head towards Jocasta and smiles and winks.

Oh my god Jocasta thinks again. There was never had any thing like this in West London. Although, on reflection, perhaps ther was and Mitchell and I were never invited.

And that gives her pause for thought.

Sherborne St John is lying in bed feeling very sorry for himself. The door to the en suite bathroom is wide open and ready for action. He has been both violently sick and crippled with diarrhoea. He is not a happy bunny. Gwendolyn sits in a chair by the side of the bed holding his hand and prepared to mop his fevered brow should the need arise.

'You poor, poor baby,' she croons.

'Bugger this diet,' Sherborne groans. 'Supposed to make me feel better. I don't think so.'

'You must go to the doctor's tomorrow, my love. It could be something serious.'

'I just want to go back to eating proper food. The kind Mrs Wellow had been making me for years.'

'It was full of cholesterol.'

'It didn't make me puke.'

'We'll get you to the doctor in the morning. You've had some Imodium. Try and get some sleep. The doctor will sort you out tomorrow.'

Sherborne closes his eyes and drifts off to sleep, exhausted, his body racked by trying to expel the poison he has ingested over the past few days.

'Marjory Hinton Daubrey!' exclaims Jocasta when they are sitting together again in Marjory's car. 'You shameless hussy, you!'

'It's a beautiful part of the ritual. Nothing actually happened.'

'And with Seth Warren, of all people.'

'He didn't *actually* shag me,' Marjory points out. 'It was symbolic of the union of the Earth Mother and the Spirit of the Wild. Anyway, Ashley would commit murder if she thought Seth was playing away.'

'But in front of all those people! How could you?'

'Jocasta, I *believe* in what we do. It's an inspiration for my life. It lets me connect with the infinite; with the passing of the years and the seasons. With all the millions and millions who have lived on this land and gone before. It's a common thread of the human experience.'

'But to stick your bum up in the air in front of all those people!'

'It was my privilege this time; next time it will be two different people. Maybe you?'

'No chance,' says Jocasta.

'Why not?'

'I'm a married woman.'

'And?'

'And it's not right.'

'It's a religious sacrament. It was symbolic of the elemental force of nature. I *didn't* actually have sex.'

'I thought you were so prim and proper. You haven't got a boyfriend or anything.'

'No, I haven't. And I don't want or need one. I'm happy as I am.'

'Did you never want to get married, have children?'

'Listen, Jocasta, I've never told this to anyone but I think of you as my good friend. I had a couple of boyfriends when I was at uni. One of them gave me a dose of chlamydia and left me sterile. I can't have children of my own so the kids at school are my kids and I have enough with them.'

'Oh Marjory, I'm so sorry.'

'I'm not. I'm very happy as I am. The worship of the Earth Mother makes me very content and gives me an inspiration for my life. My life is *full*. Can you say the same?'

When Jocasta honestly reflects on her life she is not sure she can say the same. She always thought she would like children but her job got in the way. And Mitchell never wanted children. She is very happy living here in Itchen Prior, for all its foibles, but she senses Mitchell no longer shares her happiness and feels he might have made a mistake. He is spending more and more time up in London and leaving her alone. She has never completely trusted him ever since his crush on Mary Nixon and she does sometimes wonder what he is getting up to on his overnight stays in London. As for her, she has her own work, but as long as she has good internet connections and her laptop she can do this anywhere and her visits to London are becoming less and less.

Is her life full? Can she honestly answer: yes? No.

'Did you see our little Penny?' asks Marjory, cutting through Jocasta's uneasy stream of thought.

'I can't say I did.'

'Henry must have brought her. She's his protégé. I told him I'd spoken to her when we took her out the other day.'

'I wonder what *she* made of it,' says Jocasta.

'Probably had a great time,' Marjory laughs. 'She's a country girl through and through.'

Jocasta take this as an implied dig at her, the Townie. She makes a decision.

'I'll give it another shot,' she says.

'I just knew you would,' says Marjory, true happiness for her friend in her tone.

'When is the next meeting?'

'There are eight principal festivals in the year. Four major Solar celebrations and four Fire celebrations but we also honour the full moon so there is one more before Samhuinn, which is a major event. Cernunnos himself appears for Samhuinn.'

'OK. I'll give it a go.'

They have arrived back at Marjory's cottage.

'Do you fancy a drink? You can stay over if you like. I've got a bed made up in the spare room?'

Jocasta suddenly feels that she does not want to go home to Mitchell tonight. Perhaps something of the ceremony *has* rubbed off on her. She wants to talk to Marjory some more; to probe into her religious convictions. After all, she is a researcher by profession and driven by curiosity about the world.

'Yeah, I'd love to,' she says.

'I've got a couple of bottles of Pinot in the fridge. Come on in.'

In the room once occupied by Crux Eaton over the stables at St John Hall Penny Taylor lies awake in the dark. Her eyes are open and shining as she replays the events of tonight in her mind. She pictures herself in the role of the Earth Mother, naked and submissive. But who will be her Cernunnos who strides up behind and consummates the marriage?

'What did the doctor say?' asks Gwendolyn St John when her husband returns.

'Couldn't make it out. Ran all sorts of tests on me. Took blood and pee. Asked for a stool sample which I have to take in. Couldn't perform there and then. Says he'll let me know and gave me a prescription for some tablets.'

'So he has no idea?'

'Some sort of tummy bug. Asked if I been anywhere exotic. Delhi Belly or Montezuma's Revenge. Said we'd not been out of the country for years. Complete mystery.'

Sherborne's symptoms have abated somewhat since Gwendolyn has stopped feeding him raw kidney beans but, in his own words he 'is still not right'. This is exactly the scenario Gwendolyn is working on. She is fairly confident the doctor will not be able to diagnose the source of Sherborne's illness and put his sudden death down to unknown causes brought about by complications of his gastric problem. A superbug, maybe?

So, if the deed is to be done, it best be done soonest.

'There are some men here to see you, Mr Smith,' Miss Twyford announces.

'What sort of men?' asks Smith irritably, looking up from his paperwork.

'They didn't say.'

Smith is a busy man these days; it is the beginning of October and the Christmas stock will start to arrive soon and must be stored until the Hallowe'en costumes, plastic pumpkins, witches' broomsticks, face paint and other assorted rubbish is shifted by the end of the month. Still, Hallowe'en is always a money spinner, so mustn't complain.

He is also expecting a consignment of shrubs and bulbs from Hartley's contact in the Netherlands ready for propagation for the spring. People think that the autumn and winter mean a break for the Garden Centre but they couldn't be more wrong. The work never ceases. Each season brings around preparation for the next.

It is the unceasing wheel of nature, he ponders philosophically, and he is here to help nature along and flog it to the punters who can't be arsed to do it for themselves – lazy bastards!

The door opens and three men come into the office uninvited. Smith thinks he caught a glimpse of Barton Stacy hanging about outside and is immediately on his guard. What now, for God's sake?

'Mr Jed Smith?' asks one of the men.

'Yes,' says Smith slowly; no use denying it when his name is painted on the door in fancy gold letters.

'Proprietor of Itchen Prior Horticultural?'

'What's this about? And who are you gentlemen?"

'Answer the question, please.'

'Yes. What's this about?'

'We are from the UK Border Guard and the Department of the Environment.'

'The *Border Guard*? What's that got to do with me?'

'Following a tip off from our colleagues in the Netherlands we intercepted a lorry entering the country at the port of Harwich. In it we found two young men from Kandahar in Afghanistan.' He waits for a reaction from Smith.

When Smith does not respond he continues:

'We also found a large consignment of plants and bulbs in the lorry. They were both bound for the same destination – Itchen Prior Horticultural Centre.'

'You're joking!' says Smith but a cold vice has gripped his stomach. The plants, yes. Hartley had set it up with his contact in the Netherlands. But illegal immigrants? No way. He learnt his lesson with those bloody Bosnian students. Never again.

'Unfortunately, I'm not.' says the man from the Border Force. 'Can you explain why they had this address?'

'No,' says Smith, oozing genuine disbelief. 'I've no idea.'

'We've spoken to Sergeant Stacy. It seems there have been allegations of you employing illegal workers before. This summer, in fact.'

'I explained all that to Sergeant Stacy. It was all a mistake. It was the gang master. Not me.'

'There is also the matter of the plants,' says a second man. 'Importation of unregulated plants into the United Kingdom. 'Off the book' as we say.'

'No,' Smith protests. 'There must be some mistake. I've never imported off the book. It is all kosher.'

'The paper work and the import licenses were faked,' says the man from the Department of the Environment.

Smith flounders. Hartley, you bastard, he thinks. You told me there'd be no problem.

'I don't know what to say. I ordered the stock in good faith.'

'So you admit that the plant material *was* destined for and ordered by, you.'

Bugger!

'There is another small problem,' says the third man.

Oh yes, bad luck always comes in threes.

'A number of the items were infected.'

'Infected? Whatya mean 'infected"?' Can this get any worse?

'Xylella fastidiosa was present in a number of the oleander shrubs; rose rosette virus in the rose bushes – the leaves were already turning bright red – and we found red palm weevil in the ornamental olive trees. If that little lot had got out I dread to think of the consequences.'

Smith has his head in his hands. The brown stuff has hit the fan with a vengeance. It *can* get worse.

'Have you anything to say? I must caution you that anything you say can and will be used in evidence in a court of law,' says the man from the Ministry.

'I'm innocent!' Smith wails. 'It was Hartley!'

'Who or what is Hartley?' The three men are suddenly very interested.

Hartley got me into this, thinks Smith savagely. If I'm in bother that bastard is coping for some of the blame.

'He's my partner. He set it all up. He's been dealing with this bloke in Holland for years. He arranged it all.'

'Then I think we need to have a little chat with him as well. In the mean time, we need to inspect your premises to see if you have any more infected stock. I trust you have no objection. You will be charged with the infringements of plant importation and we will investigate the charge of conspiring to traffic illegal immigrants into the United Kingdom. You are likely looking at a custodial sentence.'

149

'Hare,' says Hatch Warren, running into the propagation shed, 'the filth are in with Smith!'

'What do they want?'

'I'm not hanging around to find out. Let's scarper.'

'Mam will kill us if we loose this job.'

'But Da always says if the filth come round, get lost.'

'True,' his sister agrees. 'We can always say we had to go home urgent like.'

'Come on then!'

Barton Stacy accompanies the two men from the Department of the Environment in their search of the green houses and propagation sheds. He could have sworn the Warren twins were employed here but there is no sign of them. He is not really surprised - the Warren family seem to have a sixth sense when it comes to Authority.

'Sergeant, you'd better have a look at this,' one of the Environment men calls to him, standing in the doorway of a dilapidated greenhouse.

Stacy goes over and enters. The smell hits him as soon as he enters. A forest of cannabis plants. Hatch *has* been a busy little bee.

Oh dear, oh dear, Stacy thinks, Smith, you really are going down. You bloody idiot.

'Cannabis cultivation! Do me a favour, Barton. Have you ever known me to have any truck with drugs? I'm a drinking man.'

'I'm not saying they are for personal use, Jed. I'm saying the quantity makes it intent to supply.'

'I know nothing about any cannabis plants!' This cannot be real. This is the stuff of nightmares. Perhaps he will wake up in a minute tucked up safe in bed.

'Nevertheless,' says Stacy remorselessly, 'they are on your premises and you do run a horticultural business.'

The penny drops: 'It's those Warren kids! It must be. Look, I'm no angel but I don't cultivate drugs.'

'Can you prove it was the Warren twins?'

'No.'

'Then, Jed Smith, I'm arresting you for the cultivation of a controlled substance with intent to supply.'

Smith listens to the caution in a state of numb disbelief. This is NOT happening to him!

'Where can we find this Hartley character?' the man from the Border Force asks Stacy and Stacy gives him directions to the Hartley farm.

Stacy speaks into his radio, calling for forensics and the Drug Squad to come to Itchen Prior Horticultural Centre and arranges for the staff to attend the police station to make statements. He makes a note to chase up the Warren twins, but knows he will get nowhere with them. They sucked in the Mafia code of *omerta* with their mother's milk.

Smith appears to be in a trance as Stacy leads him to the police car.

Ragged Appleshaw leans on the bar of the St John's Arms swilling his pint round in his glass.

'Heard old Hartley got busted,' he says to Gordon Turgis, who is scowling at nothing in particular.

'Yeah?' says Gordon, struggling to feign interest.

''E were storing all sorts o' drums o' poison on 'is farm. Coulda killed us all.'

'Yeah,' says Turgis again.

'An they say 'e were bringing in them foreign chaps. People smuggling 'e were.'

'Oh yeah?'

'Him an' Smith were in it together. Smith's gone Doolally.'

'Yeah?'

'Can't see 'em coming in here no more,' says Appleshaw slyly.

'What!' says Turgis, suddenly paying close attention.

'Two o' your best customers, I reckon,' says Appleshaw and cackles.

'Bloody hell,' Turgis shouts and flings the grubby cloth he has been wiping the glasses with onto the bar. '*Bloody hell!*'

The churning in Sherborne St John's innards has subsided to an occasional rumble – from Krakatoa to Vesuvius. For this he has to thank the course of Charcodote activated carbon pills his doctor prescribed for him. He is ready to go back onto grown-up food and Mrs Wellow has promised a full roast dinner of beef, roast potatoes, Yorkshires, carrots and parsnip. With thick gravy with a touch of sherry in it.

This is what Gwendolyn has been waiting for.

Her expeditions out into the country have been in search of water hemlock, an altogether lethal plant in all its components. She has discounted using the leaves as perhaps too traceable but has discovered that the roots contain a toxic oil that apparently tastes like parsnip. The toxin attacks the central nervous system, causing fatal seizures. This is her Plan C. Having established that Sherborne is suffering from an unspecified gastric malady, she will now administer a fatal dose of poison.

Third time lucky, she thinks.

Gwendolyn goes into the kitchen where Mrs Wellow is putting the finishing touches to the meal. In her pocket she carries a tiny glass bottle of liquid. She has expended considerable time and much care in crushing the roots and extracting the oil from the plants she has gathered. She has burnt the gloves she wore during the process and scrubbed clean the chopping board she used with bleach.

She is confident that there is no trace of the oil anywhere, apart from in her bottle.

'Good morning, Mrs Wellow,' she says, bright and breezy. Mrs Wellow looks at her suspiciously. Bright and breezy is not Gwendolyn St John's default mode.

'Can I help you, Mrs St John?' she asks cautiously.

'Yes, please. Now that Sherborne is feeling much better I want to give him a treat. One of your lovely roast dinners deserves a really good wine to go with it. I'm hopeless when it comes to choosing wine. Would you be so good as to fetch something from the cellar? I know you are supposed to let the wine breathe, so if you could choose something and open it in good time for dinner I would greatly appreciate it.'

Mrs Wellow knows that Gwendolyn has no idea about fine wines, of which there is a goodly selection in Sherborne's wine cellar and, seeing nothing odd in the request, leaves the kitchen to select a bottle for her master.

The peeled vegetables are sitting on the work surface ready to go in the oven. Gwendolyn pulls on a pair of kitchen gloves (if there is any trace of water hemlock oil, then let it lead to Mrs Wellow) and with the ghost of the Empress Livia (rumoured to have murdered Augustus with poisoned figs) at her elbow, proceeds to smear the water hemlock oil onto the parsnips.

By the time Mrs Wellow returns from her errand, Gwendolyn has gone.

154

'I'm famished,' says Sherborne St John, sipping at his pre-prandial gin and tonic.

'I think Mrs Wellow has pulled out all the stops,' Gwendolyn tells him. 'I'm so sorry my attempts to make you healthier made you poorly, darling.'

'Oh, don't you worry your pretty little head. I know you only want what is best for me,' Sherborne replies and plants a loving kiss on the top of her head.

'I've asked Mrs Wellow to dig out a really good wine, to celebrate.'

'You are such a thoughtful old thing. Thank you.'

'Finish your drink and let's go in to eat.'

The knowledge that her husband will die in the course of the next few minutes and the role of the grief-stricken but helpless wife that she must play is stretching her nerves to breaking point. She consoles herself with the thought of the money she will inherit.

Mrs Wellow has made a beef consume to start the meal. Sherborne takes his time to savour the soup and sip at the glass of Chateaux Grand Faurie Larose St Emilion that she has selected to go with the meal.

'D'ya know, old girl, life can't get much better than this. Good food, fine wine and the woman I love to share it with.'

Get on with it and get it over, Gwendolyn thinks savagely. You daft old fart!

Mrs Wellow brings in the entrée and serves them both.

'Parsnips! My favourite veg,' exclaims Sherborne.

'Enjoy your meal, Mr St John,' says Mrs Wellow as she leaves the dinning room.

'I will that. Thank you so much, Mrs Wellow. Any horseradish?'

'In the dish.'

Sherborne takes a dab of horseradish, spreads a little on a slice of his rare beef, cuts a piece and pops it in his mouth. A look of pure joy spreads over his face. He chews and swallows, takes a sip of wine and then cuts a slice of parsnip.

Gwendolyn's nerves are screwed tight. *Just a few moments more. I might get myself a little place in the sun, perhaps the Bahamas. That will do nicely. Come on. Eat it.*

He chews and swallows.

She waits.

Nothing happens.

He attacks the roast potatoes.

Why isn't it working?

The phone rings.

Gwendolyn jumps.

'Steady, old girl. I'll get it.'

'Leave it!' she barks, louder than she intends.

'Might be important. You carry on.'

He gets up from the table and goes into the living room to take the call.

The cooking must have destroyed the poison, thinks Gwendolyn. *According to the internet it only takes a miniscule amount of the toxin to prove fatal.* She has a back-up. The tiny bottle is still in her pocket for an emergency just like this. She will destroy it in the confusion of Sherborne's sudden death.

She quickly uncorks the bottle and smears the blade of Sherborne knife with the oil. She picks up a parsnip off Sherborne's plate to administer another dose.

The vegetable is hot and burns her finger. She jerks her hand back and cuts her finger with the knife.

Unlike her husband, Gwendolyn St John does not have any activated carbon in her gut, an antidote to the effects of water hemlock.

Immediately her body goes rigid; her eyes roll back until only the whites show.

'That was Long Sutton on the phone,' says Sherborne, coming back into the dinning room. 'Couldn't get him off the...Gwendolyn?'

Gwendolyn lies on the floor, shakes and goes into convulsions.

Sherborne rushes to her and supports her head in his arms but he can do nothing.

Within three minutes she is dead.

There is a tiny glass bottle near her outstretched hand.

155

It is late October. There have been many changes in Itchen Prior since the death of the late and universally unlamented Gwendolyn St John.

Sherborne St John, once he recovered from the shock of his wife's betrayal and what he now realises were at least two attempts (he slept through the first) on his life has sold the horses that were a potent reminder of her; he has, however, kept Penny Taylor on as a secretary to help him manage the estate. Penny now lives in Gwendolyn's old rooms in the Hall and is devoted to her employer.

Itchen Prior Horticultural Centre is in the process of being sold to a garden centre chain; Jed Smith has not recovered from his breakdown and is happy in his own world of medication. The CPS are not convinced he will be fit to plead at his trail.

Paul Hartley is on bail and awaiting trial; he has not been seen around the village since his arrest.

Crux Eaton has moved back to the village now there is no danger of bumping into Gwendolyn St John and has made his peace with his mother. He and Sally Fairfax moved in with his mother and there is talk of marriage. Major Farleigh Wallop has given him a job as his assistant at Paintball Patrol and he has taken to it like a duck to water. Dressing up and playing at soldiers in the woods appeals to the big kid that never grew up in him. He has given up all horticultural activities.

That mantel has passed to Hatch Warren, who is now cultivating a small secluded patch of woodland in St John's Wood. Long Sutton is fully aware of his efforts but is prepared to turn a blind eye as long as the game is left in peace.

For the rest of the Warren family nothing has changed. Ashley still cleans for Farleigh Wallop and Paul Hartley, doing Hartley's shopping for him twice a week and keeping him abreast of gossip, some of it about himself but he is just an empty husk, a shadow of his former self. She is busy stealing Hartley's smaller possessions and passing them over to Seth to sell on. Hartley either doesn't notice or doesn't care.

Mitchell Dever is spending more and more time up in London. He sleeps in a spare room in the flat of his friend, Tony Highbury, now divorced from his wife. He has started seeing a new woman, a junior editor from his publishing house and they have slept together a couple of times. He thinks it might be time to tell Jocasta and put the house on the market. He might be able to buy a studio apartment in an unfashionable part of zone 3 in London with his share.

Marjory Hinton Daubrey is back at school with her new intake for the autumn term and is busy planning for Harvest Festival and Hallowe'en and then the high point of the term, the Nativity Play – always a hit with the mums and dads. She and Jocasta see each other several evenings a week, what with Mitchell being away so much.

Jocasta Dever now has a pretty good idea what Mitchell is up to, having sneaked a peek at the foolishly undeleted messages on his mobile. She is biding her time. She has no wish to move out of Itchen Prior and is in no hurry to sell the cottage that they invested so much money and optimism in. Itchen Prior, for all its foibles, is now her home. And she still has Bart the dog for company of an evening.

As for the rest, Tristram Clatford, Henry Grey, Gordon Turgis, Natalie Somerfield and Ragged Appleshaw, life goes on as it always has.

156

On the other side of Europe Mirko Knin, Vukodin Punta, Joagoda Doboj and Nevena Stolac sit in a café in Sarajevo drinking coffee and sipping glasses of raki They reminisce about their summer in England and their fortuitous escape.

Sadly, they will never know that their tormentor has had his comeuppance.

157

Samhain. The three days when the world of the living meets the world of the dead. The death of the year, herald of the hard lands of the winter. One of the four great celebrations of the Celtic year. And also Hallowe'en when children dress up and their parents take them from house to house begging for stuff they could buy them themselves.

'Tonight will be special,' Marjory tells Jocasta when she comes to Yew Tree Cottage to collect her. Mitchell is up in London. Jocasta suspects he is seeing his new squeeze and realises she does not care. Perhaps she is picking up on the philosophy of being a part of the greater whole that her new friends in the Itchen Prior Grove espouse. What was it the hippies said: go with the flow!

'In what way?' she asks.

'Cernunnos will be present.'

'Oh, whose turn is it tonight?'

'No, Cernunnos himself will be present.'

Jocasta is bewildered. Is Marjory suggesting that some primeval spirit of nature is going to manifest itself here at the Devil's Tooth. Come to think of, given what has happened over the last few months, she wouldn't be at all surprised.

'Cernunnos is the leader of the Grove. A sort of High Priest if you like. He leads the ceremonies of the Four Great Festivals.'

'Any one I know?' asks Jocasta, a little flippantly.

'Wait and see,' Marjory replies enigmatically.

158

There is a large crowd out tonight, rather like the congregation of a church for Midnight Mass at Christmas. Many people hold flaming torches and Jocasta is reminded of a mob assembled to drive the monster out of his castle. The night is chill so perhaps the torches provide heat as well as light.

The Green Man steps out of the trees and leads the procession to the stone and anti clockwise around it.

Henry Grey steps forward to lead the Grove in the invocations. These being done he calls for the Earth Mother to enter the circle.

Jocasta is stunned to see Penny Taylor strip and enter the circle but also very relieved it is not her. She is not sure whether she is ready to get her kit off and have pretend sex in front of a gang of people just yet.

If ever!

She supposes Henry Grey must have talked her into it somehow.

There is a hush. Grey lifts his torch high and calls: 'Cernunnos!'

'Cernunnos!' the circle chants, again and again.

Suddenly there is movement in the darkness, a shape caught in the flickering of the torch light. Jocasta makes out a terrifying figure at the edge of the light. It is human but seems to have a large set of antlers growing out of its head.

'CERNUNNOS! CERNUNNOS!'.

The chanting has become ecstatic; the worshippers are drumming the ground with their feet. She feels herself getting caught up in a primitive frenzy. Her blood is pounding through her body and she is becoming sexually aroused despite her earlier misgivings.

'CERNUNNOS! CERNUNNOS!'

The rhythm of the stamping feet goes faster. Jocasta is joining in, giving herself to the moment.

The figure enters the circle. She can see more clearly now. It has long shaggy hair and a wreath of oak twisted around its horns. The face is obscured by the hair but it/he is naked and supporting an erection. It/he raises his arms in the air, tilts its/his head and emits an animal like howl.

He drops to his knees behind Penny, gripping her around the waist.

This time the sex is emphatically not symbolic but a raw rutting of animal lust.

The rite over, the figure strides out of the circle and disappears back into the darkness from whence it came.

Jocasta is drained, as if she too has just had sex. Next to her she hears Marjory Hinton Daubrey sigh.

Penny Taylor lies prone on the cold ground, sated. Ashley Warren steps over to her carrying her robe and helps her up, hugging her.

'Cernunnos has come to the Earth Mother. Let there be a quickening. Let there be new life in the new year. All in its proper season. All hail,' intones Grey.

The Green Man blows his horn; the meeting is done.

159

Marjory and Jocasta drive in silence for a while, each lost in their own thoughts. Jocasta, at last, breaks the silence.

'Who the hell was that?'

'That was the Lord of the Wild Places,' her friend replies.

'Yes, but *who* was it?'

'It was who it always is in Itchen Prior.'

'Oh, come on, Marjory. Don't get all mysterious on me. Who was it?'

'The St Johns have always been the lords of Itchen Prior.'

'*Sherborne St John!*'

'Of course. Who else could it be. This land is his land. The stone is on his land. The woods are on his land. He *is* the land. And with luck, after tonight there will be another St John to inherit the land. The circle is unbroken.'

And then the penny drops.

'That's why you recruited me,' Jocasta says, stunned. 'Why you asked me about having children. You wanted *me* to, to *mate* with Sherborne. To have his child!'

'Yes,' Marjory admits. 'You were so keen to become a part of Itchen Prior. What greater part could there be? To carry on the traditions! To be the Earth Mother. But Penny loves Sherborne and he will marry her. The circle is unbroken.'

They spend the rest of the drive in silence.

160

Night and silence return to St John's Wood and the Devil's Tooth. Small animals and the night birds play their eternal game of hide or die. The land sleeps as it has slept since the dawn of time and the folk of Itchen Prior are abed. Life goes on as it always has and always will, the dramas of the people who inhabit the land play themselves out in the circle of birth and death.

THE END

Acknowledgements

Many thanks to: Fiona Collier for things constabulary; Sam Dennes for botanical matters; Zona McGlynn for her expertise about horticulture and garden centres; Milena Stajic for things Bosnian; Heather Webb for pointing me to my agent, James Essinger, to whom thanks for his support and encouragement and helping me get the book into shape.

Lastly, but certainly not least, to my wife Liane for help, proof-reading and patience beyond the call of duty.